SHATTERED Illusions

CHRISTINA SOL

To Todd, Lucy & Jackson—
I couldn't do any of this without you.

CHAPTER ONE

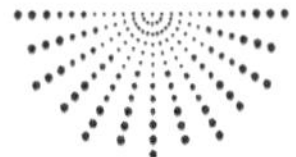

J oe Buchanan trudged up the last step to the front door of his childhood home. The wind howled, and the rain snuck under the covered porch to slap him in the face. Swiping a hand over his brow, he wiped away the icy water that stung his eyes. Dammit, this was why he avoided the Pacific Northwest during winter.

The porch lights flickered twice, and he frowned. A moment later, there was a flash of light, followed by a loud bang. Then, the neighborhood went dark.

On instinct, he reached for his holster. He came up empty. It took a split second to remember he was no longer a special agent.

Damn.

Glancing down the street, he guessed a transformer must have blown somewhere. He should go in, get dry, and pour himself a giant tumbler of whiskey while he waited out the storm.

Instead, he set his suitcase down by the front door.

He didn't deserve comfort. No. Not after all the shit he'd done.

Joe would never forget that night. Her emerald eyes had been glassy with terror and tears. The silver barrel of the gun pressed to her head. Then, his heart had completely stopped when she'd crumbled. He'd never experienced such fear and helplessness as he had in those moments. Not being able to touch her for fear of injuring her further had been agony. And the pool of blood growing around her head as she'd lain there unconscious haunted him.

Yes, she'd recovered. Yes, the bastard who'd held her captive had gotten his just dues. But that image of her was never far from his mind. A constant reminder of his failure. That what he'd done for the greater good hadn't been worth it. Not at all.

Feeling his way across the porch, he grimaced when his shin cracked against something hard.

Yeah. That's more on par with the shit I deserve.

Another lightning strike illuminated the offending Adirondack chair, which must have been new. For as long as he could remember, two ancient rockers had sat on the porch. That's what he got for staying away for so long.

He sank into the chair, resting his head against the high back. Exhaustion swept over him. He closed his eyes. The rain pelted his front with each gust of wind. A violent shiver tore through him, but still, he didn't move.

Two days ago, Joe had walked into his special agent in charge's office in Boston and handed over his resignation. His life had been a whirlwind ever since.

Two hours of his SAC trying to convince him to change his mind. Six hours of debriefing after both his SAC and assistant SAC had realized his mind was made up. Eighteen hours of travel madness, which had included a flat tire on his cab ride to the airport and then two rescheduled flights. Then, when he'd finally landed at Sea-Tac and hopped in his rental car, there had been a four-hour wait for the Hudson Island ferry.

Now he was home. Unemployed. And bone-tired. To top it all off, while waiting for the god-forsaken ferry, he'd answered his cell phone without looking at the caller ID.

Idiot.

The woman's shrill voice echoed in his head. He knew it was supposed to be sexy, but . . . it wasn't. Hell, a drill to the head would've been more desirable.

Candie. He shuddered. There was nothing wrong with her name. But when a grown-ass woman had introduced herself as "Candie with an *ie!*"? He should have known she'd be more trouble than she was worth. But he was a fucking idiot. An idiot who'd been blinded by boobs. When she'd sat down next to him on the Boston-to-Seattle nonstop, her gorgeous cleavage on full display, he'd done what he did best: ignored the noise and turned on the charm.

Self-disgust rolled through him.

It was one thing to flirt with the hot woman next to you on a six-plus-hour flight. It was another thing entirely when said flirting almost led to a hand job. On a fucking plane. In coach. With another passenger in their row. What the hell was wrong with him?

Worse yet, he'd been tempted to let her go to town. He'd had a shitty week—hell, a shitty year—so what would be the harm? Two consenting adults and all that bullshit . . .

But that's what his entire life had been for the past few years. Abject bullshit.

And he was tired of it.

With a sigh that was part weary, part self-hatred, he rose from the Adirondack and made his way back to the front door, pulling his keys from his pocket. Freezing drops of water slid beneath the neck of his jacket and down his spine. Goosebumps rose in their wake.

As he silently entered his childhood home, he set his suitcase just inside the entryway. The smell of new wood and paint surrounded him. His father had recently remodeled the entire lower level of the house. After the fiasco Joe had caused eight months ago—

No.

That clusterfuck hadn't been his fault. Well, it hadn't been *entirely* his fault. That whole case had been fucked from the start. Everything that could have gone wrong had gone wrong. In epic fashion. But like a good little minion, he'd kept his mouth shut and followed orders. And brought pain and destruction to his hometown. To people he cared about. To his family.

Sick of his own thoughts, he focused on picking a path through the pitch-black living room, not wanting to whack into anything else. When he approached the kitchen doorway, another scent caught his nose. He couldn't quite put his finger on it, but it was comforting and familiar.

The air shifted, and he froze. The hairs on the back of his neck stood at attention.

He wasn't alone.

He reached for his holster, and for the second time that night, came up empty.

Fuck.

Putting his back to the wall, he scanned the living room. It was so damn dark. He couldn't see for shit. But his gut screamed that someone was in the room with him. And he trusted his gut.

Whoever it was, they were close. A split second later, he ducked. Something hard sailed over his head and struck the wall. The crash was deafening in the silent room, and drywall dust exploded into the air.

A shadowy figure, holding what looked to be a baseball bat, loomed over him and swung again. He twisted, but his shoulder burst into flames as the bat made contact. He went on autopilot, and a lifetime of martial arts and hand-to-hand training took over.

All the built-up anger and frustration he'd been carrying unleashed. With a growl, he lunged, tackling the perp. The bat clattered to the ground, and he pinned the asshole under him. Sitting atop the writhing intruder, he easily held the fucker down with one hand at their throat while he let his other fly. With a fleshy thwack, his fist made contact. The perp grunted.

Joe hesitated at the sound, pulse pounding in his ears. His gut screamed that something was off. Something beyond almost getting his head taken off with a baseball bat.

But fuck it, there was no time to deliberate. He squeezed his hand tighter around the perp's throat and raised his fist again.

"No," a ragged voice wheezed.

He froze mid-swing, and dread turned his blood to ice.

Fucking shit.

His shoulders sagged as the fight in him vanished.

Citrus with a touch of honey. That was the scent he'd been unable to place earlier, and his gut twisted.

What the fuck have I done?

A giant boulder formed in his throat, and he could barely find his voice. "Rox?"

The painful thud of the intruder's fist on Roxie's jaw stunned her. Little white stars filled her vision, and her face throbbed in rhythm with the frantic beating of her heart. *Holy shit.* This crazy guy was going to freaking kill her. Or worse.

She tried to buck him off, but he was too heavy. Her mind scrambled. She needed to find a weapon.

"No," she moaned, scratching and clawing wildly at the hand around her throat. If she could just see where the damn bat had rolled to, maybe she could reach—

"Rox?"

In an instant, the heavy body holding her down was gone, replaced by gentle hands that helped her into a seated position. Her head swam with the movement.

"Holy fuck, Roxanne. Are you okay?"

She stilled. She knew that voice. But no—that couldn't be right. What the hell was going on? "Joe?"

"Hold on, Rox. Fuck! Let me find a light."

Joe. The intruder was *Joe*.

She exhaled, feeling around with her hands until she bumped into the back of the couch. Grateful, she leaned against it. Her dizziness settled, but she continued to tremble in the aftermath of adrenaline.

She'd been asleep when a loud boom had rattled the house. A quick glance at her bedside clock had told her the power was out. She'd left her phone charging on the dresser across the room when she'd gone to bed, so she'd gotten up to set her cell's alarm clock. Then she'd heard someone shuffling about downstairs.

Before giving it a second thought, she'd grabbed the baseball bat she kept tucked next to her bed and went to investigate. Like Nancy freaking Drew.

Dumbass.

Roxie rubbed her jaw and winced.

She could hear Joe rummaging around on the other side of the living room. A few seconds later, a beam of light shined on her face. Irritation replaced her fear, and she welcomed it. Hell, she embraced it.

"Holy crap, jackass." She held one hand up to shield her eyes and swatted him away with her other. "Are you trying to blind me now, too?"

"Stay still, Roxanne, and let me see how bad you're hurt." He crouched next to her, and when her swatting proved futile, she glared into the blinding light.

"Admiring your handiwork?" she asked.

Though Roxie couldn't see him, she felt him stiffen.

A tiny part of her felt bad for the snark. She was being a bitch. She knew it. But her nerves were shot. She was shaky and anxious and her face *hurt* . . . and bitchy was her default. Sad, but true.

Joe stood and walked away. The beam of light from his phone revealed he was heading toward the kitchen. "It never ends with you, does it, Rox?"

She sent a death glare into his back. God, they really did bring out the worst in each other.

They were freaking adults. Responsible adults at that. She owned and ran a wildly successful café and catering company. And Joe? Well, the government trusted him enough to issue him a damn gun. So yes, they were mature adults. In their *thirties*. But put them in a room together, and they reverted to being ten years old.

That wasn't even a fair statement. When they were ten—or, technically, when they were seven and ten, and then ten and thirteen—they'd gotten along fabulously. Their friendship hadn't gone to hell until a few years ago.

"Here." Joe tossed something in her lap.

She yelped at the sudden coldness. A frozen bag of peas and a kitchen towel. Mumbling her thanks, she wrapped the bag in the towel and placed it against her jaw. She winced, but the cold soothed her aching face.

"Despite what you think, Roxanne, had I known it was you, I wouldn't have hit you." He followed his words with a grumbling noise, and she pictured him scrubbing his hands over his face. "What the hell are you doing here, anyway?"

Of course the fucker was going to make this her fault.

"What am *I* doing here? Excuse me, buster, but I think the better question is, what are *you* doing here?"

"Uh, news flash, Rox: this is my dad's house."

God, he was such an ass. "So why the hell were you lurking around in the dark?"

"Holy shit, really? First off, Rox, the power is out. Second, if anyone was lurking, it was you. You nearly took my head off with that damn baseball bat."

She should have aimed lower.

"And third," he continued, "why the hell are you here again?"

Yup. Definitely should have aimed lower.

"I *live* here, you jackass. How dare you go creeping around in the dark in the middle of the night and then try to turn it around on m—"

"What do you mean, you live here?"

It was like talking to a brick wall. "It's a pretty self-explanatory statement."

"God, you're such a smart-ass. Wh—"

"Seriously? Smart-ass? Me?" She scoffed. "Pot, meet kettle, Buchanan."

He muttered a curse and took a deep breath. "Look, I talked to my dad before I left Boston, and he didn't mention you were living here. Hell, I talk to him every week, and he's never said anything."

"Well," she countered, "I had dinner with your dad literally last night, and he didn't mention you were coming back. So don't—"

She startled when the entryway table lamp flicked on and the refrigerator resumed its steady hum. Thank god the power was back on. She let out a sigh of relief.

Still cross-legged on the ground, Roxie glanced up. Sure enough, Joe was glaring at her, stance wide, arms crossed over his broad chest. Classic freaking alpha-hole caveman pose. There was a look in his eyes she couldn't quite decipher. He didn't say a thing; he just stared at her. And the longer he stared, the deeper his brow creased.

She refused to look away because she was stupidly stubborn. But his intense eye contact made her nervous. She fought the urge to squirm. There was no way she'd give him the satisfaction, dammit. But she needed something to do with her hands, so she pulled the bag of peas from her jaw, rewrapped it in the towel, and placed it back against her face.

The air left Joe's lungs in an audible whoosh. He dropped to his knees in front of her, and devastation twisted his face.

She frowned. Why was he so upset? He couldn't stand her.

Before she could question anything, his large hands cradled her jaw. "Holy Christ, Rox."

She was stunned. Speechless. And she was *never* speechless.

She racked her brain for some snippy comeback but drew a blank. It disturbed her. Completely.

Joe spitting nails, she could handle. But Joe with concern in his eyes? She had no clue how to deal with such a thing. It reminded her of a lifetime ago . . . when they'd been best friends. For the most part, she'd gotten over their implosion, but sometimes the disappointment haunted her.

"I'm sure it'll be fine." Brushing his hands away, Roxie awkwardly tried to stand. She flinched when his hands clasped her elbows and guided her up with ease. "Thanks," she mumbled, heading toward the stairs.

Space. She needed some freaking space.

"Dammit, Rox. Have some damn decency, will you?"

She spun on her heels at his tone, and her eyes narrowed. Judgmental Joe, she could handle. "Excuse me?"

He turned his back to her. "Put some clothes on or something."

She looked down at herself and flushed. Yeah, she was wearing a tank top and a pair of boy shorts, but seriously? She'd been *asleep* for crying out loud!

She stomped up the stairs, cursing Mr. Holier Than Thou under her breath.

Puritanical jackass bitch.

Slamming her bedroom door, she bit back a howl of frustration.

At least they'd reentered familiar territory. Sniping at each other was what they did best.

***

Joe scrubbed his hands over his face, cringing as a door slammed shut upstairs.

When Roxie had moved the bag of peas, he'd gotten his first glimpse of the damage he'd inflicted. The sight of her jaw and cheek—both already black and blue—had plowed into his gut like the baseball bat she'd wielded in defense.

Holy motherfucking shit.

He'd hit her. *Her!* Roxanne Elizabeth Jameson. The girl he'd known forever. And then he'd almost hit her a *second* time. His stomach rolled. It made him sick to know he'd put those marks on her face. It made him just as sick to think of how his mind had gone straight to the gutter when she'd stood up. All concerns for her safety and well-being? Poof! Gone.

Clearly, Roxie's "jackass" accusations weren't that far off.

But the way her long auburn hair had fallen in a tangled mess around her shoulders, skimming the tops of her breasts, which had been nearly visible under the paper-thin tank top . . . And the way her shorts had displayed the bottoms of her perky ass cheeks when she'd walked toward the stairs . . .

Holy fucking hell. His mouth had gone dry, and he'd forgotten his own name.

He'd had no choice but to turn away. If he'd continued to stare at her in those criminally small shorts and damn-near-transparent tank top, he'd have said something—like how fucking gorgeous she was—that would have led to disaster.

And she was living here? Oh hell no. That was not possible because *he* was living here. It was *his* damn house.

He let out a low growl and scrubbed his hands over his face again. *Fuck.* He was definitely going to have a chat with his father. And soon. Because living under the same roof as that woman would be a huge mistake. They'd either kill each other or end up in be—

Nope. Don't even think *of going there, buddy.*

They'd kill each other. Yeah. That's what would happen. That's *all* that would happen.

An image of Roxie in those tiny shorts flashed in his mind and he grimaced. *Damn.* He was in trouble. After all, wasn't denial the first sign of a problem?

CHAPTER TWO

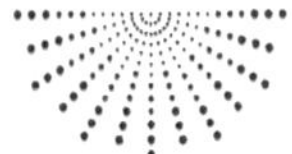

It was going to be a long day. As always, Roxie had arrived at her café, Comfort Food, at four in the morning, and the doors had opened at six. Now, at only seven thirty, they'd already served twice as many customers than usual, and the crowd didn't look like it would let up anytime soon.

The businesswoman in her was thrilled, but she wished she could attribute the traffic to something better than the rumor mill. Small-town gossip was like a wildfire—it traveled fast, could be devastating, and left a giant mess behind—and the news about her banged-up face had been no exception.

But money was money, and customers were customers. Gossipy busybodies or not. So Roxie was doing what she did best: pasting on a smile and sucking it up. Besides, she was touched by the true concern of her regulars, some of whom she considered more like family.

Nina Castillo, her lone full-time employee, turned to her. "I've got the front covered if you want to head back."

She was beyond tempted by Nina's offer, but she refused to hide. "That's okay, it's no problem. I—"

"Oh my god!"

Her molars ground together, and she winced at the shrill voice. She winced again as the slight motion increased the pain in her throbbing jaw. Sheila Lancaster, her newest part-time employee, had a *Hello Kitty* voice that was too high-pitched for this early in the morning.

"Roxie, your face! What happened?" Sheila rounded the counter, her eyes wide with concern, her hands fluttering in a helpless gesture.

Roxie forced a smile, reminding herself that one of the reasons she'd hired Sheila was because, squeaky voice and all, the customers loved her.

"Don't worry, Sheila. It looks a lot worse than it feels." Complete lie. Her jaw and head throbbed from the punch, and her shoulder ached from the tackle. She desperately wanted to lie down. Preferably on a soft surface far away from the looky-loo customers.

Glancing between her employees, a sense of calm settled over her. These two women were solid, and she knew Comfort Food would be in good hands if she decided to listen to her body and rest for once. Which was doubtful, but never say never and all that . . .

Nina had been with her for just over a year, and she was efficient, organized, innovative, and the best right-hand woman anyone could ask for. Sheila was also a great worker. It had only been a month since she'd joined the team, but Roxie had a good feeling about her.

As far as appearances and personalities went, while both women were petite, they were polar opposites in every other way. Nina was Filipino-American with long black hair and enormous dark-brown eyes reminiscent of Princess Jasmine's. On first impression, she was the epitome of sweet and innocent. While *sweet* held true, *innocent* was a complete facade. Nina's sarcastic and bawdy humor had Roxie in stitches on a regular basis.

Sheila, on the other hand, was a curvy, hourglass-figured, blond-haired, blue-eyed bombshell. If you looked up *sexy* in the dictionary, you would find a picture of her. Beneath Sheila's sultry pinup-girl looks, however, was an innate sweetness and naivety that all the customers adored.

"But what happened?" Sheila asked, her baby blues welling. "Are you really okay?"

The corners of Roxie's lips twitched. See? Sweet. "I promise I'm okay. It was an accident. I have an unexpected new housemate, and last night we had a massive lack of communication when—"

"Who the fuck did that to you, Roxie?" a low, ominous voice interrupted.

Could this day be over yet?

Roxie groaned, and her shoulders sagged. She counted to five before turning to meet the storm-gray gaze of Sheriff Quinn O'Conner.

"I want a fucking name, Roxie. Now."

Those seven little words had a small smile ghosting her lips.

Like Joe, she'd known Quinn her entire life. The three of them had grown up together, thick as thieves. But while she and Joe had grown apart, she and Quinn had stayed close. The man was the big brother she'd never had. He was her dearest friend and most favorite person. His wife, Alex, was a close second. And their little one-month-old daughter, Annie, was angling for the top spot.

She and Quinn had seen each other through both wonderful and devastating times. There wasn't anything she wouldn't do to protect him and his family. She knew he reciprocated the sentiment, and because of that, her smile slipped. She had no clue how to tell him about what had happened last night. He saw things in black and white, and no matter what spin she put on it, no matter how much she explained it had been a misunderstanding, he'd be furious.

Yes, Joe was a complete jackass, but she didn't want him to get pummeled. And yes, Joe had all sorts of combat training and could probably hold his own, but right now, Quinn looked capable of murder. Her friend had absolutely no tolerance for violence toward women—misunderstanding or not. Especially since his wife was a former victim of domestic abuse.

He'd met Alex when she'd fled to Hudson Island after her sadistic then-husband, Preston Woodsworth III, had been put in jail. Not only had the evil man been under investigation by the FBI for public corruption and extortion, but he'd terrorized Alex. The stories of abuse she'd relayed about the horror and pain she'd endured at the hands of her ex-husband turned Roxie's blood cold every time they crossed her mind.

Especially since Roxie'd had the misfortune of experiencing his monstrous nature firsthand. It had been a horrible case of wrong-place-wrong-time that had led to Woodsworth taking her captive. He'd left her with a fractured and dislocated shoulder—the same shoulder that was now throbbing, thanks to Joe—and a severe concussion.

And nightmares. Countless nightmares that she woke from in a panic, dripping with sweat, swearing she could still feel the cold barrel of the gun pressed to her head and the jut of his arousal against her back.

"Answer me, Roxie," Quinn said, interrupting her thoughts. "Who the fuck laid their hands on you?"

She closed her eyes. "Quinn . . ."

"Dammit, Roxie," he hissed, slamming his hands down on the counter that separated them.

Her eyes flew open. Quinn didn't lose his temper. He was steady. Always.

Well . . . unless you messed with his family. She internally winced because she knew he considered her to be his sister. So the frustration, concern, and rage blazing on his face made sense. And worried her.

"Tell me who this son of a bitch is, and I swear I will lock that fucker—"

"It's not what you think, Quinn." She placed her hand over his. As his eyes narrowed, she hurried on. "Really, I swear. It was just a misunderstand—"

"A *misunderstanding*? Roxie, dammit—" He took a deep breath and scanned the crowded café. Everyone's stares were glued to them. Without another word, he rounded the counter. Gently taking her by the elbow, he guided her to the back office.

Once inside the cramped room, his voice dropped to a harsh timbre. "The side of your face is black and blue. This is not a misunderstanding. This is assault. Now tell me who did this. I'll find out either way. You know that. The bastard's going to regret ever laying a hand on you. I swear it."

"Ease up, O'Conner."

They turned.

Joe stood in the doorway. His grim gaze met Quinn's furious one. "Believe me, I regret hitting her more than you'll ever know."

"You son of a bitch," Quinn roared as he pounced.

Roxie yelped and scrambled out of the way. Before she could blink, Quinn's fist smashed into Joe's jaw. Joe's head whipped backward, and he did nothing to defend himself. When Quinn's fist came flying his way again, he took it.

"Quinn! Stop it!" she shouted. When he wound up for another punch, she did the only thing she could think of— she jumped on his back. "Stop it right now!"

The room went quiet except for the sound of their uneven breathing.

"Jesus, Quinn," she said, climbing off his back. Every muscle in her body protested the movement. "I told you it was a misunderstanding, all right?"

The men continued to glare, and she knew that the moment she moved away, they would beat the shit out of each other. So, she shifted to stand between them.

"Those were your two shots, O'Conner," Joe said. His voice was calm, though his eyes blazed. "Hit me again and I will tear you apart."

She slapped both palms on Quinn's chest when he looked ready to lunge.

"Holy shit, Joe. Shut the hell up already!" Her gaze ping-ponged between them. "Both of you need to back off. I swear to god, you two are the biggest idiots." She pointed at the chair behind her desk, then at the futon on the opposite side of her office. "Sit. Both of you. Neither one of you says one damn word until I'm done talking. Got it?"

Quinn sank into the chair. Joe sat on the futon. All the while, they scowled at each other.

"Roxanne," Joe began, patting the futon, his tone suddenly casual, his expression relaxed, as if she hadn't just pulled the dumbasses off of each other, "why the hell do you have this in your office?"

"Shut. Up. Joe." She seethed, turning her attention to Quinn, who was still glaring at Joe. "Look at me, Quinn."

Long seconds ticked by before her friend met her eyes.

"I swear, Quinn, it's nothing nefarious. Joe came home in the middle of the night. The power was out. I didn't know he was coming. He didn't know I was there. We both thought the other was an intruder. I tried to take his head off with a baseball bat, but unfortunately, I missed." She glanced at Joe, mustering as much of a smirk as she could with her bruised jaw. "No offense, of course."

"None taken," he said dryly.

"Apparently," she continued, "the idiot's FBI training and all that jiu-jitsu and Krav crap—"

"Krav Maga," Joe cut in.

"Yeah, whatever it's called. Apparently, he's really good at it—"

"I *was* a hand-to-hand combat instructor at the FBI's training academy, you know."

She continued as if Joe hadn't interrupted her. "—and that stuff's the real deal because the next thing I knew, my baseball bat was gone, I was on my back, and he socked me in the face. I swear, I thought . . ." Her throat closed as remembered fear surged through her. She shifted on her feet, fighting to push it away. "Let's just say that in our struggle, I lost. Thankfully, he figured out it was me and stopped. End of story. It was just a colossal mix-up, okay?"

Quinn opened his mouth to speak, but a quiet knock on the open door halted his words.

Nina poked her head in. "I'm so sorry to interrupt, Roxie, but the mayor's wife's here. She wants to talk to you—and only you—about her catering order."

"Thanks, Nina. Please let her know I'll be right out." She shot what she hoped was a reassuring smile to Nina. Once the woman's back was turned, she stared down the two men. "I swear to freaking god, if you guys start fighting in any way, shape, or form, or if you begin acting like the stupid cavemen I know you guys are, I will kick both your asses."

As Roxie left the room, Joe worked his aching jaw from side to side and glared at his best friend. "Seriously, O'Conner, do you honestly think if I'd known it was Rox that I'd have hit her?"

Quinn let out a deep breath. "I don't know what to think, Buchanan."

Joe's hands fisted as his resentment and anger returned. "Then fuck you, Connie. If you think for one fucking second that I'd ever knowingly lay a hand on that woman, then—"

"Relax," Quinn said. "Relax, okay? I know you wouldn't ever hit Roxie on purpose. I know that." He shook his head. "But look at it from my view, man. I come in here to see if she wants to come over for fucking dinner tomorrow night, and all I see is that some asshole has pummeled her face in. Then she won't tell me who did it."

"Seriously?" Joe's eyebrows rose to his hairline. He'd figured she'd have the whole town hating him by brunch.

Quinn nodded. "She didn't say a damn thing. So that pissed me off. Then you waltz in and say *you* hit her and . . ." He shrugged. "What the hell did you expect?"

Rubbing a hand over his sore jaw, Joe nodded at his old friend. "I'd expect exactly what you did." His lips pressed into a tight line as images of his fight with Roxie filled his vision. "When I heard her voice last night and it finally registered in my brain that it was Roxanne . . . Holy fuck." Bile rose in his throat. "Trust me when I say I've never felt so fucking horrible."

After a few moments of silence, Quinn met his gaze. "How did you *not* know it was Roxie?"

That was the million-dollar question. One that had kept him up until the wee hours of the morning. Yes, it had been pitch-black, but how the hell had he not recognized her presence? They might fight and bicker like crazy, but for better or worse, he had always been in tune with her, had always sensed the exact instant she stepped into a room. And to not have known . . .

Fuck. He wasn't sure he'd ever be able to forgive himself.

He'd failed her. Again.

She was hurt because of him. Again.

"I don't know, man." Raking his hands over his face, Joe sighed. "The power was out. One second, I'm trying to find my way around the living room, and the next second, there's a baseball bat flying at my head. I didn't think. It was all gut reaction. Like she said, all the training kicked in. 'Disarm the enemy, take him to the ground, attack.' And goddamn, Connie, I hit her hard." The bile crept up a little higher in his throat.

He shook his head, hoping to clear the memories, but it didn't work. Groaning, he leaned his head back and closed his eyes. "God knows I've imagined Rox underneath me plenty of times, but it was never like that."

Quinn coughed, and Joe froze.

His eyes flew open. *Shit. You did* not *fucking say that out loud.*

One glance at the shithead across the room told him he had. Joe squirmed as amused and curious gray eyes gleamed back at him.

You're a fucking idiot, Buchanan.

His face heated, and he cleared his throat. *Dammit.* "Could you just, uh, forget I said that last part out loud? That thought wasn't exactly supposed to leave my brain."

Quinn laughed. Loudly. The fucker. "No way in hell, buddy."

"Shit," he muttered. "Is there even a point in me asking you not to mention this conversation to Alex? Because if you tell her, then she'll tell Roxanne. And the last thing I need is for Rox to know that I think she's hot."

"So, wait." Quinn's brow furrowed. "When the hell did you start thinking Roxie was hot?"

"Are you kidding me, Connie? The woman's been hot since she was sixteen."

Quinn grinned, and Joe realized he'd just taken the bait. His eyes narrowed.

Fuck.

Well, in for a penny and all that shit. "How could you *not* think she's hot? Have you never looked at her face? Have you not noticed that she's built like a goddamn wet dream? The girl's nearly six feet tall, miles of legs, and—"

"Okay, stop." Quinn waved his hands. "You're making me uncomfortable. Look, I may think of Roxie as a little sister, but she's not my sister, and I do have two eyes. Although I haven't dwelled on her body as much as you apparently have, I will acknowledge that Roxie is attractive. And she knows it, too."

Joe shrugged. "Yeah, well, it's one thing for her to know it, but it's another thing entirely for her to know *I* know it. Believe me, O'Conner, I'm not gonna do anything about it because that would just be a fucking disaster. So please, Quinn, I'm asking you—on our thirty-seven-year friendship —please don't tell Alex."

"You think you can play the friendship card?"

"You bet your ass I can play it." He stuck his hand out. "Deal?"

Quinn smirked and took Joe's outstretched hand. "Fine. Deal."

Roxie released a long breath and rubbed her temples when the front door closed behind Mrs. Bonnie Green. Getting punched in the face aside, no one could make her head throb quite like Bonnie. She was the mayor's wife, but to hear the woman tell it, she was the First Lady of Hudson Island.

Regrettably, Bonnie was also one of her best catering customers. A damn shame.

Reverting her attention to the man waiting patiently in line, Roxie bit back a groan. Jeremy Neville. *Great.*

She took back everything she'd thought about Bonnie. This man was number one on her headache-inducing list. And unfortunately for her, Sheila was busy talking with a couple of customers in the dining area, and Nina was in the kitchen prepping for tonight's catering event.

Straightening her shoulders, she put on a friendly smile. *Focus, Roxie! You're a businesswoman first and foremost, dammit.* She tried her hardest to stop her eyes from rolling at the look of horror that crossed Jeremy's face. She wasn't quite sure she'd succeeded.

"Before you say anything," Roxie began as she poured his customary cup of drip coffee, "it looks worse than it actually is."

"Yikes. Please tell me that the other person looks worse. What on earth happened?" He ran a hand through his dark-brown hair and flashed her a smile she assumed was supposed to be charming. It wasn't. It took everything she had to keep her smile in place.

Jeremy was a nice guy. She knew for a fact that lots of women on the island found him attractive. But he was like an overeager puppy. One that was neither cute nor cuddly. He reeked of douchey cologne, used too much hair product, wore tacky gold jewelry, and had an obvious fake tan. It was winter in the Pacific Northwest, for god's sake. Who did he think he was fooling?

"Unfortunate accident with the new housemate," she said, handing over his coffee as she rang up his order.

"Unfortunate, indeed. But hey, it'll take more than a few bruises to dim your beauty, gorgeous." He flashed her another toothy grin and handed over a crisp ten-dollar bill. "No change. Do you have plans for dinner tonight?"

It had been the same damn question day after day. For weeks. The guy was persistent, she'd give him that.

"I have a catering event tonight." An event she'd scheduled down to the minute and was going to be handled by Nina—*without* Roxie, for once—but Jeremy didn't need to know that.

"What about tomorrow night?"

God, if you're listening, please make this end. Make the phone ring. Let locusts descend upon the town. Flash flood. Anything. Amen.

"I'm flattered, Jeremy. But like I've said before, it's been really busy, and I just don't have the time."

"Surely you get a day off now and again?"

Her smile was beginning to hurt. "Actually, I don't. I guess that's the downside to being your own boss."

"I suppose I can see your point there. But if you let me take you out just once, I promise you'll have a great time. I can be patient, you know." He winked and headed for the door, calling over his shoulder, "I'll see you tomorrow. Same time, same channel."

At that, she couldn't keep her eyes from rolling. Hard. Luckily, he was already outside.

"You have to hand it to him," Sheila said as she returned to the counter. "The man's determined."

Roxie groaned. "More like unrelenting."

"Oh, come on. What's the deal? Jeremy's a nice guy. He obviously likes you, he's rich, and on top of it all, he's not hard on the eyes. At all."

"Then you go out with him."

Sheila's expression grew dreamy. "If only. But really, what gives? All the women in this town drool over that guy. He's got the tall-dark-and-handsome thing nailed."

Roxie blew out a breath. Not *all* the women.

Jeremy Neville was a good-looking guy. But so what?

Yes, he was tall, and as a woman who stood a little over five-nine, it was hard finding men who weren't intimidated by her height, especially when she wore heels. And yes, he was a very successful man from an even more successful family.

But, again, so what?

Jeremy was *that* guy. The one whose best friend was a bench press. The one who perpetually talked too loud on speakerphone and thought he was god's personal gift to mankind. He'd gone to the University of Washington on a football scholarship and was quick to remind everyone within earshot that he "would have gone pro, if I didn't blow out my knee" and started half his sentences with, "Back when I was playing ball at U-Dub . . ."

In Roxie's mind, having an actual conversation with Jeremy was about as much fun as banging her head against a brick wall. While having the worst menstrual cramps ever.

She wrinkled her nose as she glanced at Sheila. This was a conversation she did not want to have at her café, where anyone could overhear. Even on a normal day, Comfort Food was a main stop on the town's gossip train.

"Jeremy and I don't have much in common," she said carefully. "Besides, I prefer to spend my rare free time catching up on sleep, not jumping into the evil dating game and being obligated to make small talk with a guy who has better hair than me."

Sheila laughed. "All I'm saying is that you might be surprised. I'm sure he's a nice guy."

"Like I said, *you* go out with him then."

"Oh, believe me, Roxie, I would if I could, but the guy only has eyes for you. I think you should give him a chance."

"Who should Rox give a chance?"

Both women turned, and Roxie's eyes narrowed.

Forget Bonnie Green. Forget Jeremy Neville. Joe Buchanan was *numero uno* on her headache-inducing list. Just being in his presence filled her with agitation.

He was leaning against the archway separating the front of the café from the kitchen, his thumbs hooked into his jeans pockets, that lopsided grin on his face. At six foot two, the man was a lean, fit, blue-eyed, blond-haired Adonis. He looked like a cross between Jude Law and Matthew McConaughey, only younger and better-looking. There truly was no justice in this world.

Her annoyance kicked up a notch when Sheila's normally friendly smile turned predatory. Then like any smart predator, she pounced.

"Hi," *Hello Kitty* cooed, standing straighter to put her ample chest in plain view. "I don't think we've met. I'm Sheila."

"Hi, doll." Joe took her outstretched hand. "Joe Buchanan." He returned Sheila's smile and gave her a subtle once-over, much to the woman's delight.

It took everything Roxie had to not scoff.

Because there it was . . . the infamous Buchanan charm. She knew he could call that panty-dropping smile up on cue. *Jackass.*

"Sheila, you must be new in town because I could have sworn I knew all the gorgeous women on Hudson Island."

"Oh. My. God," Roxie said under her breath. "I think I just puked a little in my mouth." She frowned, and a sting zapped the corner of her lip.

Joe ignored her. "It was a pleasure meeting you, Sheila. I'm sure I'll see you again soon, but I need to steal your boss away for a little bit."

With one last charismatic grin at Sheila, Joe snagged Roxie's hand and pulled her toward the back office. She tried to shake him off without causing a scene, but his grip was firm.

"Holy crap," Roxie hissed. "Could you be more obvious?" She dropped her voice an octave. "'I could have sworn I knew all the gorgeous women.' Barf, Joe. Barf. That was pathetic. Surely you have better lines than that in your arsenal."

"It worked, didn't it?"

Her lips pursed, and she fought a wince at the sting on her lower lip. "Well, apparently the woman has led a very sheltered life because that's the only reason she'd fall for such a worthless line . . ." Her forehead scrunched in confusion when Joe pushed open her office door and began collecting her things. "What are you doing? I'm in the middle of work."

Joe made a sound that was part growl, part grumble as he looped her scarf around her neck and draped her jacket over her shoulders. Tucking her purse under his arm, he grabbed her hand and pulled her through the kitchen, toward the back door. He flashed his charming grin again, but this time to Nina, who was at one of the workstations, staring after them with wide, curious eyes.

He pushed open the back door, and a gust of wind rushed over her. The chilly air snapped her out of her dumbfounded obedience. She came to an abrupt halt.

"Hold up, mister. What are you doing? I have a ton of work to do today. I can't just leave."

"I don't care, Roxanne. I'm taking you to see my dad." Joe's blue eyes were flinty with anger. All the humor and charm he'd shown Sheila and Nina were gone. "Your lip is bleeding."

CHAPTER THREE

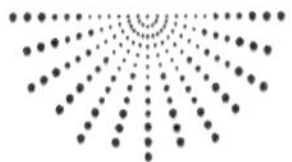

"Joseph, my boy, how are you? How was your fli—" Dr. Sean Buchanan stopped short as Joe stormed into his office, Roxie following close behind. "Oh my god, Roxie. What happened to you?"

"I'm fine, Doc," she said, hoping to reassure him. She hated it when he worried about her. "Really. It looks worse than it feels."

"Bullshit," Joe spat. He turned toward his father. "She's bleeding, and this is all your fault, Dad."

Doc squared his shoulders, and when he faced Joe, his voice was quiet. Lethal. "What the hell did you do, Joseph?"

A chill ran down Roxie's spine. In all thirty-four years of her life, she'd never *ever* seen Doc lose his temper.

Now, he stood toe to toe with his son. Both Buchanan men were the same height, and though Joe was thirty years younger and in better shape, Doc was no slouch.

She squeezed between Joe and Doc, pushing them apart. "Stop! What's wrong with both of you?" she scolded.

"Roxie, my dear girl, please step aside," Doc said, his livid gaze never leaving Joe's. "I need to speak with my son."

She wouldn't move. No way. But when Doc's voice deepened, worry turned in her gut.

"Joseph Patrick Buchanan, I asked you a question. Answer me. What the hell have you done?"

A scarlet flush stole over Joe's face. "This is all your goddamn fault, Dad."

Roxie gasped. Yes, the duo didn't always see eye to eye, but she'd never known Joe to treat his dad this way. "Joe, stop it! Don't talk to your father like that. This is not Doc's fault. This is not your fault. It's nobody's fault. It was an accident, you idiot!"

Ignoring her, Joe said to his father, "I spoke with you yesterday. We talked for nearly an hour. Not once did you mention that Roxanne was staying at the house. Hell, you even had dinner with Rox *last night*, and yet you never mentioned to her that I was coming home. These bruises on her face? If either one of us had known what was going on, they wouldn't have happened. This is on you, Dad."

Doc's face paled, and her stomach dropped.

Placing both hands on Joe's chest, Roxie gripped his shirt. "Please stop," she pleaded.

"I thought she was a damn burglar robbing the place. Why the hell didn't you tell me she was staying at the house? Because you didn't, *I* hurt her. How could you—"

Joe's words died on his lips when she moved both her hands to frame his face. She gently tugged until he tilted his head down to meet her gaze. The agony swirling in his blue eyes had her chest pinching tight.

"Enough, Joe. Please. Please, just stop and breathe. Don't be mad at your dad, okay? Don't say something you'll regret because you're angry. There's no way he could have known this would happen."

Joe exhaled and gave her a slight nod. "Dammit, Roxanne."

While the fight left him, she could see his frustration remained. She patted his cheeks, trying to lighten the mood. "Now say sorry to your dad like a good little boy."

Her attempt at humor fell flat, and his blue eyes darkened. He caressed her bruised jaw with his thumb, causing her breath to catch.

"I need to blame someone else," he said quietly, "because blaming myself hasn't done any good. I can't exactly beat the crap out of myself. If I could, I would."

The guilt painted on his face tugged at her heart. It made her want to forgive him for being such a jerk all these years.

Pulling away, she cleared her throat, which had gone thick with emotion. *Keep it light, Roxie.* "Joe, this wasn't your fault. And to be fair, I did try to decapitate you with my baseball bat."

He picked up a lock of her hair and gave it a playful pull. It had been a long time since he'd done that, and the familiar move left her unsettled. Still, she refused to admit how much losing his friendship had hurt.

"That would be *my* baseball bat, actually." Joe's small smile faded as he turned to his dad, head bowed. "Sorry, Dad."

"I understand." Doc nodded, then moved around Roxie to haul his son into a tight embrace. "But if you ever talk to me in that tone again, you'll regret it."

The corners of Joe's lips tipped up. "Yes, sir."

Doc turned to her and linked their arms. "Any of these bruises on my boy's face yours?"

She chuckled as Doc escorted her from his office. "Unfortunately not. They're courtesy of Quinn."

"Now that's a good boy."

"Thanks, Dad," Joe said, trailing behind. "I'm standing right here."

"Give me a break, Joseph. If the roles were reversed, you would've done the same to Quinn."

Doc ushered Roxie into an exam room and onto the table. After washing his hands and donning gloves, he performed a quick assessment.

"Looks like you'll need some stitches on your lip. Probably two. Three tops. It shouldn't leave a scar."

Her stomach rolled. The mere thought of getting stitches made her nauseous. But she wasn't a four-year-old, dammit. She lifted her chin. "No problem, Doc."

Damn. Had her voice shaken?

Joe coughed, and she glared at him. Did he think this was funny?

"Rox, I'll just go ahead and wait for you out—"

"Oh hell no, buddy." No way was she going through this alone. "You're the one who broke my lip."

"Jesus, Roxanne, I swear I didn't mean to."

"Yes, I know. But still." She crossed her arms. "You broke it, so now you get to sit here with me. And you have to hold my hand because you know I hate—"

"Needles," Joe finished.

As she lay down, he pulled a chair next to the table and offered her his hand. Without hesitating, she accepted, holding it in a death grip.

"You always were the biggest damn crybaby when it came to needles."

***

Joe watched Roxie's eyes narrow.

Good. Anger was better than fear.

As his dad approached, he felt her pulse quicken. She slammed her eyes shut and tightened her bone-crushing grip on his hand. It was starting to hurt, but hell would freeze over if he ever admitted that out loud.

"Now, Roxie," his dad said in what Joe considered his

'Trust me, I'm a doctor' voice. "There will be a tiny prick, and then it may sting a little—"

"Don't lie to me, Doc," she said, voice trembling. "You're going to jab that needle right into my face. Right? It's okay. Go ahead."

Damn. After all these years, it still hurt to watch her put a brave face on. He gave her hand a reassuring squeeze. "Breathe, Roxanne. Just keep your eyes closed and breathe. I've got you."

She inhaled sharply when the needle was inserted, and a lone tear trickled out from her closed eyes.

His heart constricted. He wiped the wetness from her cheek with his free hand, and the urge to continue touching her consumed him. He gave in, softly running his fingers over the line of her jaw. He knew he shouldn't, but he couldn't help himself. She needed comfort. And maybe he did, too.

Joe glanced over at his father, who was finishing up the second stitch. "He's almost done, Rox. I promise."

Joe frowned. What the hell was he doing? Why was he reassuring her? He didn't even like the woman, right? She'd fucking destroyed him. The two of them—at least in his mind—were like mortal Shakespearian enemies.

Another tear leaked out.

Fuck.

Her tears had always crushed him. Always.

"Please don't cry, Roxanne," he whispered. He knew he'd sounded a little desperate, a little frantic . . . but watching those tears slip down her face, he couldn't bring himself to care. Or to remember they were supposed to be enemies.

CHAPTER FOUR

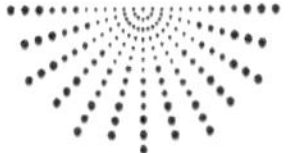

By seven o'clock that evening, the local anesthesia had long since worn off, and Roxie's lip was throbbing. She'd just returned to her mountain of paperwork and mail at the café after sneaking down to the Mullins' party, where she had peeked inside to spy on how things were going.

Based on what she'd seen, Nina had everything under control. While her second-in-command had worked numerous catering events, she had never flown solo. This was the first time Roxie had passed along the baton. The first time she'd trusted delegation. She was learning to let go of her inner control freak. Or trying to, at least.

On one hand, she was thrilled about Nina's success. On the other, she had to admit that her pride was a little dented that everything was going just fine without her. She would never ever admit that to another soul, but it still stung. Apparently, her inner control freak was a fierce bitch.

Dog-tired but not ready to call it a night, she turned on her laptop. It was slow to boot up, so she grabbed a large manila envelope from the pile of junk on her desk. There was no mailing or return address on the front, only her first and last name in tidy block letters. Anticipating some sort of article on Comfort Food, she frowned when she pulled out an eight-by-ten picture. Of herself.

"Huh," she muttered, her frown deepening.

It was an actual photograph, not a clipping from a newspaper or a printout of a magazine article like she'd received countless times before. In the photo, she was dressed in her customary catering uniform—a simple black dress—but she couldn't tell which event it was from.

Her computer prompted her for her password, and she absently put the picture in a file folder labeled, *Add Me To A Scrapbook*. Yet another project for another day. One day, she would get her tiny office organized. One day.

Turning her attention to her laptop, she dove into the bookkeeping work she tended to neglect. After what seemed like an hour of hovering over her computer, she rolled out her aching shoulder and glanced at the clock. She gasped. Eleven? Where the hell had the time gone? She eyed the accounting software on her screen, and her nose wrinkled.

There. Right there. *That* was the giant time-suck.

Alex, who'd joined the Comfort Food staff as a part-time employee when she'd arrived on Hudson Island almost a year ago, had taken over the responsibility of bookkeeping for six glorious months—until the beginning of November, when she'd been hospitalized with an awful case of bronchitis. The bronchitis had progressed into walking pneumonia, and then, before fully recovering, she'd given birth to sweet baby Annie.

A month and a half later, it was no surprise that Alex was still not 100 percent, especially since she now had sleep deprivation to contend with, too. Roxie prayed her friend felt better soon . . . for both their sakes. Alex was much more efficient with the books, hence why it was nearing midnight and she still had at least two more hours of bookkeeping to finish.

You're thirty-four years old. You graduated with a freaking business degree from the University of freaking Washington. You can't let a bunch of numbers beat you!

She slumped down in her chair, leaning her head back with a groan. *Damn.* She couldn't tell if her inner voice was trying to motivate or shame her.

So what if she'd spent more time baking for her study groups and feeding her classmates than actually studying for her exams? She'd still passed all her classes, dammit . . .

But college was a million years ago, so yes . . . maybe a bunch of numbers *would* beat her.

"Problems?"

She jerked, and her heart tried to crawl up her throat. "Holy shit, Eli! You just about gave me a freaking heart attack!"

"Sorry. Your back door was open, so I came in to check on you."

As Eli's face turned red, she willed her heart rate to return to normal. "No worries."

"Everything okay?"

Roxie waved him in and nodded. "I was having a little pity party for myself. Nothing too tragic, though." She gestured to her laptop. "But I swear, even with a business degree, the books on this business are going to be the end of me."

He took a seat on the extra chair on the other side of her desk. "Which business would you be referring to? Comfort Food's brick-and-mortar or the high-in-demand catering?"

"Exactly," she said, flouncing against the back of her seat with a dramatic eye roll for her old friend.

She bit back a frown. *Old friend* was a bit of a stretch. She'd known Eli Walker and his wife, Poppy, who was

Sheila's cousin, for years, but they weren't exactly close. Eli and Poppy owned the building at the end of the block—two down from Comfort Food—which housed both Poppy's gift shop, Rainy Day Boutique, and Eli's real estate office. While Roxie wasn't the best of friends with them, as fellow business owners in a tight-knit community, it was more accurate to say they were friendly business acquaintances.

Roxie had been thirteen when she'd first met Eli, who, like Joe and Quinn, was three years older. He'd been a stereotypical, popular, all-American boy. A class president who'd played both football and baseball. But for some reason, Joe and Quinn had never liked him. So, by default, Roxie had detested him, too. Not because she'd really known him or spoken more than two words to him, but because thirteen-year-old Roxie had accepted the opinions of Joe Buchanan and Quinn O'Conner as certified truths. If they hadn't liked someone, then neither had she.

Ahh, youth.

"I guess I shouldn't be complaining too much, huh?" Pulling her ponytail out set the waves of her hair tumbling around her in a tangled mess. She scrubbed her fingers over her scalp and stifled a yawn. "I have a business—well, two, really—that are doing well. It's crazy that the catering end has taken off as much as it has. I know I should be grateful, but you know what, Eli? I'm not."

She stilled. *Holy shit. Wow.* Exhaustion had her spewing things she'd never say to this man otherwise. She needed to shut. Her. Damn. Mouth.

Sitting up, she pasted a smile on her face that she knew only a select few could see through. Eli was not one of those select few. "But enough about me. How are you doing? How are Poppy and the boys?"

"They're all good. The boys are enjoying their freshman year at UW, and Poppy's all empty-nest crazy." With a chuckle, he rolled his eyes. Then his expression sobered. She was surprised by the concern that filled his gaze. "If you don't mind me saying so, Roxie, I think you work too hard. Have you ever heard of a vacation? Or sleep, for that matter?"

Needing to keep her hands busy, she reached for her mug of now-cold hot chocolate. "What's that saying? 'Sleep is for the meek'?"

He laughed. "'Meek'? Well, that is something you're definitely not." He nodded to the opposite corner of her office. "I see you've managed to cram that horribly uncomfortable-looking . . . thing . . . into your office so you can get at least a little bit of shut-eye. What is that, anyway? A gurney?"

She rolled her eyes. "It's a *futon*. I'll have you know that while it's uglier than sin, it's actually quite comfortable and—"

"Sure, you keep telling yourself that." He grinned. "On a different note, Roxie, you really need to get that lock fixed."

She frowned. "What lock?"

His jaw dropped, and he gestured toward the kitchen. "The lock to your café's back door? You know, the lock I've been telling you to get fixed for the past two weeks? The lock that doesn't actually lock? The lock that works so well that I just walked right in at eleven o'clock at night? The lock—"

"Uncle, okay?" Roxie raised her hands in surrender. "I get it, all right? Good god, you're beginning to sound like Quinn."

"Who's beginning to sound like me?" a deep voice asked from outside her office.

Both of their heads turned and, as if on cue, Quinn walked into her overcrowded office.

Rubbing her temples, she grimaced.

"How's it going, Eli?" Quinn lifted his chin at the other

man, then looked at Roxie, annoyance etched on his face. "What have I told you about that door, Roxie?"

"Oh. My. God." She slumped back into her chair and closed her eyes. "I'm officially in hell. All we need now to make the party complete is for Joe to walk in and start yelling at me."

"You can close your eyes all you want," Quinn said, "but how many times do I have to tell you to get that damn door fixed? It's hanging wide open. Anyone can just waltz on in here and—"

"Okay. Jeez. If I promise to call the locksmith tomorrow, will you please stop nagging me?" It took all her willpower to not bang her head on her desk. She'd truly meant to get the door fixed. But things were so damn hectic, and she kept pushing it to the bottom of her to-do list. If she could only get four more hours added to the day . . .

Eli rose. "I better get going. I'll text you that number for the locksmith tomorrow. Again." He nodded to Quinn. "See you around, Sheriff."

As the back door closed with a loud thud, silence filled the room.

Quinn stared at her.

"Don't go all cop mode on me," she snapped. "What already?"

"What was Eli doing here?"

"I don't know." She yawned. "He stops by every now and then to chat. You know, seeing as he's two doors down."

"Yeah, but at eleven o'clock at night?"

She shrugged. "I don't know. Maybe he was working late."

"Yeah, sure," Quinn said with a snort.

Excuse me? Her eyes widened, and her annoyance turned to anger. "What exactly are you getting at, Quinn?"

"I just find it strange that he's hanging around here at eleven o'clock at night when his business closes at six. And when he has a wife waiting for him at home. I just think that it's—"

"I don't think I like what you're implying, Quinn O'Conner. Not one bit." She rose to her full height—putting her a handful of inches shorter than his six-two—and crossed her arms over her chest. If he was going to insult her, she wasn't going to take it sitting down, dammit. "Need I point out that *you* have a wife and kid waiting for you at home? So what are *you* doing here at eleven o'clock at night? Your little nice-cop routine may work with other people, but it doesn't with me. Just spit out what you're trying to say. And heads-up? If you're implying that I'd mess around with a married man, then you can go straight to—"

"Oh, for fuck's sake, Roxie. Relax, will you? I'm not implying that you're having an affair with him. I'm just saying that you need to be more careful who you let into your store when you're alone."

"I didn't let him in. As you both kindly reminded me, the lock doesn't work, so the back door was open. He came in to check on me. *Only* to check on me. Not for anything else."

He looked at her like she was slow. "Roxie, sweetheart, you're kidding me, right? I know you're not dumb."

Holy. Shit. This man was so freaking frustrating. What the hell was he talking about?

"Spit it out already, O'Conner."

Shaking his head, he moved from the doorway and sat in the chair Eli had vacated. "Let's put it this way: If my sweet, non-violent little wife saw me looking at you the way Eli was looking at you? I can guarantee you Alex would kill me. Or at least cause bodily harm. To a very specific part of my body."

"You've got to be joking. Eli doesn't think of me like that, you moron. He's happily married and—"

"Hey, I'm a guy. Guys can read guys. And I know what *that* guy was thinking."

"You're crazy. Really. We've both known Eli for years, and what you're suggesting is ridiculous. As I said earlier, if we're talking about how strange it is for a married man to be hanging alone with me in the wee hours of the night, then the better question is, what the hell are you doing here?"

He smirked. "I'm the sheriff. I just got off work, and when I passed the alley, I noticed your back door hanging wide open. So, I came over to investigate." He stretched as he rose from his chair. "Now, since I am a public servant doing my civic duty, why don't you reward me with a pie or something?"

"You're so obvious, Quinn," she said, fighting a small smile. She could never stay mad at her friend for long. "Make sure you take a blueberry pie home for Alex, though."

His answering grin was downright blinding. "You don't have to tell me twice."

They walked side by side to the kitchen, Quinn's arm slung over her shoulders.

"Is she feeling any better?" Roxie asked.

He sighed. "She's getting there. Coughing a lot less, but she still gets light-headed if she goes too fast. If the dizziness doesn't ease in the next day or two, I'm going to have Doc come check on her."

Her heart pinched, and she gave her friend a squeeze. "You'd think she'd be feeling okay by now. I'm not gonna lie, Quinn. I'm worried about her."

Stepping out from under his arm, Roxie loaded a bag with two pies, plus a spinach and bacon quiche. She topped the selection off with Alex's favorite, a scalloped potato casserole with ham and gruyere. Food made everything better, right?

"You and me both. The good news is that Annie's sleeping a little longer during the night now, so Alex is getting a little more rest. Hell, we both are." Quinn's gray eyes twinkled.

"That tiny popsicle's the cutest thing ever, but damn if she isn't ten pounds of pure exhaustion."

Roxie bit back a sappy "Awww!" and chucked Quinn under the chin. "I thought marriage looked good on you, but you know what? Fatherhood looks even better."

"Thanks. It feels good, too." He grabbed the bag of food. "And thanks for these. You heading out with me?"

She shook her head. "I have a little more paperwork to do, but give Alex and Annie a snuggle for me, okay?"

"Oh, I'm planning on giving Alex more than a snuggle." He wagged his eyebrows and broke into an ear-to-ear grin.

She shuddered. "Gross, dude. Gross."

Quinn laughed, then nodded toward her office. "Promise me you'll stop working too hard?"

She raised an eyebrow.

"Fine. At least *try* to stop working so hard." He opened the back door and smacked a kiss on her forehead. "Lock up, okay? Make sure the damn thing latches."

"You're nagging again," she sang, shooing him out the door.

He paused to look at her over his shoulder. "Oh, and Roxie? You're going to have to explain to me again why you have a hospital bed in your office. Lock up."

With a final wave, she shut the door, making sure it actually locked behind him. She settled into her office chair and scanned the piles of paper on her cluttered desk. Her gaze moved to the futon across the small room, and she frowned.

Yes, she tended to work long hours and often didn't have the energy or desire to make the trek home, so it had made sense to move a futon into her office. After all, unlike Quinn, she didn't have anyone waiting for her at home, so it didn't really matter where she slept.

Her frown deepened as the tiniest hints of jealousy stirred in her gut.

Quinn had Alex and Annie and would possibly have even more kids down the road. She knew his wife and daughter were his focus, as they should be. She didn't begrudge Quinn's happiness. Not at all. If anything, she was thrilled he'd found Alex.

She hadn't been lying to him earlier. There was a sparkle in his eye that no mere friend would have been able to give him. It was all Alex and Annie. But it left her a little lonely. Which was completely selfish and petty on her part because his priority should be his family. Not his friend and neighbor.

But it still made her a little sad. For as long as she could remember, there'd been two people in her life who had always made her feel special. Joe and Quinn. Well, three. Doc Buchanan had always been there for her too. Even more than her parents. Not that her folks had been abusive or awful. They'd simply been caught up in their own thing. She'd been a needy child, and they hadn't understood her desire for attention. They'd provided for her. She'd had every toy and gadget she'd wanted, but they just hadn't been around much—

Oh my god. What are you doing?

Roxie slumped down in her chair. She was throwing a pity party for herself. That's what she was doing. Rubbing her eyes, she let out a frustrated growl.

Focus, Roxie. Focus on work.

With another giant sigh, she brought up the bookkeeping software on her computer. Working herself to exhaustion may not be the wisest or healthiest of choices, but it was all she had right now. If she wasn't going to be smart, at least she could be productive.

CHAPTER FIVE

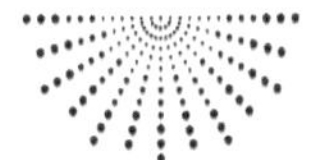

After the trip to Doc's to get her lip stitched up yesterday, by some stroke of luck, Roxie had managed to dodge her new housemate. It didn't hurt that she hadn't left Comfort Food and the evil bookkeeping until after midnight. When she'd woken up this morning, she was determined to repeat her success. Unfortunately, the sounds of Joe rummaging around in the kitchen threw a wrench in her plans. What he was doing awake at such an ungodly hour, she had no clue.

So, like the mature woman she was, she snuck out for a run.

Then again, was it really sneaking out if she ran at the same time almost every morning? Sure, she'd left before her morning coffee, which she never did, but that was a mere coincidence. Yeah. That was it.

Roxie deflated. She'd always been a crappy liar. Even when trying to lie to herself.

So yes, she'd snuck out before Joe could see her. Because she wasn't prepared to face him yet.

Her face flamed in mortification as she remembered the

way she'd cried like the little crybaby he'd accused her of being. The worst part was how he had tried to make her feel better after seeing her tears. He'd even held her hand, for god's sake.

It had been like salt in the wound.

She hated thinking about how it used to be between them. They'd been best friends their entire freaking lives. Then, in the blink of an eye, he'd turned into Jackass Joe and cast her as public enemy number one. She still didn't know why. It was a question that had plagued her for years.

But as much as she despised Jackass Joe, she was beginning to despise Nice Joe even more.

Jackass Joe was cruel, but she always knew what to expect from him. She could brace herself and spit fire right back. Nice Joe, however, cut straight through her defenses like a knife through warm butter. He ignited a little spark of hope in her chest, one that told her they could possibly find their way back to before. To their friendship. That hope made her vulnerable. Then, without fail, when she gave in and allowed that spark to grow, Nice Joe disappeared, taking all the light with him.

It was soul-crushing.

Every. Single. Time.

She closed her eyes and breathed in the salty sea air to clear her mind. Instead, memories from that day—when everything had gone to hell with Joe—invaded her thoughts.

Roxie turned just as the door to Monty's Tavern opened. She barely held back a whoop of joy when Joe entered. God, she'd missed him. It had been too damn long since they'd all been together. Calling out his name, she waved him over.

Joe's blue eyes lit up and there was a lightness to his expression that had her heart smiling. On her next heartbeat, though, it was gone. Her stomach pitched when anger, unlike any she'd seen on him before, contorted his face.

"I thought you said he wasn't showing up until later?" Paul asked from beside her, startling her.

Roxie swung her gaze to her boyfriend. Confusion had her frowning. Why did Paul sound so put out? And what the hell was going on with Joe?

Before she could make heads or tails of anything, Joe approached. Before she could take her next breath, Joe's fist smashed into Paul's face.

Surprise had her jumping from her seat.

Paul tumbled from his barstool, and Joe loomed over him. Going down to one knee, his fist flew at Paul again. The thunk of flesh hitting flesh reverberated through the bar.

Then it was chairs scraping on the tiled floor, people shouting, glass breaking. It was fast and slow, all at once. Madness. Chaos. Mayhem.

"Stop!" she cried, not knowing who to run to the aid of. Her boyfriend or her best friend.

Quinn yanked Joe up and off Paul, and she gasped. Paul's face was a bloody mess, his nose obviously broken. She moved toward him but froze when Joe turned his fury on her.

"Fucking whore! How could you? You goddamn slut!"

Joe's words were like a punch to her gut. He shouted more vile insults, but they were a blur. The only thing that was clear was the anger, the devastation, the fury that colored her best friend's face. It stopped her cold because it was all aimed at her.

Quinn hauled Joe out of Monty's, and she could only stare after them.

Dread. Shock. Confusion. Heartbreak. All warred within her.

A tear slipped down her face, and she didn't bother wiping it away. She stole a glance at Paul, who was being helped to his feet, then at the door Quinn and Joe had disappeared through. Her chest squeezed tight and panic began to simmer in her gut.

What just happened?

A rustle from the trees pulled Roxie from her memories.

She stumbled on a root but caught herself. *Holy crap, focus!* Letting out a loud exhale, she picked up her pace, concentrating on the path before her so she wouldn't faceplant. A sheen of sweat dotted her brow despite the frigid January breeze cutting through her neon-green jacket.

She was well into one of her usual morning runs—a four-mile out-and-back from her house to Fort Ripley State Park. This route was one of her favorites. The dirt trail wove back and forth, into the forest and then out along the bluff overlooking Puget Sound. The sun was still a couple of hours away from rising, making it difficult to see the water and trees on either side of the path. Still, she could hear the waves crashing below, and the crisp scent of the forest filled her nose.

Between her busy baker's schedule and her hectic to-do list, these three-in-the-morning runs were her only quiet moments. The solitude gave her a chance to be mindful, set her day, and just breathe. Unfortunately, today's run was doing little to clear her mind. But as she put one foot in front of the other, she pushed those awful memories away.

A side stitch had her slowing. She walked a few more paces, then pulled her water bottle from her running belt. Taking a long gulp, she patted herself on the back for keeping to the state park's service road. She could have picked the trail that cut deeper through the woods, but this early in the morning, with the thick canopy and the lackluster moonlight, she would have struggled to remain upright on the uneven ground.

As Roxie brought the bottle back to her mouth, she scanned the horizon. Familiar lights twinkled in the distance. Her eyes widened; she choked on her sip. Water dribbled down her chin, and she swiped it away with her sleeve.

Hudson Island was shaped like the number seven. The downtown and main residential area were located at the southern end of the island. Fort Ripley State Park ran up the middle, along the western coast. And those twinkling lights? They belonged to the Pacific View Resort, located at the island's northwestern tip.

If she could see the lights, then she had gone a full two miles farther than she'd intended. Her four-mile run had just turned into eight miles. *Damn.* It looked like she'd be getting into work closer to five, almost an hour later than usual. At least the extra distance would earn her a guilt-free splurge on a giant slice of pie and a bigger pour of wine tonight.

Roxie sent a quick text to June, who was one of her part-time employees, to let her know she was running late. Literally. Then, with a groan, she redid her ponytail and set off for home. As her feet slapped against the dirt road, she tried not to think about everything that needed to be done. But how could she not?

She'd opened Comfort Food six years earlier with a simple dream of serving delicious treats to both locals and tourists in a cozy setting. In those early days, she'd never imagined adding a catering branch, but five years into business, it had seemed like a good way to give her café more exposure and pick up some extra income.

To say the endeavor had been an instant hit would be an understatement. The amount of demand she'd received from the get-go had taken her by complete surprise. She'd hoped her catering business would be successful; she just hadn't let herself believe it. But with success came growing pains. And stress. Never-ending stress.

So, while she was grateful to see her hard work and sleepless nights pay off, she was drained. The hustle never let up. It only intensified as her business expanded. If she was going to make it all work—which she was determined to do—then she needed to hire another person or two. She was already asking a lot of her small staff. Probably too much.

But there simply weren't enough hours in the day to figure it all out.

For now, she'd make do with her one full-time employee, Nina, and two part-time employees, June and Sheila. She would have had two more part-timers, but Ella, June's daughter, had moved away to Seattle for college over the summer, and Alex was on indefinite maternity leave. Once Alex returned, everyone's load would be a little lighter. Until then, Roxie was barely keeping her head above water. She was sure her team felt the same.

She hadn't been lying to Jeremy when she'd said she didn't have the time or energy to go out with him. She didn't. Comfort Food was open seven days a week, from six in the morning to two in the afternoon—except Sundays, when they closed at eleven—and the catering side required around-the-clock attention. Granted, she didn't *want* to go out with him either, but that was an entirely different discussion.

Her body was running on fumes. Her brain was turning to mush. If something didn't give soon . . . well, she didn't know what would happen. But it wouldn't be pretty.

Usually, when life overwhelmed her—which, unfortunately, happened more than she wanted—she'd schedule an official Sunday Vegetation Day. Or, technically, a Sunday Vegetation Afternoon/Evening. She was a small business owner, after all, and there were people depending on her.

When the pre-determined Sunday arrived, she'd head home from the café after closing, lock her front door, turn off her phone, throw on yoga pants and a ratty sweatshirt, and park herself on the couch with the remote control, a pie, and a spoon. Then she'd veg. A Lifetime movie marathon with a delicious dessert always made her feel better.

But now she had a housemate, and there was no point in

throwing a pity party if there were other people around to witness your misery.

Ugh. Jackass Joe. She picked up her pace. Nothing like a little aggravation to improve her running time.

Hopefully, he wouldn't be in town for very long. She could always hide out in her office when she needed a break. She generally tried to avoid burying her head in the sand, but where Joe Buchanan was concerned, she lost all pride.

Four miles later, she jogged up the front steps of the Buchanan house and checked the time on her phone. Four twenty-two. If she hustled, she'd be showered and at the café by four forty-five. Not too shabby. Good thing it was a Thursday morning. Midweek customers were usually just locals.

After a quick stretch on the porch, Roxie plowed through the front door and came to an abrupt halt. She removed her earbuds.

Joe was blocking her way. His lips were drawn in a tight line, and his jaw muscles twitched. With his arms crossed over his chest, anger radiated from him.

It took every ounce of energy she had left to not roll her eyes. Apparently, luck was not on her schedule this morning after all.

Sure, the mere thought of Joe this morning had improved her running time, but it was way too early to actually converse with the man. Especially when he was in a pissy mood. She wracked her brain for a snarky comment about dealing with assholes before coffee, but—

"Where the hell have you been, Roxanne?"

Her right eyebrow arched in question, and irritation heated her already flushed face. Did the jackass have a death wish this morning? *Bring it, buddy.*

She slapped her hands on her hips, striking her best fuck-you pose. "Considering I'm wearing running clothes and all sweaty, I'd take a wild guess and say I was out baking cookies."

His eyes narrowed. She could have sworn he growled.

Her chin lifted.

"What the hell do you think you're doing? You can't just prance around the island by yourself in the dead of the night."

Roxie saw red. She'd always thought it was just an expression. But it wasn't. She literally saw red. And she wanted nothing more than to bash his stupid head in.

She jabbed her finger into his chest. Hard. "I *run*, jackass. I don't *prance*. I'm a grown woman and can take care of myself. Who the fuck do you think you are? You have absolutely zero say in what I do."

He grabbed her finger when she jabbed him again. "I do have a say if your stubbornness and stupidity puts your safety in jeopardy."

Yanking her finger out of his grasp, she smacked her hands on his chest and shoved.

The damn bastard didn't budge.

"Fuck you, Joe. I'm not stupid. And you gave up all rights to say anything to me the moment you decided to turn into the world's biggest asshole. That was your choice. Not mine. You don't get to be an asshole *and* concerned about me at the same time. It doesn't work that way."

Releasing a deep breath, he took a few steps back. "Dammit, Rox, I wasn't calling you stupid."

She stalked toward him and punched him in the stomach as hard as she could. If she weren't so pissed, a satisfied grin would have spread across her face when he winced. But she was pissed. Beyond pissed.

She spun on her heels and raced up the stairs, ignoring his calls after her. She didn't have time for this.

The jackass was now two-for-two in consecutive mornings he'd managed to ruin for her. Bastard.

A few hours after the fiasco with Roxie, Joe climbed the back steps to Quinn and Alex's house, which was conveniently next door to his. He hadn't texted to see if they were home; Annie's sharp cries, which he'd heard clear across the yard, were answer enough.

Peering through the kitchen window, he spied Alex standing with her back to him. He gently knocked on the door, trying not to startle her. She spun around, an unhappy, red-faced baby in her arms, and motioned him inside.

When he opened the door, the volume of the little one's shrill crying increased tenfold. Each wail was like a lightning strike to his eardrums. The urge to retreat was overpowering, but before he could take a step in either direction, Alex thrust the screaming baby into his arms.

His stomach knotted, and he froze.

Firing deadly weapons? He could handle that. Going undercover to infiltrate a circle of dirty politicians? No problem. Hand-to-hand combat? Bring it.

A tiny, shrieking baby? *Holy fuck.*

For the life of him, he couldn't remember the last time he'd held a baby.

Annie's howling intensified, and he adjusted his awkward hold on her. Supporting her itty-bitty body with his forearm, he rested her delicate head against the crook of his elbow and tucked her close to his chest.

To his absolute shock, Annie's fury dissolved into soft hiccups. Which, if he weren't so damn panicked, he'd acknowledge was the cutest fucking thing ever.

"Alex," he whispered, not bothering to hide the desperation in his voice, "are you sure I should be holding her? I don't know what the hell I'm doing."

She laughed and gave him a hug, squishing the baby between them. "Joe, meet Annie Rosalie O'Conner." Stepping back, she beamed at her baby and tickled her chubby chin. "Annie, sweetie, meet Uncle Joe."

"Alex," he whispered again. "Seriously, you—"

"You don't have to whisper. It's good for you to talk in your normal voice. She needs to get used to it. And yes, you should definitely be holding her. The little terror has been crying for the last forty-five freaking minutes. I need a break."

"But, Alex—"

"You're fine, Joe. Just keep holding her like that. If you move her into a different position, her head is still wobbly, so make sure you support it. I'm going to run upstairs real quick and change."

Alex disappeared before he could protest.

Glancing down at the little, chunky bundle in his arms, he let out a nervous breath. He could do this. Right?

"Hey there, sweet girl," he cooed. She let out a giant yawn, and he couldn't stop the smile that spread across his face. Okay, now *that* was the cutest fucking thing ever. "Aren't you just the most perfect little angel?"

Annie gazed up at him with her mama's big brown eyes, and her cute, pouty mouth transformed into a toothless grin. Just like that, in the span of one heartbeat, he fell in love with his perfect little niece.

Sure, technically, they weren't related. But Annie didn't share DNA with his best friend, either. Blood didn't make family. Quinn was—and would always be—her dad in every way that mattered. Annie was one lucky girl. Especially since she would never have to know her sperm donor, who was now rotting in hell.

Alex's ex-husband, Preston Woodsworth III, was Annie's biological father. Joe had met the crooked piece of shit while working undercover to investigate the bastard's white-collar crimes. That was how Joe and Alex had met, how he'd learned about the abuse she'd been suffering. He'd ended up saving Alex's life and sending her to Hudson Island for a fresh start. Clearly, she'd made the most of the opportunity.

"She likes you," Alex said, walking back into the kitchen.

He shook his head. Awe and amazement filled every inch of him. "I can't believe this perfect little girl . . . came from you."

"Uh, excuse me, buster, but what are you saying?" Alex asked, her tone playful. "That I couldn't produce such a perfect child because I'm somehow deficient?"

His eyes widened as he replayed his words in his head. Holy shit, he was an idiot. Looked like saying the wrong thing wasn't limited to his interactions with Roxie. "Sorry, that came out wrong."

Alex chuckled at his blunder, and the worry in him eased. He took a moment to memorize Annie's sleepy face.

"She's perfect, Alex," he said reverently, glancing over at his friend. "Truly. And you and Quinn are *parents*. I can't find the words, but . . . it's perfect. You, Quinn, and Annie. It's so damn right, you know?"

His chest clenched when Alex's eyes filled with tears.

"Sorry," she sniffed. Taking a seat at the kitchen table, she wiped away a tear. "Hormones. But you know the great thing, Joe? It *feels* right, too. It really does."

"You happy?"

Her eyes welled again, but the grin that lit up her face was radiant. "More than I thought possible. Now, what brings you over?"

"Can't I come and say hi to my two favorite girls?"

"Sure." Alex pursed her lips, and a different kind of worry

bloomed in his gut. "But Annie's five weeks old. Do you know what that means?"

By the look in her eyes, it meant nothing good. For him, anyway. Knowing it was the wisest option, he kept his trap shut and waited.

"It means I'm awake all the freaking time. Which also means I saw Roxie storm out of your place this morning, more pissed off than I've ever seen her. And I've seen her pissed a lot. So, what did you do, Joe?"

"Why does it have to be my fault?" Dumb question, but he still had to try.

Alex's brows arched. He wasn't fooling her.

Looking down at Annie, he continued to sway. After his blow-up with Roxie, he'd needed to see a friendly face. He'd hoped to find a sympathetic ear, too, but from the way Alex was glaring at him, that wasn't going to happen.

"Rox and I got into an argument this morning. I simply asked her where the hell she'd gone so early." He shrugged. "Honestly, Alex, I'm not quite sure how the conversation went to hell so quickly."

Her jaw dropped, and she looked at him like he was a complete idiot. "Really? I'd say asking 'where the hell she'd gone' was when the descent to hell began. Then, when you called her *stupid*—"

His eyes narrowed. How did she know about that?

Alex crossed her arms. "We text."

Frustrated, he ran his free hand through his hair. "Alex, she left at three in the freaking morning and was gone for over an hour. I was worried. And I didn't call *her* stupid. I called her *actions* stupid."

She shook her head, a look of disbelief on her face. "I'm not even going to roll my eyes right now because they may actually fall out of my head." She let out a big sigh. One that sounded suspiciously like she was striving for patience.

"Roxie always runs at three in the morning. Comfort Food opens at six, and she's there at four to get things going. The woman works super crazy hours, so that's the only time she can fit in a run. And your 'stupid' comment? Sorry, but it's potato, potahto on that one. And you know it."

Fine. She had a point. He was a fucking idiot.

"What were you doing up that early, anyway?" Alex asked, tilting her head in question.

"Jet lag. I'm still on east coast time." He held Annie closer, hoping her cuteness would chase away his lingering worry—his panic—over Roxie's safety. "My point is that she shouldn't be running by herself. Especially at that hour. Alex, you know her. The woman doesn't pay attention to her surroundings. She even had her earphones in and music blasting. She wouldn't be able to hear an approaching car or person or anything. Yeah, she had a bright jacket on, but the rest of her clothes were all black. It's just not safe for her to be out there. In the dark. By herself."

He knew he was right about this, so he didn't understand why Alex looked so exasperated. He tried not to squirm under her gaze.

"Why didn't you just say that?" she asked, throwing her hands up. "Your concern makes sense. Your execution, however, could use some help."

"I know." He scrubbed his free hand over his face, making sure not to jostle Annie. "I swear, I meant to have a normal, civilized conversation with her. Over coffee, even. But I took one look at her pulling her earbuds out like she didn't have a damn care in the world and got so irritated. It seems like everything she does pisses me off."

Everything he did pissed him off, too. Because Roxie had been right. He was the one who'd started their war all those years ago. He was the one who kept it going. He treated her like shit. Because in some ways, it was easier if she hated him.

When she was constantly mad and spitting nails at him, he stayed on his toes. Her wrath distracted him from the ache that had been simmering in his gut these past few years. It also overpowered the pain of what he'd witnessed eight months ago: Roxie broken and bleeding, a gun pressed to her head.

Their constant bickering drowned out how he'd failed her. How he'd hurt her. How he was *still* failing and hurting her.

Fuck.

He cleared his throat, desperate for a topic change. "Quinn mentioned you've been sick. That's why I wanted to come by. How are you feeling?"

"I'm fine," she said with a wave of her hand. He could tell she wanted to say more about Roxie but was biting her tongue. Thank god. "Quinn worries too much. The better question is, how are *you* doing? Are you okay?"

His forehead knit in confusion. "I'm fine. Rox is the one you should be concerned about. She's got the bruises and stitched-up lip." And he'd never forgive himself for any of it.

"It's just bruises, Joe," Alex said. He opened his mouth to object, so she hurried on. "Trust me, I know Roxie will be fine. She and I talked yesterday, and she knows there was nothing malicious about you hitting her. Even though you can be a complete asshole to her, she knows you'd never intentionally hurt her. Physically, anyway."

Ouch. Her jab landed. He opened his mouth to defend himself, but something in Alex's expression warned him to shut up.

"What? Are you going to stand there and deny that you constantly act like a world-class ass with her?"

No. He couldn't. What had Roxie called him? Oh yes—the world's biggest asshole.

He nodded in concession. "Go on. I feel like there's more you want to say. Lay it on me."

"Roxie will be fine. Her bruises will heal, and she won't give that incident any more thought. But I'm worried about you."

He scoffed. "Me?"

"Yes, you. I know you, Joe Buchanan. You and Quinn are like two peas in a pod. I know you feel guilty about what happened. I also know that you're not going to talk about it. You'll sit there and stew in your own guilt. It's going to eat you up inside."

"Alex, have you seen Roxie? Up close?"

She shook her head.

"I punched her in the face, Alex. I didn't hold anything back." His stomach clenched as self-disgust rolled through him. "I *should* feel guilty. When I think about what could have happened if I hadn't recognized her . . ."

"That's exactly why I'm worried about you. It was an accident. This wasn't your fault."

Yes, it was 1,000 percent his fault. Accident or not, his fist had hit Roxie's face. "Don't worry about me, Alex. I'll stew for a little bit, then things will be back to normal."

"Great," she huffed. "Does that mean you'll revert back to being an asshole every time you're around her? Because don't." She leveled him with a serious look that had his Spidey-senses twitching. "Seriously, Joe. Don't. You never heard me say this, but I don't think Roxie can handle that right now."

His brow furrowed. He didn't understand what Alex was getting at. Roxie could handle anything. Especially his asshole tendencies. She fucking excelled at taking his shit and flinging it right back at him. She was the master of snark.

"Clarify that last comment. Please."

She fiddled with the coffee mug in front of her. "Roxie's been different ever since . . ."

His stomach took a dive as her whiskey-brown eyes filled with concern. He waited, but she remained silent.

"Ever since?" he prompted.

"That night with Preston. When he took her captive." Alex's shoulders slumped, as if she were a balloon that had been pricked with a pin.

Joe scanned the kitchen and spied a portable crib at the end of the dining table. Carefully, he placed the baby down, thankful when she remained asleep. Once Annie was settled, he sat next to Alex and placed an arm around her slim shoulders, hugging her close.

"Remember that lecture you just gave me about guilt? Well, right back at you, doll. It wasn't your fault Woodsworth hurt her."

It was his.

Roxie had suffered a dislocated and fractured shoulder, a concussion, and god knew what other mental traumas. Yes, Woodsworth had inflicted the damage, but the fault lay at Joe's feet.

He was the one who'd yelled at Roxie, who'd caused her to run away from their safe and secure location. And when Roxie had been alone—because of *him*, because he'd been a raging asshole—Woodsworth had taken her hostage in exchange for Alex.

Reading his thoughts, Alex placed her hand atop his and squeezed. "It wasn't your fault, either." She sighed. "But ever since that night, Roxie hasn't been the same. She moved out of Quinn's guest house, claiming she wanted to give me and Quinn privacy. She's a horrible liar, so I know that was crap, but she wouldn't tell me the real reason. She moved in with her folks, but that lasted less than a week. They sold the house and—"

His brows shot up. "What? The Jamesons sold their house?"

"Yup. The house was snapped up within a few days, and they hopped in their RV and hit the road." Alex frowned. "Quinn and I both thought the timing was strange. Roxie had just gotten out of the hospital and her arm was still in a sling. She wasn't incapable of doing stuff for herself because, well, she's Roxie, but she still needed help, and her parents just took off, leaving her with no place to live. We offered her the guest house again, but she declined. That's why your dad rented the house to her."

Joe's stomach soured. He'd read the full report on what had gone down with Woodsworth that night. He also knew it wasn't public information that the fucker had hidden out in Roxie's place. It was there where he'd ambushed her and taken her captive. Helpless rage coursed through him knowing that she'd been alone with that fucker for close to twenty minutes. So it made sense why she'd declined Alex and Quinn's offer to move back into the guest house.

His eyes narrowed. "Wait, she's been living at my place this whole time?" According to the report, Woodsworth had ended up dragging Roxie from her place to Joe's. Surely, there were lingering memories for her at his place too.

Alex nodded. "Your dad asked her to move in as a favor to him."

"A favor to him?" His brows rose in question.

"Doc knew she needed a place to live, and he claimed he didn't have time to deal with the house repairs after all the damage Preston caused. He asked her to keep an eye on things. I think overseeing the renovation of your place was therapeutic for her. After what happened, I think seeing the whole kitchen gutted was good for her." Alex shrugged. "I'm pretty sure that was a big reason why Doc offered up the place."

Joe nodded. "Yeah, that sounds like Dad."

Alex grinned. "Of course, Doc didn't say that to her. Since he knows Roxie has a hard time accepting help—"

"Understatement of the year," he scoffed.

"—your dad framed it as her helping him out."

A matching grin grew on Joe's face. "Dad's pretty slick."

"*That's* the understatement of the year," she said, chuckling. "Roxie has no idea she's been played. But I'm so thankful she's next door."

"Then why are you so worried about her? It sounds like the move was good for her."

Alex fiddled with her coffee mug again, seeming to search for the right words. "Her excuse of moving to give us privacy is just one clue that there's a problem. Obviously, you know she's a workaholic. Well, take that workaholic you remember and amplify it tenfold. She's also holding back. You know how she would always tell you how she was feeling whether you wanted to know or not? How she'd just talk your ear off if you gave her the chance?"

Good god, yes. Roxie could talk for hours. Hours. For as long as he could remember, she'd always wanted to have deep, *meaningful* talks about emotions and feelings and crap like that.

"She doesn't do that anymore, Joe."

His jaw dropped, and his eyes grew wide. "Really?"

"I know, right? Sure, she'll still talk, but it's about inconsequential things. Catering orders or work or the stupid bits from the gossip mill. She barely talks about herself anymore and never ever about her feelings."

Had hell frozen over without his knowledge? Roxie *always* circled the conversation back to her life and her feelings. That self-centeredness was one of his guaranteed, sure-fire insults he could fall back on when he needed to throw her one last quip.

Joe scowled. How had he not noticed a damn thing?

Because he'd been the asshole who'd barely bothered talking with her since getting back. Because he'd been making every damn thing about him. *Ironic.*

"Oh, I have an idea!" Alex's expression brightened. Hell, she was practically glowing. He could see why Quinn had fallen for this little spitfire of a woman. "Roxie's always complaining about being a third wheel to me and Quinn, but you're here now."

He grimaced, not sure he liked the turn this conversation had taken. "Okay . . ."

"Swing by the shop and tell her you guys are having dinner with me and Quinn tonight. Like a 'Welcome home, Joe!' dinner."

He snorted. "That's the best you've got?"

"You're right." Alex tapped her chin in thought. "If anything, that would make her boycott our house for the entire evening, huh?"

"Ouch. Thanks for that." It was true, though.

She ignored him. "I know! Tell her I have an announcement to make."

"What's the announcement?"

Again, Alex looked at him like he was slow. "There is no announcement, Joe. It's the excuse we're using to get Roxie over for dinner so she can sit down for once and not work herself to death. Got it?"

Damn. Maybe he was slow after all.

CHAPTER SIX

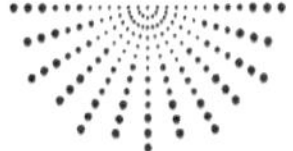

Given the terrible morning she'd had, Roxie expected the rest of her day to follow suit. Because that's how it always worked, right? One thing led to another until you were stuck in a giant debacle of crap gone wrong. But the hours passed by without drama, and soon, only thirty minutes remained until closing time.

While she still had a couple hours of paperwork ahead of her, there were no catering events to worry about tonight. She was looking forward to a nice, quiet evening alone in her office with the pie and wine she'd promised herself.

Comfort Food's front door opened, and Joe sauntered inside. Her mood plummeted.

Sheila and Nina were standing at the counter beside her. Both of them tittered, and Sheila puffed up her ample chest. Roxie ground her back teeth together.

Tucking his thumbs into the pockets of his well-worn jeans, Joe approached the three women with that half-grin, half-smirk playing on his face. His black sweater fit snugly over his broad—

Wait. Why the hell did she care what he was wearing?

Clothes, Roxie. They're just freaking clothes, and he's just Joe. Obnoxious, annoying, condescending Joe.

She sighed in time with Sheila and Nina, but while they were smitten, she was frustrated. Because Joe was only obnoxious, annoying, and condescending to *her*. To everyone else, he was magnetic and kind.

She shouldn't care. But she did. And she needed to figure out how to stop.

While her employees swooned over Joe, Roxie ignored them all. Grabbing the stack of mail she'd just retrieved, she headed back to her office. Once seated at her desk, she busied herself with the pile. Bills, bills, junk mail, and more bills.

A plain white envelope gave her pause. Her full name was inscribed on the front in neat handwritten letters. There was no return address, no mailing address, no postage. Only her name. Just like the envelope from a few days ago.

She tore the top open, and a lone picture fluttered to her desk, face down. The fine hairs on her arms rose.

Oh, for god's sake, Roxie, it's just a damn picture.

Despite her internal pep talk, she forgot how to breathe as she turned it over.

Objectively, it was a really pretty photo of her. It could have been an advertisement for outdoorsy activewear: black running pants, a neon-green half-zip jacket, and a running belt locked around her waist. She stood off the side of a dirt road, illuminated by the moonlight, her body in profile as she looked out over the horizon. The twinkling lights of the Pacific View Resort cast a magical glow in the background.

Her brain finally connected the dots. Bile rose in her throat.

Setting both elbows on her desk, she dropped her face into her trembling hands.

The picture was from this morning's run.

Alarm bells blared like sirens in Joe's head as he watched the color seep from Roxie's face. His stomach clenched when she dropped her head into her hands, her slim shoulders shaking.

"Rox?" he said quietly, not wanting to startle her.

She almost jumped out of her seat. "Holy shit, Joe! You gave me a freaking heart attack!"

She flipped over the picture she'd been staring at, and a chill crawled up his spine.

"What's that?" he asked, sitting in the tiny office's guest chair.

"Nothing," she replied quickly.

Too quickly.

He could be a patient man when he wanted, and his gut was screaming for him to be that man now. Leaning back in the chair, he crossed an ankle over his knee. "Baby, I can sit here all day and wait for you to tell me what's got you spooked."

"I'm not spooked. And don't call me baby." She glared at him. "Don't you need to go flirt with Sheila or Nina or someone else with boobs?"

A chuckle escaped him, but there was no humor in it. He kept his tone light as he said, "It warms my heart that you care, *baby*."

Annoyance flashed in her emerald eyes, replacing the fear. Just as he'd intended. He'd take her annoyance over fear every day of the damn week. And that's what had been in her eyes moments earlier: fear.

She huffed and rearranged the papers on her desk. "Of course I don't care, you idiot."

He knew a stall tactic when he saw one. "Rox? The picture?"

"I said it's nothing."

That squirrelly feeling returned to his gut. "Then why are you as pale as a ghost?"

She lifted her chin. "Don't be ridiculous, Joe. I'm not scared."

No matter how much time had passed, he knew Roxie. And her eyes were telling another story.

"I never said you were."

"It's just a stupid picture." Her gaze was everywhere but on him. "You don't know what you're talk—"

He leaned forward and placed a finger over her lips. Enough was enough. "Please, Roxanne. Tell me what's wrong."

He didn't think it was possible, but her face went even paler. With an audible gulp, she drew away from his touch and took a deep breath. As she let it out, she flipped over the picture and turned it so he could see.

He stared at it for a moment, not understanding why Roxie had reacted so badly. It was a beautiful photo of her. She looked strong, sporty, and fucking gorgeous.

Then it clicked. His blood chilled.

She fiddled with a stapler, staring at it intently. He waited. After a minute, she picked up her head and met his gaze. His heart squeezed at the confusion and terror on her face.

He already knew the answer, but he had to ask. "Is that from this morning?"

At her slight nod, trepidation avalanched over him.

"Did you see anyone on your run this morning?"

She shook her head.

"Was there a note that came with it? A return address on the envelope?"

"Neither," she said, showing him the plain envelope. "Look, it's probably nothing. I'm tired, and I'm probably blowing things out of proportion. Like usual. Making it all about me like I always do, right?"

His default accusation echoed in his head. *Everything always has to be about you, huh, Roxanne?*

Joe cringed. He really was an asshole.

"I mean, really, Joe, it's just a picture. A flattering one, actually. I'm sure whoever sent it was just being nice."

Right. With no return address, no note, no nothing. A picture that had been taken before the ass crack of dawn. In the dark. Without her knowledge.

He could see that while she was talking a big game, even she wasn't buying her bullshit.

Restless, he rose. "Let's go."

"Excuse me?"

"I said, let's go." He motioned toward the door. "Now."

Her eyebrows shot up, and she crossed her arms in indignation.

Fuck. What was it that Alex had told him earlier? Oh yes, his execution sucked.

Fine. He could play nice, dammit.

He looked up at the ceiling and counted to ten. Then, flashing her his sweetest grin, he said, "Roxanne, baby? Will you please close up shop and come with me? I promised Alex that we'd be over for dinner tonight."

She rolled her eyes. "It's two o'clock, Joe. Try again."

The corner of his lips twitched. "I swear, Alex does want us over for dinner. Apparently, she has some big announcement to make." That caught Roxie's attention. Score one point for Alex. "Also, before we head over there, I want to swing by Quinn's office. I know he has a meeting at three, and I need you to show him that picture. Maybe he has some ideas about what's going on."

"Fine." She stood and began gathering her things, heaving out a dramatic sigh.

He bit back a smile because that dramatic sigh? *That* was the Roxie he knew and lov—

Whoa, Buchanan. What the fuck?

Storming past him, she grumbled, "And stop calling me baby."

As much as he tried, he couldn't help the chuckle that escaped. Holy shit, this woman. She had him not knowing which way was up.

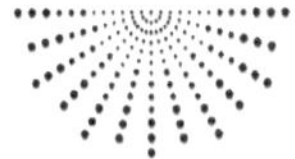

Roxie shot a save-me look at Alex in the hope that her friend would rescue her from Quinn's interrogation. God help the people of Hudson Island should they ever be on the wrong side of the law.

She rose from the table to pace the length of the O'Conners' kitchen. "Enough with the twenty questions already, Quinn. Didn't we already go over all this at your office?"

Frustration had the groove between his brows popping. "This isn't a game, Roxie."

"I know that," she snapped. Jerking to a halt, she took in a deep breath. The fact that Quinn was concerned made her even more scared. She didn't need to be more scared right now. "I don't know what else to tell you. The picture came in today's mail without any hints as to who the sender was."

"You're sure it was taken this morning?"

She nodded, and her stomach twisted. "I haven't run out to that lookout spot in a long time." God, how she wished that wasn't the case. But there was no doubt. "And my running jacket's new. I got it last week."

Fighting a shiver, she stole a glance at the kitchen table.

Three worried faces looked back. Well, Alex's face was worried. Quinn and Joe had their somber law-enforcement-officer masks on. The last thing she wanted right now was to be the center of their attention. Oh, what she would give to be baby Annie, tucked away asleep upstairs.

"Look, Quinn, like I told you and Joe earlier, it's probably nothing." She really, *really* hoped it was nothing. But something deep in her gut told her otherwise. Her gut had been wrong before, though, so she was holding out hope, dammit. "Besides, there's nothing we can do about it. I don't know who sent it."

"Sweetie," Alex said, "have you broken up with anyone recently?"

Roxie shook her head. Yeah, right. That would imply that she had a social life.

"What about Eli?" Quinn asked.

Her eyes narrowed. He did *not* just say that. "What about Eli?"

Quinn shrugged. "Eli's been sniffing around you for a while now."

Heat washed over her face, and her jaw dropped. She dug her nails into her palms to prevent herself from socking the man. "Eli's not interested in me like that, Quinn. I've said it once already, and I won't say it again. The guy's married with kids, for fuck's sake."

"Yeah," Joe scoffed.

She froze, forgetting Quinn as she swung her gaze toward Joe. Flinty blue eyes stared back at her in challenge.

"What the hell is *that* supposed to mean?" she hissed.

"Oh, please, Roxanne. Like you don't know."

Goosebumps broke out over her skin. "I have no idea what you're talking about. Why don't you enlighten me?"

The look of disgust Joe shot her was shocking. Her heart knocked hard in her chest.

"Don't play the innocent, Rox. It doesn't suit you. We all know you're no stranger to dating married men."

"What the fuck, dude?" Quinn growled, shoving Joe's shoulder.

She opened her mouth, but she couldn't find any words. The man was delusional. Fucking delusional. That had to be the only explanation.

Joe shot up from his chair and stalked toward the living room. She followed on his heels, ramming her finger into his back. "I have never *ever* dated anyone who was married, you jackass! Let alone married with kids."

"Sure," he said, his tone patronizing. He stopped walking and faced her. "If lying helps you sleep better at night, then great. Go ahead and keep telling yourself that."

She wanted to knock that smarmy smile off his face, but she could only glare. "You're insane, you know that? Totally deranged. I have no idea what you're talking about."

"Riiight." He rolled his eyes. "Does 'Paul' ring a bell?"

"Paul?" A whole world of disbelief colored her voice. "As in my former boyfriend, who broke up with me because you're an asshole and beat him up for no freaking reason? *That* Paul?"

"You're blaming *me* for that breakup?" He laughed, but there wasn't an ounce of humor in it. "Me punching that worthless fucker had nothing to do with the two of you breaking up. Paul ended things with you because you tried to ruin his family."

What. The. Fuck?

Roxie jerked back as if he'd slapped her. She opened her mouth to speak, to say she had no idea what he was talking about, but he rushed on without giving her a chance to respond.

"He told me everything, Roxie. Don't play stupid. *You* are the one who messed things up for yourself. If you hadn't tried to make him leave his wife, maybe your cozy little affair could have kept going. But you got greedy. You wanted what she had: the husband, the kid, the big house, the white fucking picket fence. So don't go blaming *me* for anything. He told me you guys were done before I ever laid a hand on him."

Roxie's chest seized. What the hell? She couldn't have heard him right. It took a couple of tries to find her voice. "What do you mean, 'he told' you?"

"I ran into him on the ferry a few hours before we all went to Monty's that day." Pain washed over Joe's face, but on her next heartbeat, it was gone. His cold, distant, professional expression returned. "I met Paul's wife. Met his kid. Hell, I even met his fucking dog."

Joe continued talking, but Roxie no longer heard him. She was scrambling to process the bombshell that had just dropped.

Paul had been *married*? And Joe had known, but she hadn't?

Nothing was adding up. How was any of this possible?

Then it all clicked into place. And bile inched up her throat.

Her mind recalled that day from three years ago. The fight between Joe and Paul, the vile names Joe had spewed at her both at the bar and when she'd cornered him privately later. She'd never forgotten the anger and loathing she'd seen on his face. It had been the turning point of her and Joe's friendship.

After that day, whenever they'd seen each other, there was always an underlying hostility that she didn't understand. Yes, she knew her anger was reactionary to him. But she'd never understood the reasoning for his. For why he'd turned on her in the first place.

Over the last couple years, and on more than one occasion, she'd tried to get Joe to explain himself. Because for better or worse, she knew there had to be a reason—people didn't go from best friends to that kind of hate overnight without a reason. However, each time she tried to talk with him, it was like a steel curtain would fall. So she'd stopped asking.

He'd never apologized. Not once. Hell, this was the first time he'd ever spoken about that day.

So she'd pushed the confusion and hurt away and had fought back the only way she knew how—by giving as good as she got. For every snarky, asshole remark Joe threw her way, she was twice as bitchy back.

Joe's revelation that Paul had been married shocked her. Repulsed her, even. But looking back, it made the quirks of her relationship with Paul click into place.

In the six months they'd been together, he'd always visited her on the island. Whenever she had offered to go to Seattle to meet him, he'd always declined, usually citing the need to get away from the city and spend quiet time on Hudson. When she'd asked to meet his friends, there'd always been an excuse about schedules.

It had all been crap. Nothing but smoke and mirrors. Because holy shit . . . she'd been the other woman.

She was a goddamn idiot. How could she have been so blind?

A wave of nausea washed over her. After three long years of confusion, she finally had an explanation for the implosion of her friendship with Joe. Even though it was the very last thing she'd expected.

Joe truly thought she was a cheating whore.

Roxie's nose tingled, and she fought to swallow past the lump in her throat. His lack of faith in her hurt more than she cared to admit. But she deserved it.

Joe could hate her all he wanted. Because right now, she kind of hated herself.

———————◆———————

For the second time that day, Joe watched all the blood drain from Roxie's face.

Doubt tugged at the back of his mind, but he pushed it away. There was *no way* she hadn't known.

He recalled the moment on the ferry when he'd spotted Paul. He'd never met the guy before, but he'd recognized him from pictures. Paul had been leaning against the railing on the upper viewing deck, taking in the fresh air and sunshine. A pretty blond woman holding a small infant had stood beside him.

Joe had never liked any of Rox's boyfriends, but he'd begrudgingly approached the man to introduce himself. He'd been absolutely floored when the woman had joined in, saying she was Paul's wife. She'd shown off their two-month-old daughter and their golden retriever with pride. When he'd pulled Paul aside, the man had said that Roxie already knew.

The admission had socked him in the gut. His disappointment in Roxie had been debilitating. Her decision to enter a relationship with a married man had felt like a personal betrayal. After all, she'd been a front-row witness to his family's destruction. She'd seen how much damage a cheating spouse could wreak.

Rage had festered inside him that day, contaminating his every thought. Then he'd walked into Monty's Tavern and seen her leaning into Paul for a kiss . . . and he'd lost it.

He still didn't regret sucker punching Paul. A guy who readily admitted to cheating on his pregnant wife was a pussy who deserved a smackdown. But what he was beginning to regret? How he'd treated Roxie. When all the vicious accusations and curses he'd spewed at her echoed in his mind, he wanted to vomit.

At the time, he'd truly believed she deserved punishment, too. But looking at her now, with her skin ashen and eyes troubled . . . Had he been wrong?

The mere thought had his stomach turning. If she hadn't known about Paul . . .

No. She had to have known. She *had* to.

Because if she hadn't, then *he* was the fucking dumbass. For blindly believing the word of a stranger. Over his life-long best friend . . .

"I didn't know," Roxie whispered, confirming his fears. A single tear trailed down her cheek.

Fuck!

Joe clenched his fists as self-hatred consumed him. He was the biggest fucking idiot in existence.

He opened his mouth to speak, but nothing came out. What the hell was he supposed to say?

Sorry I believed a douchebag over you.

Sorry I've been a complete ass-wipe for the past three fucking years.

Sorry I haven't been able to see past my own jealousy and pride so we could actually talk about this.

He scrubbed his hands roughly over his face and growled. What a clusterfuck. "Look, Roxanne . . ."

A hand settled on his arm.

"Enough, Joe," Alex said in a soft voice, her eyes brimming with tears. "Please, just stop."

Great. Quinn was going to kill him for making his wife cry.

Alex removed her hand and walked across the living room to Roxie. She wrapped her friend in a tight embrace, whispering something he couldn't make out.

After a couple of murmurs, Roxie nodded and hugged Alex back. Her eyes darted around the living room, but she refused to meet his gaze. He couldn't blame her. Not at all. *Fuck.*

"Holy shit, man," Quinn said on an exhale. He moved to stand behind Roxie, placing his hands on her shoulders. "You guys can't go on like this. You need to figure your shit out. If not for what's left of your friendship, then at least for me and Alex. Because we can't go on like this, either." He pinned Joe with a steel gaze. "Stop being a fucking dick to Roxie, okay? You need to ease up." He dropped a kiss to the top of Roxie's head, then murmured, "Ease up on him, too."

Joe shook his head, wanting to kick himself. "It's not her fault, man."

Roxie's head whipped up, shock and disbelief on her face.

"You were right, Rox. I *am* the world's biggest asshole." He didn't think her green eyes could get any wider, but they did. God, he really was a dumb-fuck.

Heat crawled over his face. How the hell did you apologize for being a horrible human being? He cleared his dry throat. "I should have just talked to you about it straight away. I should have believed in you. But I didn't. I took the word of some cheating asshole. And then I was stupid and mean and a complete asshole. I'm sorry, Roxanne."

The room was silent. Roxie simply stared at him with her mouth hanging open, a look of doubt still coloring her features.

Glancing at both Quinn and Alex, they had matching looks of shock. Nodding to them, he asked, "Would you guys mind giving me and Roxie a moment?"

"Of course," Alex said, heading back to the kitchen without hesitating.

Quinn remained in place. The muscles in his jaw twitched as he glared at Joe.

"Please," Joe begged. He had to make this right with Roxie. He had to. But not in front of an audience.

Instead of answering him, Quinn squeezed Roxie's shoulders. "You okay alone with him? Or do you want me to stay?"

Fuuuck.

The thought of Roxie being afraid of him tore at his heart. But this was his own damn fault. He'd make things right with her. Somehow . . .

She squared her shoulders and turned to Quinn. "I'll be fine. But thank you."

Quinn dropped a kiss on her forehead and joined Alex in the kitchen.

Without a word, Roxie crossed the room and took a seat on one end of the couch. She crossed her legs and folded her arms over her chest. Tilting her head ever so slightly, she said, "Well?"

Damn. She wasn't going to make this easy. Not that he fucking deserved easy.

His pulse kicked up, and his mouth gaped a few times. He truly didn't know where to begin. As his apprehension mounted, he blurted, "I fucked up."

He cringed. *You've got to do better than that.*

More. He owed this woman more of an explanation than that, more honesty, more . . . everything.

"He told me that you knew he was married and that you were fine with it. I . . . I believed him. Like an idiot."

"Yeah," she said, her tone cutting. "Like an idiot."

He took in the woman across the room. Her rigid posture. The defiant set of her chin. The obvious fuck-you curl of her lips.

And the sadness and hurt in her emerald-green eyes.

He'd done that. He'd put that pain there.

A fucking piece of shit, that's what he was.

"I don't deserve for you to hear me out. I know that. I've

said some atrocious things to you over the last few years and . . . there's no excuse." Distrust stared back at him, but he continued. "I know my word means nothing to you—and it shouldn't. I've been nothing but an asshole to you. But I promise I'll do better. I'll do everything in my power to show you that I'm sorry. You don't have to forgive me"—hell, he was shocked she was still in the room with him—"but I am sorry."

Joe closed his eyes, pulse pounding in his ears. When he opened them, Roxie was sitting utterly still, like she was holding her breath. He gathered himself before continuing.

"I'm sorry for my horrendous words, for my inexcusable actions. Because no matter what I thought was happening, no matter how angry I was . . . you didn't deserve any of that. You were my best fucking friend. You didn't deserve the way I treated you." His voice dropped to a whisper. "I'm so sorry, Roxanne. I was wrong. Completely."

He swallowed hard, trying to gauge her reaction. Nothing. Her face was unreadable. For the first time in his life, he couldn't tell how she was feeling. And that scared the shit out of him.

The silence in the room was absolute. Until she sniffed.

Roxie's eyes filled, and his heart cracked. After swiping away a tear, she recrossed her arms over her chest.

"You know," she said, her voice hoarse, "part of me—hell, *most* of me—wants to tell you to go fuck yourself. But the other part . . ." She gave a watery chuckle. "I can't believe I'm going to say this, but there's a tiny part of me that . . . misses you. Misses what we had. How our friendship used to be. I don't know if it's possible for us to get back to that, or even close to what we had. But knowing what happened with your mom and all . . . I can kinda see why you were so angry. Why you were so hurt."

His heart stuttered, and a tiny seed of hope took root in

his chest. He didn't deserve this woman. Not her friendship. Not her understanding. Nothing. But still, he hoped.

"I miss our friendship, too, Rox," he said softly. "So damn much. I'll never forgive myself for being a stupid dumbass who shot from the hip. Who didn't take the time to ask you what was going on. That's on me. I sure as hell haven't earned your empathy."

"No, Joe, you haven't." She sniffed again, catching another angry tear with the tip of her finger. "But for better or worse, you have it."

Holy shit, she was so much better than him.

After a long moment, she shook her head and leaned back into the couch cushion. "Fighting with you is exhausting. I'm tired of it. But know this, Joe." She waved a hand between them. "You and me? We're nowhere near okay. At all. What you did? How you treated me? It was not okay." Her voice broke on her last sentence, and he wanted to stab himself in the face.

"You're right. It wasn't okay. Not at all." And he'd known it every time vile shit had spewed from his mouth. But had that stopped him? No. Because he was a selfish fucking piece of shit.

She held his gaze for a moment before whispering, "I don't know how to trust you anymore."

The knife he'd imagined stabbing himself with twisted. He didn't deserve her trust. Not after everything he'd done. But damn if he didn't want it.

"I will do everything I can to earn your trust back, Roxanne. I swear it. No matter how long it takes. I know along the way I'm gonna fuck up—"

"Of course you are." She smirked, and that little twitch of her lips, that little spark of fire in her eyes, had a bit of his screaming soul easing.

"—but I promise you, Rox, that I will never *ever* treat you that way again. I'll fuck up a lot of things, but I will *not* fuck that up. I promise."

A dizzying array of emotions crossed her face. Distrust, doubt, uncertainty, and the tiniest hint of hope. He latched onto that hope with both hands.

"We're gonna be okay, Rox. And not just for them." He nodded toward the kitchen. "For us, too. It won't be overnight. But what do you say we take this one day at a time?"

The spark of fire he'd seen in Roxie's eyes now lit into a flame. She arched one brow in that way he loved and hated in equal parts.

"You're telling me you can go an entire day with me without being a sarcastic asshole?" she asked.

He grinned. "I said I wouldn't be an asshole. I didn't say anything about the sarcasm."

She rolled her eyes, and he held his breath as she rose from the couch and walked toward him. Her expression turned somber as she came to a stop in front of him.

"I think you're right. We'll get there. Eventually." She inclined her head toward the kitchen. "But first, how about we see if you can get through dinner without being a complete dick?"

CHAPTER EIGHT

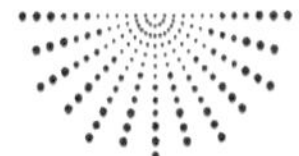

Roxie caught Alex's worried gaze as she reentered the kitchen. Her insides were vibrating, but somehow, she managed a small smile for her friend. The conversation with Joe had thrown her off balance, but she would be okay. After she had time to process everything.

Without knowing it, she had dated a married man. And Joe had condemned her for it without ever pausing to consider her side of the story.

So many emotions were swirling inside her, so many thoughts whirled in her brain. Anger at how Joe had treated her. Disappointment that he hadn't trusted her. Heartbreak because he was still suffering the consequences of his mother's countless affairs. Nervous, fragile excitement about the possibility that they could repair their friendship.

She busied herself with setting the table as Alex and Quinn finished putting the final touches on dinner.

"You okay?"

She jumped, not realizing Quinn had approached. Shooting a quick glance across the kitchen, she saw Joe in quiet conversation with Alex. She cleared her throat and prayed the flush she felt on her face was just her imagination. "I think so."

"Seeing as Joe's not bleeding, I'm guessing you guys were able to talk," Quinn said. "At least a little bit."

Roxie nodded. "We have a ways to go . . . but yeah, we were able to talk about what happened."

"You need me to beat the shit out of him? Because badge or not, I'll pummel him. Just say the word."

She chuckled and patted his arm. "Easy there, killer. Joe and I have called a truce. Of sorts."

"I don't think *truce* was the word you used, Roxanne." Joe's laugh was awkward as he set the platter of baked chicken and potatoes in the center of the table. A couple of silent seconds ticked by before he cleared his throat. "I believe you issued a challenge of whether or not I could get through dinner without being an asshole."

"Dick." She bit the inside of her cheek to keep from smiling. "The challenge was if you could get through dinner without being a complete dick, Joseph."

Quinn slung his arms around her and Joe's shoulders. Grinning, he said, "Holy shit, we're gonna make this work, guys. Because I fucking missed this."

She blinked furiously when her eyes watered. Turning into Quinn, she buried her face in his shoulder, wrapped her arms around his waist, and squeezed. He wasn't the only one who had missed this.

Was it easy bantering with Joe? Yes. And no.

Yes, because aside from the last few years, things had always been easy between them. Whether they'd been joking around, trading sarcasm, or hanging out in silence, there had never been a time when they'd been uncomfortable with each other.

And no, because she was still afraid of Nice Joe. What if he disappeared again? What if Jackass Joe returned, ready to smack her down with cruel words that would tear at her heart? She desperately wanted their friendship back, but she hadn't been lying earlier when she'd said she wasn't sure how to trust him again. Or if she even could.

On the one hand, she wanted to hold herself back, to proceed with caution, to not jump right in believing he'd be gentle with her feelings. Because no one could hurt her quite like him. But on the other hand . . . they'd already lost so much time.

All in all, she was a mess. But she'd get through this, dammit. It's what she did: got through shit. She had survived the nightmare of having her best friend turn into an enemy overnight, the trials of starting a new business from the ground up, the trauma of everything that had gone down with Alex's ex, and the apathy of her parents. She would survive this, too. One way or another.

"So, Roxie," Quinn said once they were all seated around the table. "Getting back to the picture, is that the only one you've ever received?"

Dammit.

She focused on adding a few more potatoes to her plate, then took a big bite of chicken. "What was that?" she mumbled around a full mouth.

"Roxie." Quinn placed his silverware down and leaned back in his chair, crossing his arms over his chest. The look on his face dared her to try him. "Have there been any other photos?"

She swallowed. "Um." Crap. "Sort of."

Joe's eyes narrowed. She was evading. Big time. "Care to clarify that, Roxanne?"

When she looked over at him, her smile was sweet. Too sweet. "No, Joe. Not really."

He took her smart-ass remark as a good sign, and the corner of his mouth ticked up. "Well, try, Rox. Please."

She shrugged. "It's no big deal. People send me articles and clips of press coverage from time to time."

If he hadn't been staring at her, he would have missed her slight hesitation, the flash of panic in her eyes.

He waved his hand in a circular motion. "And?"

Her gaze dropped to the table, and she meticulously pushed her food from one side of her plate to the other. "And . . . occasionally, I get a random picture or two of myself from an event. Like I said, it's no big deal."

Maybe. Maybe not.

Joe glanced at Quinn, verifying his friend looked similarly concerned.

"Are these pictures sent to you anonymously? Are there ever notes with them?" he asked.

She paused, and he caught the slight tremble of her fingers. *Damn.* More than anything, he wanted to reach over and hold her hand. But he couldn't. He hadn't earned that right. Yet. "Rox?"

She met his gaze, and the worry in her eyes was like a punch in the gut.

"Most of the stuff I get is sent directly from newspapers and magazines, or from friends outside of Hudson. Those are the clippings or printouts of articles. They have notes and addresses and stamps. The few recent ones have just been photos. And they have all been anonymous." She released a frustrated sigh, like she was blaming herself for brushing it off. "I kept everything. I've been meaning to make a scrapbook out of them."

Joe continued to hold her gaze, and he knew her well enough to tell she wanted to look away. But instead, she puffed herself up, trying to appear tough. His heart squeezed. Watching her put on her brave face slayed him every damn time.

"I guess I never really gave the photos much thought," she said. "I figured it was just someone being kind."

Of course she had. Roxie always thought the best of people, always gave them the benefit of the doubt. It made his stomach sink to know that he'd done the opposite to her for so many years. But no more. Never again.

"Roxie," Quinn said, "do you have the photos and stuff at your house or the café?"

"Café."

"Okay. I'll swing by first thing tomorrow and take a look at everything. If you still have any of the envelopes, even better. Joe and I can check postmarks and that kind of thing." Quinn turned to him. "Do you have the contact info for the fed's Seattle office?"

"Of course," Joe said. But then he stilled. *Damn*. Technically, he did. But he was pretty sure he no longer had the right to use it.

Quinn frowned. "What? They change personnel in Seattle recently or something?"

Or something.

"Yeah. About that." Cringing, he squeezed the back of his neck. "So, I, uh . . . resigned the other day."

Quinn chuckled. "Good one, man. But seriously, is there something going down at the Seattle office?"

"I wouldn't know." He locked eyes with his friend. "I resigned from the FBI on Monday."

"No shit?"

Joe lifted his chin. "No shit."

Quinn nodded. "All right, then."

This was why Joe truly appreciated their friendship. Quinn wouldn't push him to explain himself, to get into the details of *why*. Though he was pretty sure his friend had an idea. Everything that had gone down during the Woodsworth fiasco eight months ago had been . . . eye-opening.

Fidelity, bravery, integrity. He'd never questioned the FBI's motto. Not until both Rox and Alex had gotten hurt. For the first time in his fifteen-year career, he'd struggled with the integrity part. To this day, the image of Roxie lying unconscious in a pool of her own blood haunted him.

Greater good had always been the understanding. But when it had been Alex and Roxie who'd been sacrificed for that fucking greater good . . .

As the following days and months had dragged on, he'd increasingly questioned the work he'd once loved. Was it worth it? Did he still believe in the FBI enough to give them every damn thing he had? Could he continue fucking over innocent people, innocent families, in the name of the greater good?

Once you started hesitating, you got sloppy. And once you got sloppy, you put yourself and your fellow agents in danger. He'd known this. So, he'd left. For the safety of others—and for his own sanity. Maybe one day he would be able to look at himself in the mirror without seeing all the lives he'd destroyed.

"Whoa, it is not 'all right, then,'" Roxie said, pulling him from his thoughts. "What the hell do you mean, you quit?"

Quit. He fought a wince. He had never expected his tenure at the FBI to end like that . . .

"Just what I said, Rox. I resigned earlier this week."

She looked at him as if he'd lost his mind. Maybe he had.

"Yeah. I heard you. But *why*?"

He wasn't sure he could admit his reasons out loud—especially to her—so instead, he shrugged. "I just wasn't feeling it anymore."

She continued to stare at him in bewilderment. "Did you get another offer somewhere?"

He shook his head.

Her jaw dropped. "Let me get this straight. You just up and quit your job, and you don't actually have anything else lined up?"

That about summed it up. Perhaps not the wisest decision of his life, but what could he do about it now?

"Yup," he said, popping the *P*.

"Holy crap, Joe! Have you completely gone insane? What the hell are you going to do for work?"

Wasn't that the million-dollar question? Because if he were being honest with himself, he didn't have a damn clue. And since he was being honest, that kind of worried him.

All Joe knew was that he desperately needed a career change. But what the hell was he qualified for? Going undercover and investigating government officials for fraud, money laundering, extortion, and all that fun stuff. He'd been damn good at his job. He knew that. But along with the greater good doubts, he was tired of all the political crap that went along with being an FBI agent. Hell, the entire law enforcement field was full of political posturing and bullshit.

And if he didn't want to continue in law enforcement, where the hell did that leave him?

With no answers, he turned his most charming grin on Roxie. "Well, one of my childhood friends owns this café in town. We're in the process of repairing our friendship—"

Roxie arched a brow.

"—that I fucked up. So maybe I could earn some of her forgiveness by helping out around her shop."

Roxie's jaw dropped. Again. He *had* to be joking.

Did he seriously expect her to hire him—an FBI, er, *former* FBI agent—to make lattes, cut casseroles, and slice pie? Really?

She knew her mouth was gaping open, but she couldn't help it. "You've got to be kidding me, right?"

"Rox, we've been friends our entire lives—"

"Minus the last few years due to your assholery," she amended.

Doing a poor job of suppressing a smirk, he nodded to concede her point. "True. But aside from my assholery, have I ever asked you for anything? Any sort of favor like this?"

Damn. He had her there. It had usually been *her* asking for favors. Manual labor at the café. Running an errand or two for her when he'd been in town. Mailing her favorite treats from Boston. But still. Living with him was going to be enough of a pain in her ass as it was. If she had to work with him on top of it all . . . well, the powers that be might as well just kill her now.

But could she really say no? Something big must have happened if Joe had resigned from the FBI without a plan. The man was many things, but a quitter was not one of them. And being an FBI agent had been his dream job ever since he'd been a little kid.

Oh my god.

She had no choice. She had to say yes.

All of a sudden, Joe and Quinn started cracking up.

"Christ, Rox. If only you could see your face right now," Joe said, snorting.

"Holy shit, did you seriously think—" Quinn cut off when Alex slugged him in the arm, then he dissolved into a fit of laughter.

Roxie glared at them both. Jerks.

"Nah, Rox," Joe said, his stupid blue eyes twinkling. "I

have some money set aside. I'm going to take some time off and figure out what I want to do when I grow up."

"Ha, good luck with that," she said. A moment later, her eyes narrowed. "Hey, remember that challenge we made about dinner?"

Joe's grin grew wider. "Nuh-uh. Nope. Doesn't count. I was teasing you in a *funny* way, not being a dick. See?" He pointed at Quinn. "The sheriff over here is still laughing."

Roxie glared back and forth between the two idiots, biting the inside of her cheek to keep a smile at bay. She'd forgotten just how much they enjoyed ganging up on her when the opportunity arose.

Rolling her eyes dramatically—because she couldn't let on just how much she'd missed this—she stood. "Come on, Alex. Let's go check on your little angel upstairs. And leave the clean-up to Tweedledum and Tweedledumber."

CHAPTER NINE

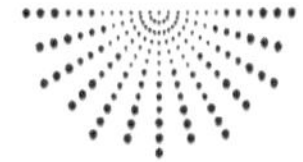

Roxie's eyes blinked open as a delicious, savory smell hit her nose.

Was that bacon? Did she smell bacon? Inhaling deep, she confirmed her suspicion. A smile grew on her face. Because really, was there any better smell to wake up to?

Rolling over, she cuddled into her body pillow and glanced at the alarm clock on her bedside table.

Her heart stopped.

Seven fifteen. Roxie shot up straight as panic surged through her body. A split second later, she relaxed.

It was Sunday. Her forced day off.

With a relieved sigh, she flopped onto her back and willed her racing heart to calm.

She'd skipped her morning run the last couple of days. In part because the mysterious photo had freaked her out, but also because Joe was acting like a caveman, insisting that if she went running, he would join her.

Okay, fine. He wasn't being a caveman, per se. Just overly cautious.

But even though she had agreed to work on mending

their friendship days ago, she was still nervous. Hence why the idea of spending the first hour of her day alone with Joe —before coffee, before she'd gotten her morning endorphins, before she'd gotten her head on right—was the last thing she'd wanted to do.

However, missing her morning runs had left her out of sorts. And being out of sorts during an unexpected rush at the café had only added to her stress. Despite the crappy January weather, a ton of tourists had descended onto their little island for the weekend. The last two days had been a blur of scrambling to accommodate the sudden influx of demand.

Not that she was complaining. The crowded café, along with two catering events on Friday and Saturday, had given her a legit excuse to avoid not only Joe, but Quinn, too. She knew the guys meant well, but the hovering was . . . a lot.

She'd been prepared to face the rush again today, but then late yesterday, she'd been ambushed by Nina, who'd insisted that Roxie take the day off.

Of course, Roxie had told the woman that she was crazy. But then Sheila and June had chimed in. Apparently, between the three of them, they'd figured out a way to cover Roxie's hours every other Sunday. Because they weren't delusional; they knew she'd never agree to take *all* Sundays off.

Pulling the duvet to her chin, she studied the swirls on the textured ceiling. She wasn't quite sure what to do with herself. It was the first full day she'd had off since . . . well . . . since she'd been in the hospital after the Woodsworth shit show eight months ago.

Her schedule since then had been ridiculous. Until this moment, she hadn't realized how much she'd needed Nina, Sheila, and June to force the issue. To make her step away and breathe. Because despite being exhausted for quite some time, the workaholic and control freak in her hated to admit when she needed help. Even though the women she employed were more than capable of taking on more hours and responsibility.

Roxie took another deep breath in, and the aroma of bacon—wait, was that coffee too?—made her stomach growl. Maybe this housemate thing wasn't such a bad idea after all.

She climbed out of bed and searched for her fluffy purple robe. After tossing it on over her pajamas, she headed down the stairs. Twisting her hair into a messy bun atop her head, she rounded the corner toward the kitchen and froze.

Whenever she heard the word *mouthwatering* in relation to a person, she always laughed. Was a gooey lasagna mouthwatering? Yes. A freshly baked blueberry pie? Most definitely. A person? Yeah, right.

Until now.

Holy. Crap.

Joe stood at the island stovetop, frying bacon. Without a shirt. Displaying broad shoulders, ripped arms, and a washboard stomach that bordered on ridiculous. There were guys with six-packs and that delicious *V* . . . and then there was Joe.

When her brain function returned, she began to worry about his chest. She'd hate to see bacon grease mar that perfection. And then an image exploded in her brain, one of the man's abs, but perhaps with . . . some whipped cream, or maybe some sticky chocolate syrup. She could li—

"Rox, baby, you keep looking at me like that, and we're going to have something else entirely for breakfast."

Her gaze flew up. The cocky smirk on his face had her flushing. She slammed her eyes shut.

Oh. My. God. I'm lusting after Joe freaking Buchanan. Right in front of him. And he knows it. Please. Kill me now. Amen.

Grimacing, she peeked one eye open. He was practically vibrating with bottled-up laughter.

She was tempted to say she'd been staring at the bacon, but she'd always been a shitty liar. Especially with Joe. Having him call her out on it would just add to her present mortification. So . . . screw it. Might as well lean into the situation.

Roxie reached for the plate of cooked bacon. Chomping down on a crispy piece, she gave a tiny groan as the salty, fatty goodness had her taste buds singing. "Don't let it get to your head, buddy. You caught me off guard. That's all. Besides"—she waved her second bacon strip in his direction —"who the hell cooks bacon without a shirt?"

"Me." He pushed a mug her way. "Do you want me to make you some eggs too?"

Taking a sip of the sweet and creamy, perfectly doctored coffee, she closed her eyes and sighed, shaking her head. "Nope. Coffee and bacon. I can't think of a more perfect way to wake up."

"I can think of a couple," he said with a chuckle.

She scrunched her nose at him. "You should get your mind out of the gutter."

"You're one to talk." He laughed. "You started it."

She gaped. "I did not. *You* started it."

Yes, she could hear the regression of their maturity.

Joe stared at her for a long moment with that half-smirk still playing on his lips. Calling bullshit on her without saying a word.

Fine. Sue her. She'd totally started it. But she'd been unable to help herself. The man was half naked and cooking breakfast. At least she hadn't said anything. Then again, she hadn't needed to. Her eyes had done all the talking for her.

"Well, maybe you should wear more clothes around the house," she said.

He grabbed his mug and rounded the island to the barstool beside hers. "I'm wearing plenty of clothes."

Roxie begged to differ. His plaid pajama pants, which rode low on his hips, were the only fabric on his chiseled body.

She had to remind herself to breathe. Dammit, this was *Joe*.

She had officially gone mad.

Sipping his coffee, he asked, "So, you've been forced to take the day off, right?" She glared at him, and he wisely coughed around a laugh. "I'll take that as a yes. Are you still planning to go to the mayor's wife's annual dinner thing tonight?"

Are you kidding me? I'm having a hard time getting enough oxygen to my brain, and he wants to talk about agendas?

She focused on his face. Like that was somehow easier. The man's early morning scruff was delicious. But the last thing she needed was for her eyes to wander down again . . . His flannel pants left nothing to the imagination.

Gah! Pull it together, Roxie!

"Yes," she croaked.

Croaked. Not good.

Roxie downed a large gulp of coffee, cleared her throat, and tried again. "Yes, I'm going. Mrs. Green holds her annual Winter Chamber Dinner on Sundays because she knows that's when most of the local business owners either have shorter hours or are closed." *Stop rambling, stop rambling, stop rambling!* "Wait, how did you hear about the party?"

"I ran into Mrs. Green yesterday. She said I *had* to go."

Her lips twitched. "Did she now?"

His brows turned inward, as if he was choosing his next words with care. "Yes. The woman is quite the steamroller."

"That's an extremely polite way to put it," she said.

Joe chuckled. "She was extremely polite, but oddly forceful."

"You have no idea. She's stopped just shy of having

everyone address her as The First Lady of Hudson Island. She truly is nice, but she's a bit . . . much."

"She's also, um, a close talker, isn't she?"

Roxie nearly choked on her coffee. "You could say Mrs. Green becomes quite enthusiastic when talking to the good-looking men in this town. Particularly the younger, good-looking men." More like she was two steps shy of creepy Mrs. Robinson territory.

"Gotcha." He nodded. "So, if she demanded I save her a dance tonight, should I be worried?"

Roxie laughed. "She's mostly all talk. You'll be fine."

Joe's blue eyes widened. "'Mostly'?"

She shrugged. "It's an official Chamber of Commerce event. It will be fancy. There's a black-tie dress code, sit-down meal, and band. So, she'll be on her best behavior. It's doubtful she'll grab your ass on the dance floor or anything."

His eyes widened even more. "'Doubtful'?"

"There'll be alcohol—and Mrs. Green does love her bubbly—so who knows?"

"Good god," he groaned. "What time does it start?"

"Six. You hitching a ride with me tonight?"

"Only if you promise to save me from The First Lady of Hudson Island. She kinda gives me the creeps. You ogling me is one thing, but her?" He shivered. "No, thank you."

"Awww." She patted him on the cheek. Probably a little harder than necessary. "Is the big, bad FBI agent scared of little ole Mrs. Green?"

He swatted her hand away. "Ha-ha, smart-ass."

She chuckled and stood up from her chair, hip checking him as she walked by. "Suck it up, stud muffin. Suck it up."

Joe glanced at his watch for the millionth time. He could hear Roxie shuffling around upstairs. She had approached the staircase on four separate occasions, then quickly pattered back to her room, faking him out over and over again.

"Rox, let's go already!"

"Be down in a minute! I promise this time."

Sure. She'd been promising that for the past ten minutes.

He flopped down on the couch with a groan and wondered why he was bothering to rush her. So what if they were late? The longer she took, the less time he had to spend at a stuffy dinner. Hell, he'd be happy to skip the entire event. Anything to avoid crossing paths with Mrs. Green again. The woman was . . . a lot. She'd eyed him like a piece of meat yesterday, and he hadn't known whether he should cover his crotch or his ass with his hands.

This morning, however, when Roxie had been the one gawking at him, he'd felt uncomfortable in a whole different kind of way. It had taken everything in him to keep his dick in check. Because the pajama pants he'd had on wouldn't have hidden a damn thing.

Footsteps sounded at the top of the stairs. By some miracle, he heard Roxie descend all the way this time. Joe dragged himself off the couch and headed for her, prepared to make some smart-ass remark about women and their primping. He couldn't let her know that her delay was working in his favor this time.

But as he caught sight of Roxie, he froze. All thoughts left his brain; his mouth turned to dust. *Holy shit.*

His gaze traveled down the length of her. She wore a simple black dress that hit her mile-long legs at mid-thigh and hugged her figure like a second skin. The two tiny straps holding her dress up were flimsy at best. Not that he was complaining. Not at all. She looked fucking stunning.

"Sorry that took so long," she murmured, fixing an earring. "I couldn't find the right shoes."

On her feet were shiny red stilettos. He wasn't quite sure how she'd survive the night in those sky-high heels, but who the hell cared? They did fabulous things to her already fabulous legs.

She turned toward the coatrack, and his breath left him in a silent whoosh.

Holy fuck. Had his eyes just bugged out of his head? Because it certainly felt like they had.

The front of her dress was high-necked and modest, but the back? *Damn.* It didn't exist. All that covered the smooth, bare skin above her hips was her auburn hair, which cascaded over her lean shoulders in soft, sexy waves.

His dick twitched. *Shit.*

He couldn't even think about the fact that she wasn't wearing a bra. If he did . . .

Nope. You're wearing dress pants, Buchanan. Do not *think about that.*

Rox was more than gorgeous. He didn't have a strong enough word in his vocabulary to describe her beauty.

Speechless, he helped Roxie into her coat. Then he grabbed her keys from the entryway table, held the door open for her, and followed her out.

It was going to be a long damn night.

CHAPTER TEN

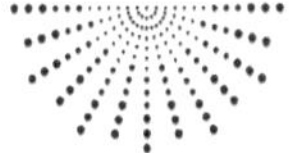

As the Pacific View Resort's valet drove her car away, Roxie checked the grand clock in the foyer and smiled in smug satisfaction. "See, we're not *that* late."

Joe popped his elbow out for her to take. She studied him with one eyebrow raised. What was his deal? He hadn't said a word since they'd left the house. Hell, he'd barely even looked at her. Was he pissed that she'd taken so long to get ready? Annoyance began to simmer in her gut. Good freaking god, if he was going to give her the silent treatment all night, then—

"Roxanne," he said, and her brow hitched higher at the gravel in his voice. "I don't know what's going on in your head right now, but stop. Let's go already."

She took his elbow. Her stilettos had them almost eye to eye, but he still wouldn't look at her.

Clearing his throat, Joe covered her hand with his own. "You look fucking amazing, by the way."

The corners of her lips twitched. "Ahhh! So you *are* capable of speech and not just growling."

"Shut it, Jameson." He cleared his throat again, shooting

"

her a quick look. "You know how you said I caught you off guard this morning?"

She nodded, not bothering to hold back a smirk now. Why would she? Watching Joe squirm was the best.

"Well, consider us even."

She chuckled. "Not even close, buddy."

They turned the corner and entered the resort's ballroom.

"Holy shit," he murmured, coming to a sudden halt.

One look at the décor had Roxie cringing. Mrs. Green's idea of *fancy* tended to lean more toward *gaudy*. The walls and tables were decked out in some sort of snowflake theme with a crap-ton of tulle and glitter, and the dance floor showcased a silver and white balloon archway, presumably a backdrop for photos. However, the balloon archway was anything but Instagram-worthy. It looked like it had traveled through time, straight from a prom. In 1992.

Roxie scanned the crowd, and her gaze locked with Mrs. Green's. The woman's eyes lit up, shining like the glitter that had been poured over every damn thing in the ballroom.

"Don't look now, Buchanan, but Mrs. Man-Eater has spotted you and is about to descend." She gave his arm a squeeze, then let go. "Oh look, I see Quinn and Alex."

Before she could take a step, his arm snaked around her waist. He pulled her to him, bringing her back snug against his front. Her breath caught.

"Don't even think about it, Roxanne," he murmured, his breath tickling her ear. "You promised you wouldn't ditch me tonight."

"I did no such thing, buster." She turned her head, ignoring the flutter in her belly when his lips accidentally brushed her cheek. "I said I'd save you from dancing with her. That was it." Slipping out of his hold, she gave him her sweetest smile. "Have fun!"

Roxie heard Mrs. Green's twittering giggles echo behind

her as she walked over to Alex and Quinn. Glancing back, she saw the older woman wrap Joe in a smothering hug. Mrs. Green's hands drifted down the former FBI agent's backside, and the utter horror that flashed on her friend's face made Roxie grin from ear to ear. Only then did it truly sink in how much she'd missed the damn guy.

Today, for the first time in forever, they'd had an actual conversation without barbs flying. It had been amazing.

Roxie wouldn't fool herself into thinking everything was fine and dandy now. They still had a lot of hurt to get over. Several years of constant arguing and bickering meant the trust between them was tenuous at best. But she felt hopeful about the future.

As long as this new, flirtatious element of their friendship didn't complicate things.

She wasn't blind; she'd always acknowledged that Joe was attractive. However, until this morning, his appearance had never stopped her in her tracks.

Her cheeks heated as memories of their kitchen encounter flashed in her mind. That face, that *body*—

"You okay, Roxie?" Quinn asked. "Your face is all red."

She closed her eyes, and the heat spread down her neck and chest.

Kill. Me. Now.

She peeked her eyes open. Only to find Alex staring at her with a knowing smirk.

Damn.

"I'm fine." Roxie fanned herself. "A little hot in here, isn't it?"

"Nope," Alex said. "Not one bit, actually."

She glared at the woman. *Brat.*

"Quinn, could you get me something to drink?" Alex asked, her gaze never leaving Roxie. "My throat's a little scratchy."

"Sweetheart, do you actually want something to drink? Because I can just leave if that's what you're getting at."

"Just leave then." Alex grinned up at him, then pulled his head down for a kiss.

Roxie had to remind herself that gagging noises were not appropriate at a Chamber of Commerce dinner. But sometimes those two were just too mushy.

As Quinn left, Alex steered her to a quiet corner.

"Spill it, missy."

She aimed for casual. Blasé, even. "I have no idea what you're talking about."

The noise Alex made in response was part scoff, part snort. "Please. I'm not sure what exactly you were thinking about when you were ogling Joe a minute ago, but I know it was dirty. So, what gives?"

It was one of those rare moments in Roxie's life when she truly had no words. She couldn't articulate how this morning had somehow flipped a switch on inside her. One that she desperately wanted to turn back off. The fluttering stomach, the racing heart, the out-of-control nerves . . . It was all unexpected and unwanted. Well . . . unwanted-ish. Or maybe not?

Gah! Get it together, woman!

"Joe and I called a truce," she said, stalling, racking her brain for a way out of this conversation.

"No kidding. But how, in a mere seventy-two hours, do you go from calling a truce to looking like you want to devour him?"

Holy hell, wasn't that the question of the century? "I wasn't—"

Alex crossed her arms over her chest, and Roxie slammed her mouth shut. The air around them grew thicker and thicker as the seconds ticked by.

"Fine," Roxie huffed, breaking under her friend's stare. "But it's all his fault."

"Meaning?"

"Meaning that the first sight that greeted me this morning was that jackass cooking breakfast—*half naked*—in the kitchen."

Just thinking about Joe sans shirt had her heart beating a little faster. *Damn.* Who was she trying to fool?

"And?"

Roxie sighed. If she couldn't be honest with Alex, then what was the point of having a best friend?

She glanced around to make sure no one was within earshot before she blurted out, "Oh my god, Alex. The man is freaking gorgeous. Holy shit. His chest, his arms, his abs, which form that perfect, perfect *V*—"

"And?"

"And, well, it's weird. Really weird. I mean, come on. It's *Joe.*"

Recalling the delicious tension that had hovered over them all day, her stomach flipped.

"Jeez, I'm starting to feel like a broken record here," Alex muttered. She made an impatient motion with her hand. "Annnd?"

Roxie scrunched her nose. "I'm not sure what you're getting at."

Liar. She had an idea, but the first stirrings of panic from these new feelings were pushing her back into denial mode.

"Ladies, there you are."

She looked over and was grateful to see Mrs. Green heading their way. That, in itself, said everything.

"You lovely girls shouldn't be hiding in the corner like little wallflowers." Mrs. Green squeezed herself between Roxie and Alex, linked her arms with theirs, and led them toward the crowd. "Let's go show the men of Hudson that we still have it."

———————

Joe hated to admit it, but he was having a good time. Once he'd managed to escape Mrs. Green's groping, he'd made the rounds and reacquainted himself with some old friends. He was now standing with his father, nursing a glass of whiskey and getting the scoop on the people he didn't recognize.

"Who's the douchebag?" he asked, nodding at the guy talking with Roxie.

"Excuse me, son?" There was more amusement in his father's voice than censure.

"Come on, Dad. Look at the guy. It's Sunday night, the whole town is in this freaking room, and the guy has an AirPod stuck in his ear. If that doesn't scream douche, then what does?"

His dad chuckled. "Jeremy Neville. He's Matthew Bellerose's nephew. You remember Matthew?"

Joe nodded. Matthew was the founder and patriarch of Hudson's award-winning Bellerose Family Cellars, which was just down the road.

"From what I understand," his dad continued, "Jeremy got his MBA a few years back and was working at some fancy consulting firm in Seattle. About six months ago, he decided it was time for a 'life change,' and so he moved here to work with the family."

Joe raised his brows at his dad's use of air quotes.

In response, his dad shrugged. "Rumor has it that Matthew handed over some of the winery operations to Jeremy, but within a month, he took them all back. Damn shame, too, because I know Matthew's been talking about retiring. But now . . ."

"Isn't anyone else in the family interested in taking over?" He knew Matthew had three kids who were all involved in the business.

His dad shook his head. "You didn't hear it from me, but apparently, there's been a lot of infighting happening ever since Jeremy joined the mix."

Joe covered a laugh with his whiskey glass. "Well, Dr. Buchanan, aren't you just a wealth of Hudson information?"

"Son, my knowledge is nothing compared to Roxie's." His dad nodded toward the woman in question and smiled. "It's a toss-up on whether Comfort Food or Ray's Diner is the official town hub for gossip."

Across the room, Roxie's smile was dazzling. She gestured at something with her glass, and the douche leaned closer to her. Joe frowned.

With his gaze ping-ponging between Roxie and Jeremy, he asked, "Are they together?"

His dad choked on a sip of whiskey. Alarmed, Joe pounded his father's back.

"Jesus, Joseph." His dad coughed, waving him off. "Have some faith in the girl."

Joe looked across the room again, and his eyes narrowed as he saw Jeremy take another step toward Roxie—and then Roxie take another step back. "So, no?"

The disbelief on his father's face was like a reprimand. He winced.

"Do you really think Roxanne Elizabeth Jameson would go out with a guy who wears a headphone thing in his ear at a party, reeks of cologne, and alternates between driving a Hummer and a Miata?"

It was Joe's turn to choke. Instead of trying to save him, his father simply glared.

Clearing his throat, Joe slapped his chest. "Wow, Dad, tell me how you really feel about the guy. Do they even make

Miatas anymore? I thought they were reserved for crusty, mid-life-crisis dudes like you."

Laughing, his dad threw an arm around his shoulders. "Tell me, are you going to stand here all night talking to a 'crusty, mid-life-crisis dude' like me, or are you going to go over there and save your girl? She's close to the wall, and if she keeps stepping away from Jeremy, she's going to run out of room."

Joe's jaw dropped, and his heart tripped. *Shit.* While he scrambled for something to say, his dad laughed again.

"I'm not blind, Joseph, and neither is anyone else in this room. If you keep looking at her the way you are, the gossip train will have you two married with a brood of kids by next weekend." Winking, his dad stepped away. "I'll catch you later, son."

Jeremy Neville was making it damn hard to be polite. All Roxie wanted to do was roll her eyes and walk away.

Good freaking god, the guy was practically standing on top of her. And he smelled terrible. Why was it that closet smokers always thought that five more squirts of cologne would make everything better?

"Just one date," Jeremy said, trying to sound playful. "I'll even let you pick the place. Come on, Roxanne."

She bristled. "Don't call me Roxanne."

He frowned. "Why? Other people call you that."

Seriously? Yes, it was her full legal name, but for as long as she could remember, she'd hated it. No one—not even her parents—called her Roxanne. Ever. "No, they don't," she said.

"Joe calls you that."

Okay, so there was one exception.

She lifted her chin and met his gaze head-on. "And he's the only one."

"Why?"

She was so done with this guy.

"It doesn't matter, Jeremy. That's the way it is." Scowling, she tried to step around him.

His hand circled her forearm with a firm grip, bringing her to an abrupt stop. She closed her eyes, tamping down her irritation. He'd just moved from being a slight annoyance to a creepy jerk-wad.

"Okay, okay," he said, tone placating. Like he was appeasing a kindergartener. "You win, *Roxie.* I must say, though, even a little temper tantrum on you is gorgeous."

Temper tantrum? She yanked her arm free. The guy was lucky she didn't throat-punch him.

Jeremy leaned forward, and his slimy eyes ran up her body. "Have I mentioned how you look especially sexy tonight? Let's dance, gorgeous."

Correction: the guy was lucky she didn't punch him in the crotch.

"Sorry, buddy, but the lady's dance card is full tonight," Joe interrupted, shoving Jeremy away from her. "And every night from here on out. So fuck off."

Roxie's mouth fell open as Joe took her by the hand and stalked over to the dance floor. A part of her wanted to protest his alpha male antics. But the other part was thankful for the timely rescue.

Once they reached the center of the parquet floor, Joe pulled her into his arms. Face to face, she noticed his jaw was clenched.

Worry turned in her stomach. She needed to diffuse the situation. Stat.

"Thanks for that. I'm not sure what's going on with Jeremy. He's usually not so—"

"The guy's a dick, Rox. I swear, if he fucking touches you again, I'll demolish him."

She opened her mouth to make some sort of sarcastic comment about Joe being a macho neanderthal, but the raging fire in his eyes gave her pause. The man was practically pulsing with anger, and it hurt her heart.

"Hey," she said softly, drawing out the word. Lifting her hands from his broad shoulders, she framed his face. "Calm down. Please. He didn't hurt me."

"He had his goddamn hand on you," he hissed, blue eyes alight.

"But he didn't hurt me." She ran a thumb over his pursed lips. "He's not worth your anger, Joe. Don't give Jeremy another thought. Please." After a moment of silence, she flashed him a teasing grin and linked her fingers behind his neck. "Instead, think about how you—the mighty, anti-dancing Joseph Buchanan—are on the dance floor this very minute. In the center. *Willingly*, I might add."

He sucked in a long breath, and on his exhale, a grin spread across his handsome face. Just like that, the tension drained from his shoulders. "Yeah, well. It was either dance with you or Mrs. Green. I chose the lesser of two evils."

She chuckled. "Surprisingly, you're not *that* bad of a dancer. You've only stepped on my toes twice."

He scoffed. "In your dreams, baby."

It was on the tip of her tongue to tell him not to call her baby, but before she could, he pulled her closer. His arms tightened around her waist, and for the second time that day, she had to remember how to breathe.

They danced to a slow song in comfortable silence, heads tucked together. His fingers began tracing lazy circles on the small of her back, just above where the material of her dress ended, and goosebumps erupted over her bare skin. She relaxed into his chest, begging her mind to be quiet. To let her enjoy this moment.

She didn't want to think about how comfortable it was to be wrapped in his arms. She didn't want to think about how the soft, woodsy scent of his aftershave soothed her. But most of all, she didn't want to think about how he'd been looking at her right before he'd tucked her into his warm embrace.

Roxie did not understand what was going on between them. This newfound attraction unnerved her. And yet, at the same time, it sent butterflies fluttering about her stomach in anticipation. Of what, she wasn't quite sure.

Taking a deep breath, she molded her body more completely to his. He held her tighter, and heat bloomed low in her belly.

They were playing with fire. And she had a feeling they both knew it.

CHAPTER ELEVEN

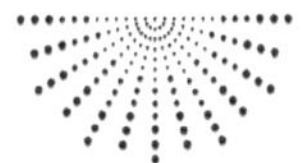

What the hell were you thinking last night?

Biting back a groan, Roxie pulled her neon-green running jacket over her head.

Dancing with Joe had been amazing. Flat-out exhilarating. And despite the ballroom's tacky overabundance of glitter and tulle, there'd been an electric charge in the air. The entire night had had a magical quality to it that she would never forget. Especially since, without saying anything out loud, she and Joe had acknowledged this ridiculous new attraction between them.

After their dance, they had stuck together for the remainder of the evening, invading each other's personal bubbles in very non-friendly ways. Like his hand lingering on her lower back. Or her leaning against him as she'd grown tired.

Now it was a new day. There was no live band, no balloon archway, no fancy clothes. Now, she had no idea how the hell she was supposed to act around the man.

She felt awkward. And she *hated* awkward. But even worse?

She was nervous. Stupidly nervous. Avoid-him-for-the-rest-of-her-life nervous.

A bit dramatic? Absolutely. But it was also the truth.

With unsteady fingers, she laced up her running shoes. Her plan for the day was to avoid Joe at all costs—because the for-the-rest-of-her-life bit was unfortunately unrealistic.

The first step? Sneaking out for her morning run. Because she was mature like that.

Roxie queued up her loudest playlist, then slipped her phone into the leg pocket of her running pants. After taking care to silently shut her bedroom door, she crept toward the staircase.

Her blood hummed in anticipation. She'd missed her morning runs, the peace and solitude of only having to concentrate on putting one foot in front of the other. The cold, crisp air of the sea and the earthy scents of the forest always worked wonders on resetting her mind. Afterward, she'd tackle whatever the day threw at her.

Running made everything better. Well, except for the other day.

She paused mid-step.

A shiver tore through her.

Nope. Do not *think about that photo!*

Fine. Running was *supposed* to make everything better.

At the bottom of the stairs, she yelped and skidded to a halt. Her jaw dropped.

"Oh good, you're ready," Joe said, straightening from a leg stretch. "Four miles, right?"

A mile into their run, Joe's muscles were all warmed up and feeling good. They hadn't spoken since they'd left the house, so the only sounds were their breaths and steady footfalls on the packed dirt, plus the occasional rustling of the animals they were disturbing. Because it wasn't even three thirty in the damn morning yet.

Joe glanced at the woman next to him. He had the distinct impression that she was doing everything in her power to ignore him. So, he broke the silence. "Are we going to talk about what happened?"

"I hate to break it to you," she huffed, her gaze never wavering from the path ahead, "but I'm not one of those let's-talk-and-run people. If I don't actively concentrate on my breathing, I might actually hyperventilate and die."

His lips twitched. Damn, she was cute. Even at this god-awful hour. "Okay. I'll talk and you can listen."

They'd been keeping a fast pace, so he eased up a fraction. Roxie's speed was no surprise. After all, the woman was only a few inches shy of six feet and all leg.

Speaking of which, her legs were currently wrapped in snug pants that left nothing to the imagination. Too bad they weren't running in the daylight. Or doing hills. Yeah, they should definitely do hills next time. He'd be more than happy to follow her up *any* hill—any time, any day.

Focus, Buchanan. Focus.

Right. He cleared his throat. "So, Roxanne, about what happened—"

"What exactly are you talking about?"

Her voice was strained, so he slowed a little more.

"When I started being a dick to you," he said. Something that looked like relief flashed across her face. But that didn't make sense. In any case, he pushed on. "I want to apologize."

It took him a split second to realize she'd stopped running. He pivoted and found her standing with her hands on her narrow hips, confusion on her face.

"You already apologized."

"I know, but I need to do it again. And I can apologize and

run at the same time." He grabbed her hand, turned, and began jogging, pulling her along with him. "You can run and listen. Please."

Roxie set the pace, and they jogged in silence for another quarter mile.

The truth was . . . he was nervous. He'd hoped the run would take the edge off, but that wasn't proving to be the case. Perhaps nothing could take his mind off the importance of this particular apology.

"Rox, I really am sorry. I just . . ." He felt her gaze on him, but he couldn't look at her. Not right now. "I should have talked to you about the whole Paul-being-married thing. But I didn't." *Instead, you decided to be an asshole, Buchanan.* "I chose to believe him and didn't even give you a chance to explain your side. And I hurt you. Over and over again, I hurt you."

On purpose. Because he'd wanted to make her feel just as shitty as he had.

"I'm so sorry, Roxanne. For all of it."

He startled when she pulled him to a stop.

"You've said this before, Joe, but you haven't said *why*."

Even in the dim moonlight, he saw the hurt glistening in her eyes. It tore at him. He'd do whatever he could to atone for his many screwups with her.

"Why were you so damn cruel to me, Joe?"

Because it had been easier than facing reality. Or what he'd thought was reality at the time.

Seeing her pick such an asshole had disappointed him to his core. And the knowledge that Roxie would choose to involve herself with a married man had been horrific. It had shattered his impression of the woman he'd thought he'd known, the woman he'd held up on a pedestal. The Roxie he'd grown up with, the one he'd cared about his whole damn life, wouldn't do *that*.

But Paul had told him otherwise. And the news had hurt him in a way he'd never imagined, breaking something delicate inside his soul.

He'd been attracted to Roxie since, well . . . forever, but the timing had never seemed right, and he'd never been sure how she felt about him. And frankly, the thought of messing up their friendship had terrified him. Still, he'd always dreamed that one day, things would work out between them.

He hadn't truly grasped how much he'd wanted that relationship with Roxie until all potential for it had been wiped away. Because he could never be with someone who knowingly destroyed families.

After Joe had learned about her breakup with Paul, he'd forced himself to stay mad. He'd constantly reminded himself what kind of person she really was. Again and again, he'd cut himself deep with thoughts of her betrayal. It had felt so damn personal.

He'd been raised by a single father from an early age. His mother had flitted in and out of their lives, jumping back and forth between his dad and other random men. As a child, it had messed with his head. Every time she'd returned, she'd promised that *this* time was going to be different, that *this* time she was staying for good. Then, without fail, she'd meet someone else and leave, often going radio silent and disappearing for months.

It was safe to say he'd been a confused and angry child.

To this day, Joe wasn't sure what exactly had happened with his parents—hell, he wasn't sure he *wanted* to know. But he remembered the evening his dad had finally put his foot down and demanded that his mother choose: stay or leave.

She'd left.

Roxie had been his best friend through all of it. She *knew* his history, knew how important trust was to him. And that's why her choosing to be with Paul had absolutely gutted him.

"Answer me, Joe. Why?"

"Because I'm a goddamn coward, Rox. Because it was easier to believe him." He scrubbed his hands over his face, then clasped them together atop his head. "I didn't give you a chance to explain yourself because I didn't want to hear you admit it. Having those words come out of your mouth . . . Hearing them would have destroyed me. It was too much like what she did. My mother, I mean. And that ruined—"

Joe tilted his face up to the sky. *Shit.* He'd just opened a can of worms. Hell, he'd opened his own fucking tackle store.

"Ruined what?" Roxie asked, her voice trembling.

He exhaled. It was time to lay it all out on the line.

Looking at the woman before him, he waited for her emerald eyes to meet his. "The possibility of us ever being more than friends."

CHAPTER TWELVE

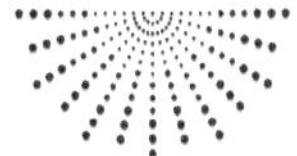

Two hours later, Roxie poured the blueberry pie filling she'd just made into its crust. Thank god the morning baking routine was second nature to her because her mind was in a damn whirl; she was moving on autopilot.

The possibility of us ever being more than friends.

A shiver ran up her spine. What the hell had Joe meant by that? A second after those words had passed his lips, he'd grabbed her by the hand and taken off running. She'd thought that when they got back home, he'd explain himself.

But no. He'd simply nudged her in the direction of the front steps, said he'd be by the café later, and mumbled, "I'm gonna put a few more miles in." Then he took off.

That had been it. No backward glance, no other explanation. Nothing.

Now here she was . . . stewing. Overthinking and overanalyzing. Replaying every single word he'd said in her mind. Over and over and over again.

After weaving a lattice crust atop the blueberry pie, she put it, along with an equally gorgeous apple pie—and a not-quite-as-gorgeous huckleberry pie—into the oven and went to join Sheila at the front counter.

She needed a distraction. Now.

Five minutes and a handful of lattes later, Roxie got it.

The bell on the front door chimed, and a new customer—a *male* customer—walked in. The lecherous anticipation that consumed Sheila's blue eyes had Roxie laughing.

"Down, girl," she whispered.

"Who *is* that, Roxie? And why on earth have I never seen him here before?" Sheila licked her lips, and Roxie held back a grimace at the production. The woman looked like she'd have no qualms about hopping over the counter to devour the newcomer.

Not that Roxie could blame her. Cade de la Rosa was truly one fine specimen of a man. He was a delicious cross between Channing Tatum and Mark Consuelos. A few years back, he'd been one of the top mixed martial arts fighters in the world, and though he no longer competed, the man was still ripped. Nope, she took that back. He was *beyond* ripped. Simply put, the guy was six-plus feet of pure sex appeal. Then if that weren't enough, Cade was a genuinely nice guy.

She grunted when Sheila's elbow connected with her ribs.

"Seriously, Roxie, who is that? You know him, right? I mean, you know everyone. You *have* to introduce me." Sheila gasped. "Oh my god, ohmygod, he's coming this way!" She gave her hair a quick toss and then did some sort of shimmy thing that magically produced more cleavage. "How do I look?"

Roxie blinked. Twice. Wow. She definitely needed to learn that trick. "You look great. Also, you do realize that he's probably coming up here to order, right?"

Her sarcasm was lost on Sheila, who said in a frantic whisper, "For the love of god, Roxie, introduce me."

The poor guy didn't stand a chance.

"Hey, Cade," Roxie called out with a wave. "It's been a while."

"Yeah, it has," he said, approaching the counter. "Happy New Year. Sorry we didn't catch up last night at the mayor's party."

Her eyes widened. How in the world had she missed him? "You were there?"

"I was." He chuckled, as if privy to some inside joke she didn't know about. "I didn't stay long, though."

She paused a moment to take him in, noting the dark circles under his brown eyes. Granted, the man was still smoking hot. He just looked . . . tired.

"Everything okay?" she asked.

He nodded. "The last few weeks have been nuts. We had some issues over at the Seattle gym—a couple busted pipes and a ton of water damage. Of course it had to happen right around the holidays, so it was a massive pain in the ass to get everything fixed. But things are wrapping up, so I was able to finally come home."

"Yikes." Building issues—on top of her hectic schedule— were a nightmare she didn't want to imagine. "How about some caffeine and calories?"

Sheila cleared her throat. Loudly.

Roxie sighed. "Cade, I don't think you've met Sheila yet. She started about a month ago. Cade, Sheila. Sheila, Cade de la Rosa." As the two shook hands, Roxie added, "Sheila is Poppy's cousin."

His head tilted ever so slightly to the side. "Really? Poppy as in Poppy Walker?"

"Really," Sheila said. Her smile was blinding. "Poppy wasn't always so lean and willowy. When her boys were little, people would mistake the two of us for sisters instead of cousins. She looked exactly like me"—slowly, she ran her hand from the curve of her waist down over her hip—"only older and a brunette."

"Wow." Cade scratched his head, still looking at Sheila in wonder. "I never would have guessed. You guys seem like complete opposites. Shows you how crazy genetics are, I guess."

"Sure does," Roxie said with a snort. Not only were the cousins complete opposites figure-wise, but personality-wise as well. Sheila was Sheila in all her flirty, bubbly, over-the-top sweetness. While Roxie admittedly didn't know Poppy well, the lean brunette was friendly, but on the reserved side. Quiet demeanor or not, Poppy was a savvy businesswoman who also managed to raise and launch into the world twin teenage sons who were respectful, helpful, and charming. As a childless woman, it was a feat Roxie couldn't imagine, especially considering she and Poppy were roughly the same age.

"So, Cade," Sheila said, leaning her elbows on the counter and plumping up her boobs, "are you from Hudson originally?"

Cade shot Roxie a wide-eyed and amused look, and she bit the inside of her cheek to keep from laughing. "Cade's grandparents are Hudson old-timers, but he's fairly new to the island."

"Hey now," he said, his hands raised, "I've been full-time here for over two years."

Roxie arched a brow. "And where did you stay while you were dealing with your Seattle gym's issues?"

"My condo in Seattle," he grumbled, his eyes dancing with humor. "But I spend way more time out here than over there, so I'm basically a Hudson Island local."

She scoffed. "I wouldn't go that far, buddy." Turning to Sheila, she added, "Cade and his brother run the big fight gym at the north end of the island."

"I didn't know the island had a gym. I'll have to sign up."

Sheila gave Cade a very obvious, very lascivious once-over. "Maybe you could . . . spot me."

Oh. Good. Lord. Roxie cringed.

Catching Cade's eye over Sheila's head, she mouthed a heartfelt apology. The corners of his lips twitched. Thank god he had a sense of humor.

"An Americano with room, Cade?" she asked.

At his nod, she nudged Sheila toward the register.

Starting his drink at the espresso machine, Roxie said, "Sheila, it's not a gym like an athletic club. It's a training facility. Cade's one of the coaches." She looked back at him. "Right?"

He hesitated. "Sure. In a nutshell, yeah. We do offer classes and—"

"What do you teach? What's your specialty?" Sheila interrupted, her voice going extra breathy on the word *specialty*.

Roxie rolled her eyes when Sheila flipped her hair over her shoulder again. It was painful to watch. But Cade, bless him, seemed unfazed by the whole affair. He was probably used to women falling all over him. And then some.

"I'm the head MMA coach at the gym. We do offer some introductory classes to the public—boxing, MMA, jiu-jitsu, that kind of thing—if you're interested. I don't teach all the classes, but me and the other coaches rotate."

"Oh my," Sheila said with a gasp. "There's more of you?"

Cade grinned, and the move took him from smoking hot to tear-off-your-panties hot. "There's a handful of us. Like I said, I'm MMA. My brother is the lead for boxing, and we have a few other coaches."

Roxie skirted past Sheila to hand Cade his coffee. "Here you go. Anything else? Pie? Scone?"

"I'll take something," Sheila said, fanning herself.

"Nah, I'm good." Cade scanned the customers at the tables, then returned his attention to Roxie. "I was hoping to run into Joe. We talked briefly at the party last night. He mentioned he'd be stopping by the gym, but I forgot to tell him we redid the entrance. When you see him, can you let him know that we're the third turn now and not the first?"

"Um. Sure." Roxie frowned. "Do you want his number so you can text him or something?"

Cade shook his head and turned to go. "Nah, just let him know when you see him."

"Wait," Roxie called. "I'm here until closing, so you'll probably see him before I do."

Chuckling, he stepped back toward the counter. "Trust me, Roxie," he said, voice low. "I was at the party last night. He's definitely going to be seeing you before he sees me." With a wave to Sheila, because he was a nice guy like that, Cade left out the front door.

Roxie's frown deepened. Seriously? What was with all the cryptic talk today? Weren't guys supposed to be the blunter of the genders? And did this mean that Joe had mentioned her to Cade last night?

Great. Now Joe was back in her brain.

She sighed. Let the overanalyzing commence.

CHAPTER THIRTEEN

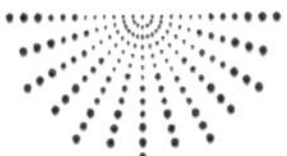

The odor of sweat, testosterone, and industrial-strength cleaner filled Joe's nose. Rancid blared from the overhead speakers, and the constant pop-pop-what-what-whap of fighters hitting pads was as steady as a heartbeat. The sounds and smells of the gym were familiar and soothing. They settled something inside him. Dissipated the antsy feeling that had been gnawing at his gut.

When Joe had swung by Comfort Food earlier, Roxie had mentioned that Cade had come around looking for him. So, instead of staring at the walls and contemplating his future, Joe had hopped in his car to go pay his old friend a visit.

He let out a low whistle as he scanned the facility. Three boxing rings. Four MMA cages. Loads of mats, bags, cardio machines, weights, and equipment. It truly was a world-class gym. "Holy shit, man. This place is huge now."

Like a lord surveying his land, Cade put his hands on his hips and looked around. The pride he held for his gym practically radiated from his pores. "Yeah. We went from twenty-five hundred square feet up to twenty-five thousand—and that's just training space. It doesn't include the locker rooms, sauna, office, and dorm."

Joe's jaw dropped. "You have a *dorm*?"

"In case you missed it, bro, we're in the middle of bumfuck nowhere. The island has some B&Bs, but the only real lodging option is the Pacific View Resort, and that's way too expensive for the fighters. Training camps run anywhere from eight to sixteen weeks. Besides, a hotel isn't very realistic since the guys need kitchen access to prep their food if they plan on making weight."

"Your fighters could stay with you," Joe suggested with a smirk. "You've got a big place."

"Oh *hell* no. I see these bastards ten-plus hours a day. That's plenty. More than plenty." Cade shuddered. "Hence why we decided to build a dorm. Eight rooms with two fighters in each, a couple living areas with TVs and gaming systems, and a big-ass kitchen. Nothing fancy. It's great for training because there's not a lot of distractions out here. The guys can really focus."

Joe looked out at the gym and couldn't help but be impressed. He noticed a wall of framed photos and upon taking a look, the display showed Cade and his coaches with their fighters, many of whom were highly decorated in their various disciplines, along with a handful of Olympic medalists. He looked over at his friend and shook his head. It was hard to reconcile the guy who he'd done keg stands in college with to this world-renowned former MMA champion and highly sought-after coach.

Though he had been a couple of years ahead of Cade at the University of Washington, they'd become fast friends once they'd realized their Hudson Island connection. Cade and his older brother, Dante, had spent most of their summers and holidays staying with their grandparents on the island. It was a wonder Joe hadn't met them prior to college.

"You've done good, man." Joe slapped his friend on the back. "Really freaking good. Do you only focus on training out here, or is this gym open to the public?"

"We have a community class program. Fighters move around a lot, so it isn't wise to rely solely on the fight purse." Cade grinned. "See, I learned a thing or two in college, after all."

"Aside from banging chicks?"

"Right, Buchanan. Like you were a monk." He nodded to a couple of guys as they passed. "All in all, it's taken a whole lot of hard work and an equal amount of luck to get here. The land we're on is family property passed down from my grandparents. And between me and Dante, we did pretty well off our endorsements when we were fighting—"

Joe chuckled. The guy was being modest. During their heydays, the De la Rosa brothers had been household names. *International* household names. Cade had been the poster child for MMA, while many critics and analysts still credited Dante for giving boxing its most recent resurgence.

"—so we were able to put a chunk of those funds toward our facility expansion. We run classes here and at our Seattle gym to cover the day-to-day expenses. We do MMA, boxing, Muay Thai, and jiu-jistu—all levels for both adults and kids. Obviously, there's more class traffic in Seattle, but we have a women's cardio kickboxing class that does really well here."

"Cardio kickboxing? Seriously?"

"I know, man. But don't knock it." Cade shrugged. "What can I say? Women love that shit. It's one of our most popular classes. We even partner with the Pacific View Resort for that class. Since there's not much traffic on the island, especially in the winter, we do a lot of weekend and camp-type programs. We work with schools on all the islands, and we do a whole lot of training for law enforcement. Which brings me to my ulterior motive for getting you out here, bro."

Curious, Joe waited.

"As you know, MMA, boxing—combat sports in general —are great things to know if you're a crime fighter. When we train law enforcement, we touch on all those aspects— standup, grappling, striking, all of it. But the problem with combat sports is that they're just that: sports. They have rules. But as I'm sure you know firsthand, the bad guy attacking you isn't going to drop his weapon or avoid kicking you in the nuts in a show of sportsmanship."

Joe laughed. "That's for damn sure."

"Yeah. So Dante and I have partnered with Gavin and his crew to create a whole new program specially designed for law enforcement and security types."

Gavin Frazier ran Hudson Security, a distinguished private security firm. They handled a wide range of security work, from risk consulting and cyber security to private protection and hostage negotiation and rescue. The only reason Joe knew any of that was because of his work with the FBI. There had been plenty of whispers about Gavin's team, a group of former special ops guys, all in hushed awe. Because they were efficient. And effective.

He had to admit, his curiosity was piqued.

"Since Gavin's company operates on our land," Cade continued, "and since Dante served with a lot of those guys, it's a natural collaboration. We want this new program to not only teach hand-to-hand and different styles of fighting but also provide tactical training. You know, weapons, marks- manship, outdoor survival, that kind of thing."

A grin spread over Joe's face. "Not gonna lie, man. That sounds like a shitload of fun."

Cade laughed. "I'm glad you think so because we're looking

for someone to head it up. Ideally, this person will also act as the program's lead hand-to-hand combat instructor. And they'll work closely with Gavin's guys on the tactical end."

"Why is that?" Joe asked.

"We want whoever's leading the program to be in the trenches, so to speak. Which makes it a hard spot to fill. We have a jiu-jitsu coach for the fight side of the gym, but he's not familiar with weapons disarming and that sort of thing. You, my friend, with your jiu-jitsu *and* Krav Maga background, would be a great fit. Your reputation precedes you, you know. You're a damn good instructor. Hell, you were *the* top instructor at the FBI Academy."

Pride bloomed in his chest. "I was."

"I also overheard a certain little red-headed birdie whispering to Alex last night about you being currently unemployed."

"That little birdie talks too damn much."

A slow smile spread over Cade's face. "Yeah, but with legs like that, bro, she can say whatever she wants. Hell, she can *do* whatever she wants to me, if she's ever so inclined."

Joe's jaw clenched, and he glared at his supposed friend. His irritation was immediate. And completely irrational. Because even though he'd spilled his feelings to Roxie that morning—granted, in a murky, roundabout way—he had zero say in what she did. But his hackles rose, nonetheless.

Cade's smile grew, and he barked out a laugh. "Hit a nerve there, did I?"

"I don't know what the hell you're talking about." *Damn.* Probably not the best comeback, but fuck it, it would have to do.

"Whatever you say, man. I'm a lot of things, but blind is not one of them." Still chuckling, Cade slapped him on the back and walked deeper into the facility. "Come take a look at the rest of the gym, and I can tell you what we're offering for compensation."

They set off on their tour, and Joe's brows hit his hairline at the six-figure salary and extensive benefits package Cade rattled off.

"Cade, man, I'm no rocket scientist or anything, but isn't that a bit steep for a hand-to-hand instructor?"

His friend shrugged. "Like I said, you'd not only be the lead instructor, but you'd also be working closely with Gavin's guys on the tactical end. You'd basically be running this program. All the training will be on-site, but there's still a bit of traveling involved. We work a lot with the local military bases, and we've got a number of law enforcement groups throughout the Pacific Northwest and all the way into Montana. There's also a whole shitload of paperwork. But since you're a fed—"

"Former fed," he interrupted.

Cade laughed. "Former or not, you should be used to paperwork. Besides, not to sound like a pompous dick or anything, but you *are* standing in one of the top gyms in the fucking world. Think about it. If anything, like you said . . . it'll be fun."

It would be fun. Everything in the job description was right up Joe's alley. His first few years with the FBI had been spent as a defensive tactics instructor at the academy in Quantico. With his extensive background in jiu-jitsu and Krav Maga, as well as a few other disciplines, he'd been part of the team in charge of training countless FBI agents in hand-to-hand combat—and for a whole lot less than what Cade was offering. Then, for some dumbass reason, Joe had traded in that job to work in the field. To go undercover and rub elbows with the slime of humanity. To get shot at.

Idiot.

A generous salary plus impressive benefits to teach and

not get shot at? Hell, he'd deck himself out in spandex and be the cardio kickboxing class instructor for that deal.

The thought of squeezing into skin-tight clothing sparked a memory of Roxie's running pants. Which then made his mind drift back to those damn pictures.

He turned to Cade. "Have you done a self-defense class before?"

Cade looked at him like he was a moron. "Wow. Rocket scientist, you are not. Hate to break it to ya, bro, but you do realize this is a fight gym? That's kinda what we do."

"No, smart-ass. I meant a self-defense class for women, specifically targeting your cardio kickboxing clientele."

"Huh." Cade's brow furrowed. "I don't think we've ever done that. Our beginner MMA and jiu-jitsu classes have self-defense aspects, but not specifically catering to women. That's smart. I mean, not rocket scientist-level smart or anything, but still."

Joe chuckled, and a plan began to take root in his head. If he could get Roxie to attend, if he could teach her some basic, real-life moves, he'd feel a little better about the whole picture ordeal. Not a whole lot better, but a little was better than nothing.

"If you think there'd be interest, I'd be more than happy to lead that class." Joe shrugged. "That way, you can also see if my teaching style jives with what you've got going on here."

"Sure," Cade said. "If that makes you feel better, we can do that. But I don't need any convincing, Joe. You're the man for the job. How long have we known each other?"

"Too long," Joe said with a grin.

They continued walking around the gym, pausing here and there for an introduction.

"I told you I swung into Roxie's café this morning, right?" Cade said after a while. "Dude, have you met that Sheila chick?"

"Oh yeah."

"Is she really Poppy's cousin?" He looked baffled.

"Hard to believe, right?" Joe wagged his eyebrows. "You interested?"

His friend grimaced. "I don't think so."

"Come on, I figured Sheila would be right up your alley. Busty, blond, and perky. If that's not your type, brother, then I don't know what is."

"You'd think, right? But, man, that squeaky Minnie Mouse voice is a bit too much."

"*Sheila's* a bit too much," Joe said, shaking his head. "I'd steer clear of that one."

Cade sighed. "Fuck, man. As much as I love small-town living, being a single guy on an island—with a shit-ton of other single guys—fucking sucks."

Joe slapped his friend on the shoulder. "Well, at least Seattle's just a ferry ride away, my friend."

"Thank fuck for that." Cade blew out his breath and nodded toward a floor-to-ceiling glass wall. "Now let me show you the offices."

CHAPTER FOURTEEN

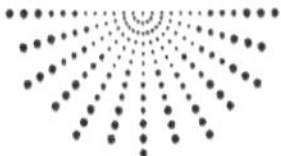

A soft knock sounded on her office door. Roxie glanced up from her computer screen, working her neck from side to side. "Hey, Eli. How's it going?"

"Your back door lock is still broken, Roxie."

She winced. Right. She'd completely spaced on that. Again. *Shit.*

Was she a real-life version of those too-stupid-to-live characters she read about in suspense novels? Maybe. Who else would leave the lock on their back door broken when they had creepy-ass pictures being sent to them?

Stepping into her office, Eli placed a business card on her desk, then tapped it for emphasis. "The locksmith. I went ahead and called them. They'll be out at closing time today."

She could only blink.

A tiny part of her appreciated him for calling the locksmith because, let's face it, she'd forgotten to do so for the past month. She'd planned to call today, but the task had slipped her mind when she'd run over to see Doc on her break so he could remove the two stitches from her lip. *Shit.*

However, another small part of her bristled. This was *her* problem, dammit. It took a lot of freaking balls to step in and make calls for someone else's business. *Shit. Shit.*

The biggest part of her, though? It screamed that something wasn't right about this situation. She was now ridiculously uncomfortable and more than a little bit creeped out. *Shit. Shit. Shit.*

Quinn's warning about Eli kept replaying in her mind.

Were the man's actions and attention more than him simply being friendly? She couldn't be sure. But she didn't want to find out.

Skin crawling, Roxie shifted in her seat and cleared her throat. "You didn't have to do that, Eli."

He smiled, and her stomach turned. Until tonight, his smile had always seemed kind. Neighborly. Now it looked downright sleazy. Had she been blind? Or had something in him changed?

"It wasn't a problem at all, Roxie. I worry about you, ya know?"

Well, don't.

The passive-aggressive in her pasted on a bright, shiny smile. "How are Poppy and the boys? You know, the twins came in over the holidays and mentioned they were invited to join a study abroad program over the summer. Have they decided where they want to go?"

If she hadn't been watching for it, she would have missed how his smile dimmed. It was just by the tiniest little bit. But it was there. *Damn.* Quinn was probably right.

"Not yet," he said, the warmth gone from his tone.

"Well, I'm sure wherever they pick will be great." She rose from her chair. Time to move the show along. "That was kind of you to call the locksmith about my door. Thanks for stopping by." *You could have just called, though.*

"Hold on a second, I've got one more thing." He shook his

head and laughed, like he thought she was being coy. "I'm planning a surprise party for Poppy next month. Her birthday is on Valentine's Day, so sometime around then. I was hoping to talk to you about catering it."

Of course. She wanted to roll her eyes, but she kept her expression neutral. "What did you have in mind?"

He flashed another off-putting smile. "Why don't we chat over dinner tonight?"

Holy. Crap. Did she have a sign on her forehead that said, *If you're married, I'm available?*

"Sorry, Eli, I'm busy tonight. This week is a bit crazy." You're *a bit crazy.* "Why don't you look at your calendar and pick the day you'd like to have Poppy's party? We'll go from there. You said it's a month out, so we should be fine."

His smile vanished, and he pressed his lips into a tight line. "Okay. Good. That sounds like a plan."

"Oh hey, Eli! How's it going?" Sheila came to a stop in the doorway, her gaze darting between the two of them. After a moment, confusion entered her blue eyes. "Wait. How did you get back here? I've been in the front this entire time."

Eli's face flushed. "I, um, used the back door," he mumbled. "I was just talking to Roxie about some business stuff."

Roxie's brow furrowed. Really? Now he was going to act all awkward and embarrassed? And guilty? She wanted to reach across her desk and strangle him.

Instead, she said, "Eli is planning a surprise party for Poppy's birthday."

Eli studied his shoes, and Sheila glared at him with what looked like suspicion.

It took everything in Roxie to not groan. The very last thing she needed in her life was additional drama. Mind racing, she latched onto the first idea that came to her.

"Oh! Sheila, why don't you work with Eli on some menu

concepts? You know your cousin better than I do, so you'll have a better feel for what kind of theme she'd like for the party. That work for you, Eli?"

"Yeah, sure. That would be fine." His throat bobbed as he swallowed. "I've got to go, but I'll see you both later." Moving faster than she'd ever seen, he disappeared outside.

"Huh," Sheila said as they watched the back door close. "That was strange, don't you think?"

"You have no idea." Rubbing her temples, Roxie dropped back down on her chair. "How are things going out there?"

"Slow." Sheila placed a stack of mail on the desk. "Did you need me to stick around after close? Prep for tomorrow or anything?"

"No, that's all right. It's an easy week on the catering end. I think people are still sticking to their New Year's resolutions. Give it another week and the catering orders will start rolling in."

"Ha! All right, well, I'll be up front for the next half hour if you need anything."

"Will do. Thanks," Roxie murmured, her attention already focused on a plain manila envelope. No stamp, no addresses. Just her name.

Her pulse raced as she opened it. And then the blood drained from her face when she saw what was inside.

Another picture. This time, from the evening before.

Her back was to the camera, and she was looking off to the side. Jeremy was standing close, his hand on her arm. And the look on his face? There was no mistaking his romantic interest.

A stranger viewing the photo would assume they were lovers having an intimate moment, not a man who didn't know how to take a hint and a woman searching for an escape route.

But the false narrative was not what had her breathing

faster. What had her heart threatening to beat out of her chest.

No, that was the single word scrawled over the picture in thick red marker.

Whore.

CHAPTER FIFTEEN

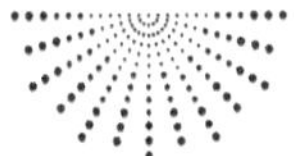

Joe parked his truck in his driveway. Well, technically, both the truck and the driveway were his dad's. Sean Buchanan had two vehicles, a Tesla because this was the Pacific Northwest, and a Ford F-150 because this was island living. When his dad had offered up one of the vehicles, Joe had happily swapped out his rental for the truck. His dad was far more generous than Joe was deserving. That was for damn sure.

Killing the engine, he snagged his phone and checked the text message he'd heard ding while he'd been driving. He grimaced at the message.

Hey, it's Candie from the plane. It looks like I'll be on Hudson Island sometime in the next few weeks—still finalizing my schedule. My firm's looking at investing in some property there and I was hoping to meet up so I could pick your brain about the area. Let me know if you're free and what your schedule looks like.

Joe had zero desire to see her again, but he didn't want to be a dick. He gave his reply a few moments of thought before he texted his response.

My schedule is currently in flux, but if the timing works, I could meet you for coffee to talk about Hudson.

Satisfied with his polite and professional text, he tossed his phone onto the passenger seat and closed his eyes, taking a minute to decompress. Today had been a good day. When he'd arrived on Hudson Island last week, he'd been an unemployed, angry shithead who'd been throwing a massive pity party for himself. Now, he was just a shithead.

Joe had stayed at the gym for a few extra hours after finishing the tour with Cade. He'd met the other coaches and some of the fighters, then he'd donned protective gear and stepped into a ring for the first time since before the Woodsworth case, breaking the longest stretch he'd ever gone without sparring. He had kept up with his running and typical strength exercises, but there was nothing quite like two grown dudes beating the shit out of each other to show you just how out of shape you were. In comparison to the guys he'd sparred with today? He was freaking out. Of. Shape.

But even though his body was sore and tired, he felt good. Not only because of the hard gym session or the potential to get paid to do something he loved, but because of Roxie, too.

Running with her beneath the moonlight this morning, he'd finally felt whole. And he'd realized that what had really torn him apart all these years, what had caused him to be such a massive asshole, was the knowledge that their friendship—and any chance of more—had died with Paul's admission.

But Paul had lied, and now Joe knew the truth. Now his anger and bitterness and pain were gone. In their place was a lightness, a growing hope of possibility.

Yeah, for all he knew, he could walk in the front door tonight and Rox could tell him to go fuck himself. Hell, she could decide AirPod Douche was the man she wanted to be with.

Or she could tell him she felt the same way he did.

The same way he'd always felt about her but was too stupid and immature to realize it. Until it was gone. Until *she* was gone.

Joe smiled into the darkness. *Possibility*. It was a damn good word.

Grabbing his duffle bag of dirty, borrowed gym clothes, he climbed out of the truck. As he stepped through the front door, he heard hushed voices coming from the kitchen. He dropped his bag on the ground and headed that way.

Rounding the corner, he saw Quinn and Alex milling about. Little Annie was strapped to Alex's chest in some sort of pouch contraption, fast asleep. Rox was leaning against the kitchen island, arms wrapped tight around her middle. Her green eyes were bloodshot and overly bright. She'd been crying.

Joe was next to her in a heartbeat, wrapping one arm around her shoulders while tilting her face toward his with the other. "Roxanne, what's wrong?"

A tremble racked her body, and she shook her head, eyes welling with fresh tears.

His heart clenched. He pulled her close, murmuring nonsense in her ear. Over her head, he shot Quinn a questioning look.

"She got another picture this afternoon," Quinn said.

"I don't want to talk about it anymore," Roxie mumbled into his chest.

"Okay, baby. You don't have to." He rubbed her back. If only he could get her to stop shaking. "Everything's going to be okay."

"Here, sweetie." Alex held out a mug of hot chocolate.

"Let's go sit on the couch. Quinn needs to fill Joe in on what's going on. Come on."

"Rox, everything's going to be fine," Joe said, cradling her face. "I promise." He brought his lips to her cheek, a hair's breadth away from where he truly wanted to kiss her.

Her breath caught as he leaned back and held her gaze. The rest of the room faded away. But dammit, this wasn't the time or place. She needed comfort, not him mauling her.

He dropped another kiss on her forehead. "Let me talk with Quinn. We'll join you guys in a sec."

Eyes wide, Roxie nodded and moved out of his embrace. Already, he missed her heat, missed having his arms around her.

Once the women had linked arms and moved to the living room, he turned to Quinn. Keeping his voice low, he asked, "What the hell happened?"

Quinn told him about the photo and the message scrawled on it. His hands clenched into fists, and he forced himself to take in a couple of deep breaths.

When they found out who this bastard was . . .

"What have you got?"

Quinn remained silent. His gray eyes were clouded with worry.

Dammit. "Nothing?"

"Nothing at all," he confirmed, frowning.

Joe exhaled. *Fuck.* He'd figured Quinn didn't have much, but that didn't make the news any less maddening. "What do we do now?"

"I remember when the shit with Alex's ex-husband was going down and I asked you the same damn question." Quinn scrubbed a hand over his face, his frustration evident. "The answer's the same now as it was then: we keep her safe. I know we can't have Roxie in sight twenty-four seven, but—"

"But I'm going to do my best to try. When I can't, I'll make sure someone else can. You don't need to worry about that, O'Conner." He locked eyes with Quinn, and the two men traded solemn nods.

For a few minutes, they stayed quiet, thinking, listening to Annie's babbles and coos coming from the living room. Roxie's and Alex's voices were a soft, indiscernible hum in the background.

"Look," Quinn said at last, breaking the silence, "I don't know what's going on with you and Roxie." He grimaced. "Well, actually, yeah, I do. But . . . sorry, it's weird for me. Alex says it's a long time coming, and I know she's right, but still . . . it's weird."

Joe patted his friend on the shoulder. "Don't worry about that. Nothing's happened on that front—"

Quinn scoffed. "Bullshit. I have eyes, Buchanan."

He chuckled. "Well, nothing *like that* has happened yet—"

"Ugh. Dude, come on. She's like my sister, for Christ's sake."

"Yeah. And I'm like your brother."

"*Exactly*. Do you see why this is all kinds of fucked up for me?"

"Yeah." Joe grinned. "I can see that. But don't worry, man. We're not there. We're just getting to know each other again. That's it."

"That's not all of it, but whatever." Quinn hesitated, then added, "I know you already know this, but she's really special."

In an instant, Joe sobered. He heard the unspoken threat. "I know, Quinn. Believe me, I know."

"Thanks again for coming over, Alex. I really appreciate it," Roxie said, pulling her friend into a hug, careful not to squish

Annie, who was expertly tucked into her carrier-wrap-thing. Even though she was an honorary aunt, she wasn't up to speed on all the baby accessory terminology yet. And holy crap, there was a lot of it . . .

"What am I, chopped liver?" Quinn asked, slinging a heavy arm around her shoulders.

She smirked at the man, who was like a brother to her. "In comparison? Yes."

He chucked her on the chin and then turned to give Joe a brotherly hug.

Roxie waved to her three favorite people as they walked to their house next door. "See you guys tomorrow."

"Lock up, Roxie," Quinn called out.

With a salute, she shut the door and turned the deadbolt. As soon as she heard the lock click into place, all her energy evaporated. Like a balloon that had been pricked, her head and shoulders sagged. She rested her forehead against the door and closed her eyes.

What a crappy end to an already muddled day. Her brain hurt.

First, there'd been the confusing conversation during her morning run with Joe. Next, Eli had gone all weird on her. And then she'd found the picture.

Whore.

A shiver ran down her spine. It was one thing to suspect the photos were coming from someone who had it out for her. It was another thing entirely to know for sure.

Strong hands settled on her shoulders and squeezed. "Sit with me, Rox."

One glance behind her revealed Joe's blue eyes were filled with concern. For her. She followed him to the living room couch. As much as she wanted to ignore everything and wish it all away, she knew that was dumb. And dangerous.

Curling up on one end, she gave Joe a grateful smile when

he handed her a glass of red wine. A very full glass of red wine. She took a long gulp as he sat at the other end of the couch.

Joe didn't say anything. He didn't push. He simply watched her with a gaze that said she could trust him, that he cared, that he had her back.

She swallowed past the growing lump in her throat and looked down at her wine, blinking fast to stay the stream of tears.

More than anything, she wanted to toss the wineglass aside and snuggle into Joe, to have his arms wrap around her just like they had earlier. The security she'd felt in his embrace had surprised her. It hadn't been the first time he'd hugged her. He'd done so countless times before. But he'd never *held* her. Not like that. Like he would hunt down the source of her fear and make everything better.

Roxie took pride in being a strong, independent woman. But there was a part of her that wanted to retreat, hoist up the white flag, and let Joe slay all her bad guys. Well, this one bad guy in particular.

He moved over to her and took the wineglass from her hands. Setting it down on the coffee table, he said, "Talk to me, Rox."

She looked into his eyes, and her heartbeat tripped. He tugged her to his end of the sofa, adjusting their positions, so she sat between his legs, her back to his chest. When his arms wrapped around her, she finally allowed herself to relax.

"Tell me what you're thinking." His soft voice soothed her frayed nerves.

Her throat knotted again, and a lone tear escaped. She closed her eyes. Then told him the truth. "I'm scared, Joe."

She bit her lower lip to keep it from trembling. That damn photo—all the random, anonymous photos she'd received over the past few months but had never paid any attention to—kept appearing in her mind. Were they all from the same person? Had someone been watching her this entire time? But why? Had she somehow brought this upon herself? The endless questions nagged at her.

"I don't understand why anyone would do this." She shifted in his arms so she could see him. "It doesn't make any sense."

Joe readjusted their position, so she now sat across his lap. One of his arms was still wrapped around her back; the other was tucking a stray lock of hair behind her ear.

"The crazies rarely do, Rox. Right now, we just have to stay alert. I promise I'll do everything I can to keep you safe."

Joe traced the line of her jaw with his finger, and everywhere he touched tingled. When the hand that had been resting on her back came up to knot in her hair, she struggled to find her voice. His name left her lips on a sigh.

Tilting her head to the side, he traced a line from her jaw to her ear with his mouth. "Roxanne," he whispered between little kisses. "I've made so many mistakes with you. I've lied to myself . . . and to you. But this right here . . . God, you mean more to me than you'll ever know. More than I'll ever deserve."

Her heart thumped an unsteady beat. She could barely believe this was happening. With Joe. It was thrilling. And petrifying.

She framed his face in her hands. And then she simply took him in.

His was a face she'd known her entire life. But unlike Quinn, she'd never seen Joe as a brother. He was her confidant, protector, tormentor, partner in crime, and best friend, all wrapped up in one. If she were being honest with herself, he'd been her first love. She just hadn't known it.

As a child, she'd envisioned them living happily ever after with a couple of kids, a dog, and a house with the proverbial white picket fence. As she'd grown older, remnants of her crush had lingered, but she'd never thought they would ever toe that line.

And here they were. With the line begging to be crossed.

Roxie knew they were teetering on the edge of something that could be wonderful . . . or absolutely devastating.

"We have to be sure," she said, tracing his bottom lip with her thumb. "The past few years without you were so damn hard."

She didn't like giving voice to her pain, but she needed him to know. Their bickering over the years had left a wound in her heart that was still raw and aching. It would be a while before it healed.

Sighing, she dropped her gaze to her lap. "Now that we're getting our friendship back on track, I don't want to do anything to jeopardize it."

"Roxanne, look at me," he murmured.

She obliged. His blue eyes were dark now, and they burned with an intensity that left her breathless.

"I can't go back to the way things were," he said, catching her hand and placing a kiss on the inside of her wrist. "I treasure our friendship, Rox. You have to know that. But I want to be more than just your friend, baby. I want to be your partner, your lover, your . . . everything. And I think deep down, I always have."

Joe held his breath. *Shit. Say something. Anything. Please.*

He prayed he hadn't just pushed her too far. His timing was shit. He knew this. But he'd waited for the right moment all his life and it had never arrived. There never *would* be a perfect moment. There was only the here and now.

Yes, he was also concerned about ruining their friendship,

but he'd meant what he'd told her. He could never go back to how things had been. He couldn't. No way. Not when this amazing woman fit so damn perfectly in his arms. The mere idea of her being with someone else—like *this*—had the caveman in him howling.

She wasn't his. He had no right to feel possessive of her. But he couldn't help himself. He couldn't deny how he felt. He was going to do everything he could to prove his worth. To make her *want* to be his.

But first, she had to give him some kind of response. The silence coming from her was deafening. Had he shown his hand too soon? Maybe. His stomach turned at the thought. *Damn.*

A single tear rolled down her cheek, and fear clutched his heart. Gently wiping the wetness away with his thumb, he drew her into his chest. "Rox, baby. Please tell me I didn't just screw everything up."

She shook her head against him. The tension in his muscles eased. But only a little.

"No," she said with a watery laugh. She pulled back to look at him, and her big green eyes were shiny and rimmed with tears. "I'm just overwhelmed by everything. The photos, work, you . . ."

Two more tears broke free, each a punch to his gut.

He released a breath he hadn't realized he'd been holding. If he could kick himself in the nuts, he would. He was an asshole. "I'm so damn sorry, Rox. I didn't mean to make things more confusing for you."

She shook her head, and the tears came faster, forming a steady stream. "Ignore the tears, Joe."

Yeah, right.

"And don't apologize." She sniffed. "I cry in times of confusion, you know that. But you're not the one making this confusing. I'm doing all that on my own."

His eyes narrowed in question. He'd thought he was fluent in Roxie-speak. Apparently, he'd been wrong.

"This?" She waved her hand between the two of them. "This feels good. It feels right. And instead of going with it and trusting it, I'm being crazy and overanalyzing it."

"No, Roxanne, you're not being crazy. Your feelings are real. They're valid. It's *my* fault you're overwhelmed right now."

"Did you send me those photos?"

His lips pressed together. Stubborn, stubborn woman. "Fine, but I'm *partially* responsible for your confusion."

"Joe, it's not—"

"No, Rox. It is. I'll own up to it. I treated you like shit for so long. This about-face, this truce, this honesty between us? It *is* overwhelming. I know you don't trust me fully. And I completely understand and respect that."

Her eyes widened. "But?"

"No buts. Like I said before, I will do everything in my power to earn your trust back. Because this?" He mimicked her earlier hand gesture. "This scares me, too. It scares the absolute shit out of me, actually."

She laughed, and that small green light gave him the confidence to keep going.

"I don't want to ruin what we've already built. At all. We have so much history. We go so far back. But now . . . I want more from you. From us. I'm not going to push you to do anything you're not ready for. I just wanted to let you know how I feel. I want to be honest with you because I haven't been for so long."

Amusement flickered in her eyes. It made him squirm. He *did* want to be honest with her, but he didn't know what he would do if she told him, *Thanks, but no thanks.*

Seconds seemed like hours as she stared at him.

Joe opened his mouth to speak. To say what, he hadn't a

clue. Then he froze when her hands framed his face. God, he loved it when she did that.

Nerves danced in his stomach, however, as she remained quiet.

"Say something, Rox. Please." He heard the desperation in his voice, but he didn't care. "You're killing me, baby."

She brought his face to hers, and he stopped breathing. Something inside him exploded with hope. She'd made the first move. In doing so, she'd told him that he had a chance. He would make the most of it because it mattered too much.

She mattered too much.

Roxie's mouth claimed his, and the kiss was like heaven and hell all at once. Heaven because her lips were as soft as he'd imagined, sweeter than he'd thought possible. And hell because he wanted to take this slow, wanted to savor every millisecond, but his primal instincts were begging him to take more.

Cupping her face, he changed the angle of their kiss, then traced her lower lip with his tongue in a silent plea for entrance. She parted for him, and his heart tripped. He didn't bother holding back a groan of pure fucking bliss as their tongues intertwined. She ran her hands through his hair, and he lost all thought.

"Wrap your legs around me," he murmured.

Roxie straddled his lap, and he hauled her close. When she rocked on his straining cock, his eyes nearly rolled to the back of his head.

She chuckled. The deep, throaty sound had him going impossibly harder. "You gonna be all right there, Buchanan?"

Joe grinned at her. He could hardly believe this was happening. God knew he'd fantasized about being with Roxie like this for far too long. Now here he was, sitting on the couch, feet planted on the floor, Roxie on his lap.

Gripping her hips—because thank you, Jesus, he finally

could—he pulled her flush against him, so she could feel what she did to him, so she knew just how hard she made him. "I'm doing good, baby. You?"

Her eyes widened, then darkened with arousal. A sexy grin played on her lips. "I'm good too, but . . . I think I could be better."

She pushed on his shoulders, and he settled back against the couch. Leaning over him, she rocked her hips harder, and they both groaned. He fused his mouth to hers as she dug her hands in his hair. Their tongues danced, and his hands itched to explore her body.

Slow down, Buchanan.

Roxie rocked against him again, and all thoughts of taking it slow flew out the window. He slipped his hands beneath her shirt. The feel of her hot, silky skin made his eyes cross. She broke away from their kiss and trailed her mouth down his neck. His brain caught up with his body, and some of his good sense returned. He placed his hands on her upper arms and ever so gently pushed her back.

Blazing green eyes questioned him.

He kissed the tip of her nose. "I just want to look at you."

Roxie's lips parted in a smile as old as Eden.

Damn. He was a goner.

She reached for the hem of her shirt. "In that case—"

"Wait." He covered her hands with his, holding them still. Hurt and embarrassment flickered in her eyes. His hands flew to cradle her face, and she averted her gaze at his touch. *Shit. Fuck. Shit.* "Rox, baby, look at me."

A moment passed before she complied. The insecurity he saw when she met his gaze had his insides stilling. The hateful names he'd called her over the years echoed in his mind, and he wanted to gut himself. *He'd* caused that worry, dammit. Well, he sure as fuck was going to work his ass off to make sure she never felt insecure with him again.

He caressed her jaw, careful to be extra gentle as he touched the almost-healed bruise. "Roxanne Elizabeth Jameson, do *not* doubt how much I want you. Because you have to know I do. Hell, you can feel how much I do." He hurried on when she opened her mouth to speak. "But I want to take this slow. I need to. I've made too many mistakes with you already, and I don't want to fuck this up."

The swirling emotions in Roxie's eyes faded, and he sighed in relief. Bringing her face closer, he kissed her lightly on the lips. "You matter to me, Rox. So damn much. I want to do this right."

Her answering smile went straight to his heart. He wrapped his arms around her and turned so they lay flat on the couch with her still atop him. "Let me hold you tonight."

"Of course," Roxie said against his lips.

She reached over him to grab the blanket that had fallen from the couch, rubbing against his cock in the process. For a moment, he rethought his noble intentions. But then she straightened, blanket in hand. She fluffed it out over them, and he caught the sly smile on her face as she snuggled into his side.

He smacked her delectable ass, and she yelped. The little minx knew exactly what she was doing to him. And hell, he was more than okay with that.

CHAPTER SIXTEEN

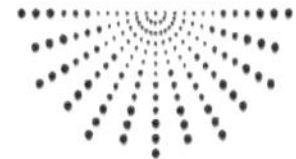

"Penny for your thoughts?"

Roxie jumped and spun around, her hip slamming hard into the prep station. "Holy crap, Alex. Are you trying to give me a heart attack?"

Her friend tsk-tsked. "Seems like the boss lady is off in la-la land."

She looked down at the pie filling she'd been working on and cringed. Judging by the smooshed blueberries, she'd been mixing for a while. Heat spread across her face. It was times like these when she hated being a natural redhead.

"Well, well, well," Alex teased, wagging her eyebrows. "What do we have here?"

Her blush deepened. *Damn.* She shoved the bowl of pie filling aside. "Shut it, Mrs. O'Conner."

Alex laughed. "Oh no, you don't, miss. Spill it."

"I don't know what you're talking about." She wrinkled her nose. That hadn't sounded very convincing.

Her friend snorted. Legit snorted. Obviously, she wasn't buying the lie, either. "Sure, Roxie. Whatever makes you feel better."

Clearing her throat, Roxie concentrated on tossing the ingredients for a new batch of blueberry filling into a bowl. "Why are you even here? Shouldn't you be home with Annie? Or resting?"

"I've got some payroll stuff to knock out. And Nina asked me to cover for a couple hours while she goes to the doctor. Annie's with Mrs. Abbot and Mrs. Yoshida. And I'm feeling much better, thank you."

Of course Alex would have an answer for everything. So aggravating. "Well . . . can't you process payroll and do the Nina stuff remotely? Like, anywhere but here? Away from me?"

Alex gave her a saccharine smile. "Never took you for a coward, you know."

Bristling, she opened her mouth to reply. Then quickly shut it. Her eyes narrowed. "Aren't you the tricky one?"

"If you're not going to tell me what has you all dreamy, can I at least guess?"

Roxie pinned her friend with a glare that usually made people steer clear. "No."

Alex grinned, then rolled her eyes. The woman was immune to her glares. "You're no fun at all. But fine. I'll lay off for now. You do know I'll get it out of you later, though, right?"

"Believe whatever you want," she said, shaking her head and focusing on the pie filling. But she knew Alex was probably right. The woman would somehow manage to get the full story out of her.

Well, maybe not the *full* story. Right now, Roxie could hardly process what had transpired in the last eighteen hours herself, let alone relay the details with any sort of clarity.

Last night, after cuddling and making out on the couch like teenagers, Joe had surprised her by insisting they retire to their rooms. Their *separate* rooms. When he'd kissed her goodnight at her bedroom door, it had taken all her willpower to not drag him inside and tear off his clothes.

Who was she kidding? *He* was the one who'd had the willpower to stop their make-out session. Not her.

Then, this morning had been like every other workday. She'd been dressed and downstairs for her morning run by three fifteen. And Joe had been right there waiting for her.

For the most part, they'd run in silence. But it hadn't been awkward. Much to her surprise, it had been quite comfortable. When there had been talking, he'd done most of it. He'd convinced her that until they figured out what was going on with the photos, she should drive to and from work. Though the distance was short—a little over half a mile—she'd agreed it was a risk that wasn't worth taking, particularly since she walked the same route at the same time every day.

After a four-mile loop and a quick stretch, Joe had walked her into the house. Right when she'd begun to think she'd imagined the previous night's intimacy—because he hadn't even *hinted* at it once during their entire run—he'd laid a kiss on her that had been so hot, so sexy, she'd expected to ignite on the spot. She'd even thought about calling in sick to see if she could change his mind about the whole taking-it-slow thing. She *never* called in sick. Ever.

Then he'd ended the kiss, said he'd stop by Comfort Food later, and taken off for some extra mileage.

Now here she was. Hours later. Her body flushed and aching from the mere recollection of their kiss. Her mind doing yet another play-by-play of the entire morning.

She sighed and glanced down at the bowl. Then groaned. Crushed blueberries. Again. She pursed her lips in thought. Looked like she would have to add macerated blueberries to today's menu. Maybe over a lemon chiffon cake? Or maybe—

"Roxie?"

She startled when Alex peeked her head through the

archway separating the kitchen and customer area. "Could you come up front?"

Holy crap. When had Alex even left the kitchen?

Roxie set the bowl of destroyed blueberries next to its twin. Wiping her hands on her apron, she headed to the front to join Alex and Sheila. "What's up?"

"Oh Mylanta," Sheila said. "It's like I've died and gone to heaven. A heaven filled with delicious, yummy men."

Alex frowned. "Uh, excuse me, Sheila, but one of those delicious men you're referring to happens to be my husband."

"Your point is?" Sheila asked in a dry tone. She arched a brow in challenge.

"Play nice, ladies," Roxie said, cringing.

While Alex and Sheila were both famous for turning anyone into a friend, they clashed like oil and water when mixed together. It was the strangest thing. Alex was by far the friendliest, most patient, and most tolerant person Roxie knew, but there was something about Sheila that rubbed her friend the wrong way. The two simply didn't mesh.

Since having Annie, Alex had come in a handful of times to help out when they'd been short-staffed. Every time, having Alex and Sheila work together had been awkward, uncomfortable, and beyond tense. In other words, a total disaster.

Roxie had made a mental note to make sure, going forward, that the women's schedules didn't overlap too much. But with Nina out, there wasn't much she could do to mend the current situation. Alex and Sheila would just have to figure out how to deal with one another for the next few hours.

Scanning the seating area, she found the dreamy men in question: Quinn, Joe, Cade, Gavin, and Matt. The men were huddled together at the café's lone six-top table.

"Oh my god." Sheila sighed. "Who are those other two?"

Alex rolled her eyes. Hard.

"Gavin Frazier is the guy with brown hair," Roxie said, pointing. "He runs Hudson Security—and before you ask, yes, his company employs a group of super-hot alpha dudes." She could have sworn she heard the woman whimper. *Good. God.* "The guy with black hair is Matt Alvarez. He's a friend of Cade's. He's a detective with Seattle PD, but he's out on medical leave."

"Great," Sheila said, talking over Roxie's last words. "Are either of them single?"

"Um . . ." *Universe, please give me patience.* "I'm not sure."

Sheila's response went unheard as Joe caught Roxie's gaze. Without a word to the guys at his table, he rose and stalked toward her. Her pulse skittered at the predatory gleam in his blue eyes. He rounded the counter, winked at the other women, and snagged her hand. A hot flush stole up her face as more than a dozen prying eyes locked on them.

Unbothered by the attention, Joe led her to her cramped office. Once inside, he shut the door and pressed her against it. Before Roxie could catch her breath, his hands were buried in her hair and his lips were crashing down on hers.

Her toes curled. Bliss. Complete bliss.

She wrapped her arms around his neck. He stepped closer, removing any remaining space between them. His lips trailed over her jaw, then her neck, then her ear. A shiver tore through her. This man. He made her feel so alive, so wanted.

"Sorry," Joe murmured, his breathing uneven. "But you looked so damn pretty standing there in your apron. I just had to kiss you."

She smiled at him as her insides melted. And because she could, she tugged his head to her for another kiss.

After a while—it could have been five seconds or five minutes for all she knew—he released her with a groan.

"I should get back to the guys," he said, eyes twinkling. "Do I have a stupid grin on my face?"

Laughing, she nodded. "I'm sure it's just as stupid as the one on mine."

He caught her hand and raised it to his lips, brushing a kiss over her delicate skin. The gentle touch sent tingles down to her toes. "I hope you don't mind that I probably just outed us."

"Probably." She gave him the once-over, and her face grew hotter. "Well, I'd say *most definitely*, considering you have flour and blueberry guts all over your shirt. Sorry about that, Buchanan."

"Yeah, right, baby," he said with an amused shake of his head. "You're not sorry one bit."

She grinned. Nope. Not one bit.

He gestured to the door. "After you."

On her way past him, he swatted her rear.

"Seriously, Joe," she hissed over her shoulder, fighting a smile. "You need to behave yourself."

He swatted her again. "Pot? Meet kettle."

Once they reached the counter, Joe flashed that ridiculously charming Buchanan grin at Alex and Sheila. "Ladies."

Both women stared after him, mouths agape, as he returned to his table.

She shook her head. The guy was incorrigible. There was no other way to describe him. Well, that wasn't quite true, but she'd keep those other delectable descriptions to herself.

"See?" Alex said in a hushed voice. She had a smug smile on her lips.

Roxie raised a brow. "See what?"

"I told ya I'd get it out of you." Alex nodded toward the guys' table. "By the amount of blueberry that's now on Joe's shirt and your someone-just-ran-their-hands-through-my-hair hair, I'd say I have my answer."

Roxie tried to smother a grin but failed. "Alex, we need to have a girls' night. Stat."

―――――

Joe resumed his seat at the table and hoped the grin on his face wasn't as dopey as he suspected.

His friends stared at him with varying levels of amusement.

Yup. The dopey grin was most definitely in place. Oddly enough, he wasn't quite sure he cared.

"What'd I miss?" he asked, trying for casual. He doubted he was fooling anyone.

Matt nodded in the direction of the counter. "I take it if I asked Roxie out for dinner and drinks, that wouldn't fly with you?"

Joe tensed, and his grin disappeared. "You're damn right that wouldn't fly with me, Alvarez." He glared at the other man. Despite crossing paths on several occasions, he didn't know Matt well. Cade vouched for him, but that wouldn't stop Joe if this fucker tried to make a move on his—

The table erupted with laughter.

"Man, you're such a sucker, Buchanan," Quinn said.

"Seriously, man?" Matt snickered. "You have her fucking blueberry shit all over your shirt."

Damn. He should have seen that one coming. Rather than acknowledge his gullibility, though, he did what every guy would do in his situation: flip them off. *Assholes.*

"You should have seen your damn face, bro," Cade said, wiping away a tear. "So, you and Roxie, eh?"

Ignoring the question, he swung his narrowed gaze back to Matt. "You weren't serious about asking her out, were you?"

The table broke into laughter again.

Joe cringed, shaking his head. "You guys are fuckers."

Of course, his crappy comeback had them laughing even harder. Again, he should have seen that coming. Biting back a smile, he waited for their raucous guffaws to subside.

"Hey, fellas!"

Sheila's shrill, squeaky voice immediately killed the table's mirth. The five men glanced at each other, then uttered awkward hellos. She didn't seem to register their discomfort.

"Gorgeous men like you need to stay fueled," Sheila said, treating them all to a bright smile. A large platter filled with various treats and goodies sat balanced on her palms. Leaning forward to set the platter down on the table, she gave the group a full display of her impressive cleavage. "It's all on the house, boys. *Anything* you want is on the house."

Joe suppressed a snort at her breathy and obvious invitation.

"Thanks, Sheila," he said, reaching for a blueberry scone. He sure did love Roxie's blueberries. "Are you having a good morning so far?"

"It's a much better morning now, handsome," she cooed, squeezing his shoulder.

He stilled, the warm blueberry scone halfway to his lips. A flicker of unease surged through him, and his appetite evaporated. Only when she let go did he relax.

The woman's over-the-top flirting was embarrassing and, frankly, a bit unnerving. A glance at his buddies proved he wasn't the only one who felt that way.

Joe liked women. Hell, he loved women. He happily flirted with all legal ages, shapes, and sizes. It wasn't something he consciously did. He just loved to see what made them smile.

However, there was one exception. Well, two.

Women who were catty and mean? He didn't give them the time of day.

Women who tried too hard and reeked of desperation? That was dangerous territory that he didn't mess with. Ever. Because flirting with desperate only got you into trouble.

Joe watched Sheila smooth her hands down Cade's back. As much as he empathized with his friend, he was glad he wasn't the only one in her sights.

"Now, you boys just holler if there's anything you need. *Anything* at all," Sheila said, throwing the table a wink before heading back to the counter.

"Holy shit," Gavin muttered when she was out of earshot. "God help the poor bastard she ends up with."

Quinn elbowed Matt. "You could put us all out of our misery and ask her out. It'd be like community service."

Matt choked on his coffee. He shook his head as he tried to recover. "Oh no. There's taking one for the team and all, but hell no. I may be fucking stupid, but I'm not fucking crazy." He reached for a muffin and paused, his lip twitching. "Literally."

Joe laughed—the twelve-year-old in him couldn't help it —and shook his head. "Man, we're all going to hell. You know that, right? Here we are, eating the free food she brought out and we're slamming her—"

"Pretty sure she'd prefer you banging her," Gavin snickered.

"—and I'm sure she's a very nice woman," Joe continued, ignoring the man. "We shouldn't be such dicks."

Cade nodded, polishing off the last bite of his muffin. "You're probably right, oh moral compass, but I'm not asking her out, either." He reached for a slice of banana bread. "Damn, Roxie sure can bake. You better make a decision about joining my team, Buchanan, and you better make it fast. Because if you keep hanging out here, you're going to turn into a fat fucker."

Quinn looked at him. "You're joining Cade's team?"

Joe shrugged. "I'm thinking about it."

"*Our* team, fuckers," Gavin corrected.

"Wait." Quinn's brows turned inward. "As what?"

"A hand-to-hand instructor."

"There he goes, being all modest and shit," Cade mumbled over a bite of banana bread. It took him another half second to wolf down the rest of the slice. Once done, he wiped his mouth and leaned back in his chair, patting his stomach. He lifted his chin at Gavin. "We're teaming up to do a new training program targeting law enforcement and private security folks."

"Hand-to-hand, weapons, marksmanship," Gavin said, nodding. "Tactical training, outdoor survival, and all that shit. We know there's a lot of interest, but with Cade's workload and mine, we're looking for someone to take the lead on the program. And our favorite fed here just became unemployed at the perfect time."

Joe flipped off his potential business partner.

"Huh." Quinn pursed his lips in thought. "I take a couple classes at your gym, and I know a couple of my deputies have talked about joining me. With the tactical aspect you're talking about, it could be beneficial if we did it formally through the department. Let me talk to the mayor and see if we can find some funding for it. Why the hell haven't you guys mentioned this to me before?"

"Believe me, I've thought about it." Cade shrugged. "But I didn't want to offer something we didn't have the manpower to deliver. Depending on what Buchanan decides to do, we still may not."

Joe laughed. "You can save your guilt trip for someone

who doesn't know you as well, De la Rosa. We've done two-story beer bongs together, remember?"

Cade grimaced. "*That* is something I'd like to forget."

"Tell me about it. I still can't look at a PBR without feeling queasy. But like we talked about earlier, let's do this women's self-defense class first and see if my teaching style jives with your crew. We'll go from there."

"What women's self-defense class?" Quinn asked.

"Cade's got a weekly women's cardio kickboxing class they do. In light of the photo shit that's happening with Rox, I was thinking of offering a self-defense class. I'd like to get her, Alex, and the rest of Rox's staff to go. I figured if we did it right after the cardio class, hopefully, we could get those women to stay for it too."

Gavin frowned. "What's the photo shit with Roxie?"

Joe gave Cade, Gavin, and Matt a quick rundown of the situation, and Quinn chimed in with any details he missed.

Cade let out a low whistle. "That's fucking creepy."

"She's got a stalker," Matt said, crossing his arms over his chest. His jaw muscle ticked. "My sister-in-law had one. If you need help, man, count me in."

Stalker. A chill crawled down Joe's spine. He'd used the word in his head, but hearing the Seattle PD detective say it out loud had his blood running cold.

"I'll keep my eyes and ears open for sure," Cade said. "As far as the class goes, I like the idea of doing it after the cardio kickboxing class. Since those ladies will be tired, we should keep it to about forty-five minutes, definitely no longer than an hour." He eyed the women at the counter and something dark flickered over his face. "I definitely think attending is a must for the ladies who work here. With the shit going on with Roxie, it's non-negotiable. I'll happily waive their fees."

Joe nodded. "I don't think Rox or Alex will have any

problems with going. But what about the others? I don't really want to broadcast what's happening with the photos."

"That's understandable," Cade said. "June already goes to the kickboxing classes, so that shouldn't be a problem."

Gavin rolled his eyes. "I'm sure Sheila will jump at the chance to go. I don't know about Nina, though." A sly grin spread across his face. "For her, though, I'd be willing to take one for the team. If need be, of course."

"Oh, would you now?" Joe asked with a chuckle.

Gavin shrugged. The picture of innocence. Well, as innocent as a six-two, two-twenty, former special ops guy could look. "What can I say? I'm a good friend like that. If I need to take Nina out for drinks, dinner perhaps, in order to convince her to come to the class, I'd be willing to do that. For her safety, of course."

"Well, aren't you just a fucking saint?" Quinn laughed. "Because I'm sure it has nothing at all to do with the fact that Nina's smoking hot."

"Nah, I haven't noticed," Gavin said, though his wide smile indicated otherwise. "Aren't you married, Sheriff?"

"Sure am, my friend. My wife is even more smoking hot, and she's the goddess I plan on worshiping until the day I die. But I still have two eyes."

Joe laughed, then lowered his voice. "What about Minnie Mouse over there? What if she needs extra convincing as well?" He nodded to Cade. "You in?"

Cade froze like a deer in headlights. Then his slick smile was back. "If she balks, let me know. I'll send a couple of my fighters down to do the convincing. I'm sure all parties will see it as a win-win."

CHAPTER SEVENTEEN

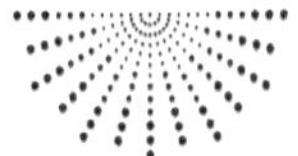

At eleven thirty that night, Roxie finally walked through the front door of the Buchanan house. With Nina out sick, she'd had to work a small catering job that she'd originally planned to delegate. The event had been a five-year anniversary party for the local yarn store, Knit Wits, which was three doors down from Comfort Food.

Most of the women who'd attended were regular customers at the café. Roxie had been surprised to find out the knitting shop drew in such a wide range of ages. Since she had the knitting ability of a rock, she'd always thought it was something only grandmas did.

Roxie had learned three very important lessons tonight. The first—which she really should have learned in kindergarten—was not to judge a book by its cover. The second was that *craft night* was code. It was a decoy that convinced significant others that the women in their lives were getting together to trade secrets of domestic and crafting bliss.

In reality, it was a bunch of women getting together to drink heinous amounts of wine, gossip like raunchy sailors, and *maybe* get a couple of rows knitted. Or purled. Whatever.

As for the final—and probably most important—lesson Roxie had learned?

When a grandmother of four merrily calls out that it's time to do shots? Just walk away.

Now here she was, leaning heavily on the front door, trying to fit her key into the damn lock. If only it would stop moving . . . Squinting, Roxie tried again.

The front door flew open. She bolted upright with a yelp.

"Where the hell have you been, Roxanne?"

Joe stood in the entryway, hands on his hips, mouth pressed into an angry line. Even in her alcohol-addled state, she could see the frustration radiating from him in waves.

It took a few moments for her to realize he'd spoken because there was something really, really yummy about an irritated Joe these days. The way his shoulders tensed and his expression got all broody had heat flooding low in her belly.

She cleared her throat. "Sorry. What was the question again?"

"Where. Have. You. Been?"

"Working, of course."

Joe's eyes narrowed as she sailed past him.

It was damn near midnight, and instead of being tucked in bed and sound asleep after a long-ass day of work—the woman had woken up at *three*, for fuck's sake!—Roxie was . . . giggly.

He frowned. Something was off. The Roxie he knew was sarcastic, exasperating, stubborn, impulsive, scattered, gorgeous, and sexy . . . and smart, loyal, hilarious, beautiful, and kind. But giggly? That didn't make the list.

He looked out at the empty driveway. "Rox, where's your car?"

"June dropped me off."

"Okaaay . . ." He scratched his head. "But where's your car?"

"At the café," she called from the kitchen. "Are you hungry? Because I'm starving."

He shut the door and headed in her direction. Coming to a stop beneath the kitchen archway, he watched her pull a pie from the fridge. His eyebrows hit his hairline and his jaw flat-out dropped when she took a bite. Directly from the dish.

Shit. Something was definitely off. Any other day, she would have his head if she caught him eating from the pie plate. For as long as he could remember, she'd spouted nonsense about respecting her pies and eating them "off a plate like a civilized human."

"And why, Rox, is your car parked at your shop?"

With a spoonful of blueberry pie at her lips, she looked at him like he was an idiot. "Because I have a parking spot there."

He closed his eyes and took a deep breath in, counting to ten before releasing it. Feeling more centered, he made the time-out signal with his hands. "Let's start over, okay? I thought you had a catering job tonight?"

She nodded, mouth full of pie.

Damn, she was cute. But still. "So why didn't you drive your car home from it then?"

She held up a finger as she chewed.

He waited. His patience was being held together by a frayed string as she gulped down a glass of water.

Finally, she said, "Well, I couldn't drive now, could I?"

He counted to ten again. "Why not?"

"Because after the first round of shots, Mrs. Abbot broke out Sylvester Stallone's shot ski." She shuddered. "Good god, can those women drink."

His mouth opened, then closed. *Sylvester Stallone's shot ski?*

Shoving another spoonful of pie into her mouth, she covered the dish in plastic wrap with an efficiency that was borderline scary and placed it back in the fridge. When she spun around to face him, she staggered. Before he could blink, however, she caught herself on the counter and flashed him a blinding smile.

Holy. Shit. A wide grin consumed his face.

Roxie was wasted.

"A shot ski, you say?"

She nodded, and her eyes grew animated. How had he not recognized that cute, glassy, loopy look?

"What were the ladies shooting this evening? Whiskey?"

"Uh, no. And barf. These are the *knitting* ladies, Joe. They don't shoot straight whiskey."

"Oh, pardon me," he said. His sarcasm was lost on the drunkard. "Then what, pray tell, is the drink of choice for the *knitting* ladies?"

"Washington Apple shots, of course. And yeah, there's whiskey in it, but all the other stuff makes it taste like a Jolly Rancher."

He laughed. He couldn't help it. She was so damn cute. "And the Sylvester Stallone shot ski?"

"Mrs. Abbot won them at an auction. He signed them, too, so that was cool, but it's not like you can put them on display or anything, right?" She shrugged. "So she had Mr. Abbot weld metal shot glasses to them. There's four per ski, so they break them out at parties. I mean, who doesn't love a friendly shot ski competition, am I right?"

Joe shook his head, dumbfounded by all parts of her explanation. "Okay. But why didn't you call me to pick you up?"

She busied herself refolding the kitchen towel on the counter.

"Roxanne?"

Her head shot up. "Why don't you ever call me Roxie? You always call me Rox or Roxanne. Why is that?"

He crossed his arms over his chest. "Because I'm the only one who gets to call you Roxanne."

"True." She pushed the towel aside and trailed her gaze down his body. Judging by the wicked gleam in her eyes, she liked what she saw.

The little voice in his head warned that she was up to something. When she got that look on her face, she was *always* up to something.

She sauntered toward him, and he held his breath.

"You know what, Joe?" She looped her arms around his shoulders. "You sure are yummy when you're annoyed."

All the blood in his brain rushed south. He uncrossed his arms, then gripped her hips to pull her flush against him. "Is that so, baby?"

"Yeah," she said against his lips, raking her hands through his hair. "You do this broody thing that's so hot. Makes me want to—"

His mouth crashed down on hers. Her lips parted at once, and their tongues explored. Moving his hands from her hips, he cupped her ass and lifted her. As she wrapped her legs around his waist, he turned them and pressed her back to the kitchen wall.

The smooth, soft skin of her neck drove him mad as he kissed along it. *Damn.* He couldn't get enough. He wanted to taste every single inch of her. When she arched into him, a soft moan on her lips, he fought the urge to take her right then, right there.

Because she'd been drinking. *Dammit.*

"More, Joe," she whispered, her legs tightening around him. "Please."

He leaned his forehead against hers, heart racing.

Roxie's hands smoothed over his face. "What's wrong? Why did you stop?"

He let out a breath. "Baby, you're drunk."

"No, I'm not." Her legs tightened even more, and her lips went to his neck as she rubbed herself against him like a cat. "I'm totally fine."

She found a particularly sensitive spot by his ear, and his eyes crossed. "Rox, baby, you ate pie straight out of the dish."

For a split second, she froze. Then she resumed her exploration of his neck. "Don't be ridiculous," she murmured against his skin. "I'd never be drunk enough to do something like that."

"Sorry, baby, but you did. Spooned it out of the dish and everything."

Her head shot up and her kiss-swollen lips formed a perfect O.

He nipped at her bottom lip and laughed as her legs hit the floor. "How many of those classy Washington Apple shots did you have tonight?"

She glared at him, but he knew it was just for effect since her hips were still flush against his. "Are you really gonna stand there, Buchanan, and tell me you don't want me?"

"What do you think?" He nudged her with his hips, making his erection obvious. "I absolutely want you. But I want you sober."

She rubbed against him, and a gleam of satisfaction flashed in her eyes. "For the record, Boy Scout, I think your let's-take-it-slow thing is stupid."

He laughed and took her face in his hands, memorizing her features. Sparkling emerald-green eyes. Kiss-swollen lips. Pale skin flushed with arousal and alcohol. Damn, she was gorgeous. He returned his lips to hers and took his time, savoring each little nip, each little taste.

When he came up for air, they were both breathless.

Dropping his mouth to her forehead, he said, "I want you so much, baby. It's ridiculous. But you're going to be stone-cold sober the first time we're together. I want you to remember every second of it." Slowly, he pulled away from her. "But that's not happening tonight."

She fisted her hand in his shirt, disbelief etched on her face. Her mouth opened and closed a couple of times before she spoke. "You've got to be kidding me, Buchanan, right?"

He shook his head. "Sorry, Rox."

Letting go, she stepped out of his reach. "You, Joe Buchanan, are gonna leave me here—all hot and bothered—and just go to bed for the night? That's it?"

Well, when she put it *that* way, it did sound really stupid . . .

Focus, Buchanan. Think with your brain, *not your dick.*

"Not tonight, Rox. Not like this."

She narrowed her eyes at him. The only sounds in the kitchen were the hum of the refrigerator and the tick of the clock. He squirmed under her stare. Then, as if someone had snapped their finger, a brilliant smile appeared on her face.

"Okay, fine," she said. "We can do it your way tonight."

She smacked him on the ass as she walked into the hall. At the base of the stairs, she stopped and turned back to him. Her bright smile morphed into a sly grin. A grin he knew couldn't be trusted.

Dammit. He was about to get fucked over. And not in a good way.

"Oh, and FYI, Joseph? If you happen to hear some strange noises tonight, don't worry about it. It'll be me and my vibrator taking care of what you won't. You're more than welcome to watch, but just know that you won't be invited to participate. You know, since we're going the let's-take-it-slow route and all."

His jaw hit the floor. *Holy. Fuck.* The visual of Roxie

getting herself off almost had him exploding in his pants. The little minx.

"You have a good night, Boy Scout." She blew him a kiss and headed up the staircase.

Groaning, Joe slumped into the wall and thunked his head against it. Once. Twice. Then a third time.

It was official.

He was the biggest dumb fuck ever.

CHAPTER EIGHTEEN

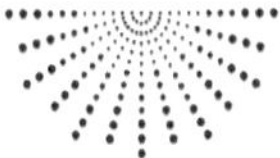

"Good morning, sunshine," Roxie called out with a smile, making her way down the stairs. "It's a glorious Wednesday morning, don't you think?"

Joe scowled at her from his position by the door. "It's still dark out, and it's colder than fuck this morning. I'm going to freeze my balls off out there. Let's just get this over with already."

"Awww. Did someone have a rough night?" She bent over to lace up her running shoes. So what if she happened to aim her backside in his direction?

When a growl emanated from behind her, she bit her lip to smother a laugh. The bastard deserved all the misery she was planning to dish out this morning. Because leaving her high and dry last night had not been cool. At all. Well, he might not have left her *dry*, per se, but whatever. It was still a dick move on his part. Or dickless, technically.

Her eyes widened at her own thoughts. *Why, good morning, sex fiend.*

Yes, she'd been a tiny bit drunk last night. And sure, looking back, it had been very noble of him to not let their first time be a drunken sex fest. However, she begged to differ with his reasoning: she *would* have remembered every moment of it. She knew this for a fact because she sure as hell remembered every single second of last night. Particularly the events that had occurred after she'd closed her bedroom door.

Like how she'd stayed awake until she'd heard him settle into his room, which shared a wall with hers. And how she'd waited to hear the click of his lamp, an indication that he'd climbed into bed, before turning on her toy. She especially recalled how she hadn't bothered holding back any of her moans as she'd worked her trusty rabbit vibrator and imagined Joe touching her instead. Knowing he'd been listening had turned her on more than she'd thought possible.

After going two rounds with her vibrator, she'd conked out. Those three hours of sleep had been some of the most restful she'd had in a long, long time. It was no wonder she had sex on the brain this morning. If she'd had that much fun with only her vibrator and thoughts of Joe, she couldn't imagine what the real deal would be like.

"Get your ass moving, Rox," the real deal barked as he held the front door open. "Let's go."

She straightened, stretching her arms over her head. "You sure are sexy when you're all bed-headed and grumpy."

Joe pointed at the porch steps. "Go. Now."

As Roxie walked by him, she stopped to pat his cheek. "Don't worry, this'll be fun."

Grumbling, he locked up and followed her down the steps. "I'm setting the pace today, Rox. Try and keep up."

It was torture. Every damn step. Every damn breath.

Fucking. Torture.

Joe set a punishing pace for the first mile. It didn't surprise him that Roxie was able to keep up, but it annoyed him. He wanted her as uncomfortable as he was. When the running app on his phone signaled they'd completed their first mile, he slowed down. There were some icy patches on the ground, and the last thing he needed was a broken ankle to go along with his damn blue balls.

It pissed him off that this was all his own doing. Joe knew that if he'd gone into her room last night, she wouldn't have kicked him out. Hell, he'd probably be buried deep inside her right now instead of out in the freezing cold for a fucking four-mile run.

Goddamn, he *had* to stop thinking about last night. It was making the run miserable, not to mention painful. But the only things looping in his head were the steady hum of Roxie's vibrator and her sexy moans. When she'd screamed out his name as she'd come, he'd almost lost his mind. He sure as hell had gotten himself off, too, but it had been the most unfulfilling orgasm of his life.

Enough already!

Checking their mileage on his phone, he groaned when he saw they hadn't yet reached the mile-and-a-half point. He didn't know how much more of this torture he could take.

Fuck it.

He stopped, turned around, and began the return run home.

"But we haven't gone two miles yet," Roxie called, pivoting to stay with him.

Joe didn't reply. Instead, he pushed their pace a little faster. Being the competitive little soldier he knew she was, Rox stopped talking and matched his stride.

Nine minutes later, he slammed the front door shut behind them.

"What the hell, Joe? Are you done being pissy now?" She

bent at the waist, hands on her knees as she tried to catch her breath. "Holy crap, I haven't run that fast in years."

He should apologize. But he didn't. Instead, he grabbed her hand and hauled her up the stairs with him.

She tried to tug free, but he didn't let go.

"What's your deal?" she snapped. "I have to get ready for work, so whatever kind of tantrum this is? Hurry it up."

"Fine," he said, guiding her through her bedroom and into the master bath. Letting her hand go, he reached into the shower and turned the water to hot.

"Seriously, Joe, what are you doing?"

He dragged his fitted running shirt over his head, then dropped it on the ground. "What I should have done last night."

Roxie's eyes widened at the sight before her. She wanted to spend all day drinking in this delicious view of Joe's sculpted chest, but his mouth crashed onto hers. He tugged at the elastic band in her hair, loosening her ponytail so he could bury his fingers in her tresses.

Clinging to him, she ran her hands over the strong muscles of his back. They were taut with frustration, and she sensed the pent-up need humming through him. His hands left her hair, and then they were everywhere, pulling and tugging until their clothes were in a heap on the floor.

When he gripped her bottom and lifted her, she eagerly wrapped her legs around him. The heat of his hard cock pressed to her core, and she rubbed her wet pussy against him. Moans of pleasure escaped her lips as she lost herself to the moment.

Holy hell.

She'd wrapped herself around him before, but there'd

always been the barrier of their clothes. Being skin to skin was more amazing than she'd imagined. And she'd imagined plenty. Electricity sparked everywhere their bodies touched, and yet still, it was not enough.

More. She needed more.

"I want to feel you inside me, Joe. Please." Roxie was begging, but she couldn't find it in her to care. Not one bit. All that mattered was him. Them. Now.

Joe squeezed her ass, then pulled away. She groaned at his sudden absence.

"Gotta get a condom, baby," he said between pants. "I think I have one in the other room."

"No," she murmured, trailing kisses along his neck. Then she met his gaze. "I'm on birth control and I'm clean. You?"

He nodded, but his expression was nervous. "I've never . . . Not without a condom."

"Me either." But she wanted this with him. Had to feel him inside her with no barriers. "I want you bare. Nothing between us."

A growl rumbled deep in his throat, reverberating against her chest. Then his mouth claimed hers, and he walked them into the shower. Warm water cascaded over them as he backed her up against the cool tile.

Desperation clawed at her, and she tore her mouth from his. "I need you inside me, Joe. Now."

Pressed against the wall, she dropped one of her legs to the ground. He hooked her other leg over his elbow, holding her open, and caressed his fingers over her slick folds, first swirling, then plunging inside. She gripped his shoulders and cried out as he finger-fucked her.

"That's my girl," he said in her ear, thrusting deep and hard. "You're so fucking wet, baby. That's it."

She broke apart at his words. Her orgasm had her limbs trembling and her pussy milking his hand.

"You're so fucking beautiful, Rox," he said with his lips against her ear. A moment later, his thick cock nudged at her entrance. He leaned back, and she saw his blue eyes were dark with need and longing. "One more time, baby."

Her heart squeezed, and an emotion she couldn't put into words washed over her. They really were going to do this.

Holding her gaze, he filled her, stretching her in one long stroke. She gasped, and her breath locked in her lungs.

"Rox, baby," he moaned, capturing her mouth once again. His tongue mimicked each deep thrust of his cock.

Tingling heat threatened to envelop her entire being. "More," she pleaded, nails digging crescents into his back.

He set a punishing rhythm, just as he'd done on the trail a half hour before. And she loved every moment of it. The sounds of their skin slapping together filled the shower.

"Harder," she moaned, gripping his shoulders. All she could do was hold on.

His deep thrusts took her closer and closer, and then he ground against her clit just right, and she screamed out his name. A moment later, he followed her over the edge.

"Baby," he whispered. "You okay?"

Roxie might have nodded; she wasn't quite sure. Every bone in her body was limp. It was as if a train had run her over. A delicious, sexy, orgasm-inducing train.

Lowering her leg to the ground, he helped her regain her balance. After soaping up her body, he eased her under the warm spray to rinse. He quickly washed up, then shut off the water. Wrapping her in a fluffy towel, he dropped a kiss to her lips and scooped her up into his arms. The grin he flashed her on the way into the bedroom made her toes curl. Good lord, what was it about this man that had her turning to goo?

With a delicious, lingering kiss, Joe laid her on her bed.

He then retrieved something from the nightstand. "You're calling in sick," he said, holding her phone out to her.

"So bossy." She rolled her eyes as she stretched. She'd never felt so relaxed in her life. It was freaking glorious. "I don't call in sick, so try again."

"Fine." He sighed. "Can you please text whoever it is you need to text and let them know you'll be coming in much, much later today?"

The corners of her lips twitched. God, he was cute. "Why is that, exactly?"

"Brat." He tugged at the corner of her towel but stopped short of removing it. "Unless you want me to text them?"

She could only stare at the gorgeous, chiseled man. Her mind was a muddled, foggy mess.

He climbed onto the bed and hovered above her, droplets of water clinging to his skin. Droplets she wanted to lick off.

She cleared her throat. "What's the reason I'm going to be late again?"

Ever so slowly, he trailed his fingers from her bare calf to her inner thigh. "Because, baby, I plan on tasting every single inch of you this morning."

Her mouth went dry, and her heart hammered in her chest. *Oh god. Yes. Please.*

"In fact, Roxanne, there are some parts I plan on tasting a few times." His fingers stilled just millimeters away from dipping inside her throbbing pussy, and every part of her screamed in protest. With a mischievous grin, he withdrew his hand and stood from the bed. It took a few seconds before she registered that he was holding out her phone again. "Call it in, Rox."

"Bossy," she scolded again, though she secretly loved it.

His grin grew wider, and the corners of his eyes crinkled.

Grabbing her phone from him, she fired off a text to her employees.

Sorry for the short notice, but I'm going to be late today. Very late.

Her gaze traveled down Joe's hard body, filing away each and every detail. She turned her attention back to her phone, and her thumbs flew across the screen.

Actually, may not make it in at all.

Once the texts successfully delivered, she powered down her phone and tossed it aside. In all the years she'd owned and operated Comfort Food, this was the first time—aside from when she'd been admitted to the hospital—that she had missed morning prep. Looking at the man in front of her, she knew the sacrifice would be worth it. She was going to enjoy every damn minute of it.

Leaning back on her elbows, she let the soft terry cloth fall to her sides. Color flooded Joe's cheeks, and his eyes blazed.

That was all it took. One smoldering look from him, and her body responded. Breathing became harder as the wetness between her legs grew. The need to have his mouth on her, devouring her, left her trembling. She spread her knees, exposing herself to him.

"Now, I believe you mentioned something about . . . tasting?"

The air left Joe's lungs in a whoosh.

Perfection. Roxanne was absolute fucking perfection.

Lying against the pillows, auburn hair spread like a halo around her bare shoulders, rosy nipples pert atop her perfect breasts, she watched him with stubborn challenge in her eyes.

How the hell had he gotten so damn lucky? Part of him

wanted to pounce. But no. He would take his time appreciating the beauty and fire of the woman laid out before him.

His gaze moved down her flat stomach to the exquisite folds that he knew would be wet for him. He licked his lips in anticipation.

Hot damn.

Rox was all smooth skin—*everywhere.* A slow, devilish smile spread across his face. He hadn't been lying earlier. He planned on tasting every last inch of her.

Moving to the end of the bed, he caught her ankle and tugged so she rested flat on her back, then kissed the arch of her foot. His free hand traced circles up her leg to her inner thigh, and his mouth followed, licking and nibbling. Inch by glorious fucking inch. He was nearly out of his mind, his cock heavy and aching, by the time he reached the juncture between her thighs. And by the sounds coming from Roxie, she was close to delirious as well.

He traced his fingers over her, teasing through her wetness, and circled the tight bud that pulsed beneath his touch. She arched toward him, moaning his name. He slipped two fingers into her heat and lowered his head to taste her, putting them both out of their misery at last.

Holy fuck, yes. Her sweet and spicy musk filled his nose. One taste, and his mouth watered for more. Her cries filled the room as he feasted.

He was officially in heaven.

CHAPTER NINETEEN

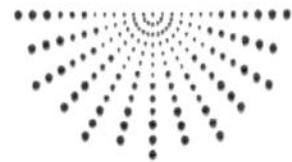

Five hours later, Joe walked into Ray's Diner and scanned the tables. Seeing his dad in the corner booth, he headed over. As much as he'd wanted to keep Roxie captive in bed for the rest of the day, her inner workaholic had prevailed.

"Mornin'." He leaned in and gave his dad a hug, then slid onto the bench seat across from him. He nodded to his dad's half-full coffee cup. "Have you been waiting long?"

"Not at all. I had a couple cancellations this morning, so I headed over here a little early." His dad paused mid-sip and looked him over. "You look good, son. A lot more relaxed and well-rested than the last time I saw you."

Oh, you have no idea, Dad.

Joe bit back a grin and busied himself with the menu as heat crawled over his face. "It's been good being back on Hudson. Relaxing."

"Is Roxie doing okay?"

Joe's head shot up from the menu. "Why?"

"I swung by Comfort Food this morning, and the girls said she was coming in late, maybe not even at all. I think they were a little worried. Truth be told, so am I. That's not like Roxie. Did you talk to her this morning?"

Yup, he sure as hell had. In fact, he'd done a lot more than just talk with that hot little mouth of hers. He swore he'd seen stars when he'd fed his cock into her sweet, hungry mou—

Fuck, Buchanan! Think of something else. Anything *else!*

Wincing, he shifted in his seat and cleared his throat. "I did. Rox is fine, Dad."

She'd been a whole lot more than fine, actually. She'd been screaming his name and making a valiant attempt at suffocating him between her perfect thighs. Not that he'd minded. He'd risk asphyxiation any day if it meant he got to taste her sweet pussy.

Holy. Motherfucking. Shit. Not *the time nor the place, buddy. Focus!*

He cleared his throat again and resumed studying the menu.

"Joseph?" His dad was looking at him expectantly.

Crap. Had he missed something? "Sorry, Dad, what was that?"

His father's eyes narrowed. "I said, I'm sorry for not telling you Roxie was staying at the house."

That comment killed all thoughts of his early morning antics. He still felt like shit for hurting her. "Why didn't you?"

Rubbing the bridge of his nose, his dad said, "Look, it's no secret that the two of you have problems. You guys are Hudson Island's version of the big fat elephant in the room. Would you have come home if you knew she was staying at the house?"

Joe crossed his arms over his chest. "No, I sure as hell would not have."

"Exactly." His dad pointed a finger at him. "That's why I didn't say anything."

"Was this your version of exposure therapy or something?"

His dad scoffed. "More like I was hoping the two of you would start acting like adults and fix your friendship, and if not, then at least talk it out and put it all behind you."

Joe glanced out the window and sighed. He knew there had been a shit-ton of gossip that had arisen after their fight all those years ago. And he'd hightailed it out of town and left Roxie to deal with the aftermath on her own. "Dad, I said awful things to her back then. In front of a whole damn bar. Then, when it was just the two of us, I said even more horrible shit."

"You did. That was the most disappointed I have ever been in you."

Joe's heart squeezed, but he nodded. His father's disappointment was warranted.

"Did you apologize? Did you make it right?"

Again, Joe nodded. "I did. But as for making it right?" He blew out a breath, his mind drifting back to earlier this morning. Passion and mind-blowing sex were one thing. Trust and true intimacy were another entirely. "I'm trying to. I have a long way to go, but I do want to make it right with her. I have to."

"For you or her?"

"For her. And for everyone—Quinn, Alex, you. But mostly for Rox. She didn't deserve any of my shit."

"What about you, son? What do you want?"

Joe shrugged. "I started this mess. It doesn't matter what I want."

His dad stared at him for a quiet moment. "You did start it all, Joseph. However, it's in the past and can't be changed. Now, what have I always told you?"

Joe's lips twitched. "The only things you can control are your actions and reactions."

His father's blue eyes twinkled. "And how have your actions and reactions been so far?"

He scoffed. "They've been shit. You know that."

"Yes, son. Yes, they sure have. But do they need to continue to be shit?"

Joe considered the man across the table, the man who was a million times smarter than him. He needed to heed his words. "Message received, Dad. Message received."

"Good. Because you need to set aside your differences, Joseph. You need to look out for her."

"I know. We're working on it." He hoped to hell he wasn't blushing, but he knew it was hopeless. He could feel his face heating.

"Are you sure? Because with her calling in sick in light of what's going on . . ."

Joe shook his head. "She didn't call in sick. She just took the morning off. She's at the café as we speak." He held up his hand as his father opened his mouth. "Seriously, Dad, Rox is fine."

"Is that so?" His dad's voice dropped low, and his tone turned sharp. "You're saying she's completely fine with having a stalker? *You're* fine with some deranged person harassing her?"

Joe closed his eyes and took a deep breath. Jesus, how the hell had he forgotten about that?

Because you've only had sex on the brain this morning, dipshit.

He met his dad's angry gaze.

"You're right. I wasn't thinking." And he wanted to kick himself for it. Roxie's safety should be front and center. Not them tearing up the sheets. If he didn't stay vigilant, she could get hurt. Just like last time.

Joe grimaced.

He'd dropped the ball, and Roxie had gotten a gun pressed against her head as a result. Thankfully, she'd ended up in the hospital and not the morgue. Still, he would never forgive himself for causing her to get hurt.

"So, Joseph, I'm going to ask again. Is Roxie okay?"

"She's handling the photos as best as—" He frowned and set his menu down on the table. "Wait. How do you even know about this?"

"I ran into Quinn."

That made sense. Quinn trusted his dad completely, and he knew the good Doctor Buchanan cared about Roxie as if she were his own.

With a nod, Joe continued, "As I was saying, she's handling it the best she can. Right now, there's not a lot she can do except be careful. Quinn and I have both spoken to her about not being alone and not putting herself in any risky situations."

"What about this morning?"

"What about it?"

"She was late to work this morning, and that's very unlike her. Do you know where she was or what she was doing?"

Joe swallowed. He needed to get control of this conversation. Fast.

"Yes, Dad. I do know where she was this morning." He also knew what she'd been doing—or rather, *who* she'd been doing.

"And?"

And it wasn't any of his damn business.

"Joseph?"

Frustration swept over him. He raked his hands through his hair and let out an exasperated sigh. "And nothing. Yeah, she hasn't called in sick or missed work in . . . well . . . ever, but why does it have to be a national fucking crisis if the woman decides to take *one* morning for herself? Give her a damn break."

His father stared at him, eerily calm. "You may be a grown

man, but you *will* remember who you're talking to," he warned.

Joe scrubbed his hands over his face and groaned. "Sorry. Look, I know you're worried about her, but she's fine. All things considered, she's doing good."

"Well, would you look at that?" a voice interrupted.

Joe glanced up and found Martha smiling down at him. She, along with her husband of sixty-plus years, Ray, owned Ray's Diner. The couple was hilarious and surprisingly spry for being in their eighties. They were also easily two of his favorite people. He grinned. "Hey there, Miss Martha. You're looking lovely today."

She fanned herself. "Oh my lordy. Not one, but *two* sweet-talking Buchanan boys."

He fought a cringe as she pinched his and his father's cheeks. Like they were both three years old.

"Lordy, lordy. God must have been having a good day up in Heaven when He was making the two of you. Mm, mm, mmm." She pulled out her pen and pad of paper. "Now, what'll it be, boys?"

They placed their orders, and in two minutes flat, Martha had them updated on the latest town happenings. She was, after all, the conductor of Hudson Island's gossip train. Joe was just thankful that he and Roxie hadn't been mentioned in the woman's latest press release.

Martha turned to leave, then paused to look each of them in the eye. "A little unsolicited advice because, well, we all know I like to stick my nose in other people's business. You boys talk too quietly for my old ears to get any information, which is probably a wise thing on your parts, but there's nothing wrong with my vision, and the two of you looked about ready to clobber each other earlier. Now, you boys be good to each other, you hear? You're father and son. Don't forget how precious that is, all right? That's it. I'll go and get your food going."

After Martha left, they sat in silence for a few moments.

"Dad, I didn't ask you to breakfast so we could squabble about Rox. I wanted to catch up. Let you know about a job opportunity that's come up."

His dad reached across the table and patted his hands.

"I know, son. I just tend to get a little worked up where Roxie's concerned. Did I tell you I ran into her parents the other day? Rich and Julia have been vacationing over at the Pacific View Resort for the past week."

Joe's brow furrowed. "That's strange. Rox hasn't mentioned it."

"That's because Roxie doesn't know they're here. They haven't bothered to stop by Comfort Food, let alone call Roxie to inform her they're in town."

Disgust turned his stomach. "Why the hell wouldn't they call her?"

"'Because we've been so busy,'" his father mimicked with air quotes. "Apparently, yoga, massages, golf, and wine tasting take up *so* much time. And do you know *where* I saw them?"

Joe shook his head.

"The ferry dock. They were leaving. Their stay at Pacific View was done, and they were heading back to Arizona or New Mexico or wherever the hell it is they live now. The little shits had to have walked right past Roxie's shop on the way to the ferry. And did they bother to stop in to say hi? No."

Joe could see why his father was so furious. He felt the same burning anger. However, he also wasn't surprised. Roxie's parents had always been neglectful. For as long as Joe could remember, the world had revolved around Rich and

Julia Jameson. If Roxie's schedule happened to fit in, then great. If not? Oh well.

His heart ached for Roxie. A long time ago, she'd claimed she'd stopped caring, that she knew her parents' interest in her ran about as deep as . . . well, it simply didn't run deep. But if she found out that her folks had been in town—for a whole damn week—it would hurt her. She'd never admit it out loud, but he knew her better than he knew himself.

"I don't think you should tell her. It'll only upset her."

"I agree." His dad sighed. "I know you don't fully understand why Rich and Julia make me so damn mad, but one day you will. When you have your own kids, you will." He shook his head and scrubbed his hands over his face, and the gesture was so familiar, Joe couldn't help but smile.

"Dad, I know how much you care about Roxanne, and that's what matters." He met his father's gaze. "She means a lot to me, and I promise you that I'm going to do everything I can to keep her safe."

"I should hope so."

"I'm actually teaching a self-defense class on Saturday night over at Cade's gym. I'm hoping to have all the Comfort Food ladies go. You should come check it out." He hesitated, and nerves had him fidgeting with the silverware. "It may turn into a regular gig for me. Cade's offered me an instructor position of sorts at his gym."

"That's great, son."

He peeked up at his dad. "Really?"

His father looked at him in question. "Is this *not* a good thing?"

"No, it is—but are you okay with me going from an FBI agent to a hand-to-hand combat instructor?"

"Sure. If that's what you want to do. It sounds like fun." He shrugged. "Besides, you won't be getting shot at. As a parent, that makes me feel a lot better. And if there's a chance you'll be sticking around for the long haul, then even better. I've missed you, son."

Joe let out a breath as an enormous weight lifted from his shoulders. A weight he hadn't realized he'd been carrying. No matter how old he got, his dad's opinion meant so damn much. Hell, if he could be half the man his dad was, he'd be fucking honored.

Coming back to Hudson Island, he'd been nervous that his dad—the successful *doctor*—would look down on him for quitting the bureau and starting a new path. A ridiculous fear, really, because all his life, his father had supported him in everything he'd done. Always.

"Thanks, Dad. I've missed you, too." He swallowed over the lump in his throat. "It's good to be home."

"It's good to have you back, son." His dad smiled. "Now, spill the beans about this position at the gym. Something tells me it's more than just teaching a class or two."

CHAPTER TWENTY

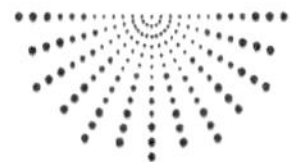

"Are you all right, Roxie?" Nina asked as she popped her head into the office.

Roxie jumped. She'd been blankly staring at her computer screen for the past five minutes. Just zoning out and replaying her ridiculously amazing morning with Joe over and over again in her mind. "Yeah. I'm good. Why?"

Nina's brow scrunched. "Because you've never really been late before. June and I are worried. Is everything okay?"

Had Roxie known that being a few hours late would cause such a ruckus, she wouldn't have—

What the hell was she thinking? Of course she'd do it all again.

"I appreciate the concern, but I'm fine, Nina. Really. Better than fine, actually. I had some personal stuff I had to . . . figure out."

"Okay, just checking." Nina nodded. "Did you want to carpool to the self-defense class?"

"What self-defense class?"

"The one on Saturday over at Cade's. It's after the cardio kickboxing class."

She shook her head. "Since when?"

"Since this week. I think he said something about it maybe becoming a monthly thing? But whatever. June will be at the kickboxing class already, but I'm only doing the self-defense one. You want to carpool?"

Roxie held up her hands in a *T*. She needed a moment for her brain to catch up. "The self-defense class sounds interesting, but I work on Saturday. As do you."

"It's *after* work, boss lady. I also checked the catering schedule, and we don't have anything planned for that night, so relax. Cade and Quinn came in earlier to talk about the class, and *wow*. I know Quinn's married and all, but man, I would give a lot to be the meat in a Cade and Quinn sandwich."

"Oh my god, you sound like Sheila." Roxie laughed. "And I think Alex would have something to say about that."

"You're probably right." Nina's face scrunched for a second, then brightened. "Well, there's always a Cade and Joe sammy. I sure as hell wouldn't have any objections to that option."

Yeah, but I would, missy. Roxie bit her lip.

"Anyway, the guys invited us to it. The self-defense class, I mean. Quinn said Alex was going, so I figured you were on board. I think they said Joe was going to lead it, too."

Roxie's brows rose. Why was this the first time she'd heard of it? "This is all news to me."

"Don't you and Joe live together?"

She nodded.

"Huh." Nina shrugged, then leaned against the doorframe. "Anyway, the point is we should carpool. Then after, we should go get some drinks. Girls' night at Monty's Tavern?"

"Ooh, a girls' night. That sounds perfect. I'm *so* overdue for one of those." Roxie smiled. She was beginning to like the sound of this. "How about instead of going out, I can pick up a bunch of wine and snacks? I'll send Joe over to Quinn's, and we can have girls' night at my place. We have extra rooms, so you and Sheila can pass out safely."

Nina chuckled. "Maybe getting Sheila and Alex drunk together will make them tolerable to be around."

Roxie rolled her eyes. "I know, right?"

"What about June?"

"I'll absolutely invite her, but I doubt she'll come. She and her crazy knitting ladies have a standing 'craft night' on Saturdays. With or without June, I'm going to call this a team-building exercise so I can write off the costs of the alcohol and food."

Nina laughed. "Always the businesswoman, aren't you?"

"Always. Now get back to work, missy."

It was eight o'clock by the time Roxie shut her computer down. Closing her eyes, she stretched her arms over her head. She was exhausted, but she could see the light at the end of the tunnel. And it wasn't a train coming to plow her over.

Her workload was finally stabilizing, and she had Nina to thank for that. While she hated letting things go—okay, fine, she was a bona fide control freak—Nina was more than capable. The little dynamo had been taking over the catering end bit by bit, and Comfort Food's numbers had never looked better.

Soon Roxie would be able to hire another full-time staff member. That would bring her one step closer to having normal hours. Maybe even taking a full day off every week. However, she wasn't going to lie to herself. It dented her pride to know that Comfort Food did just fine without her whenever she chose to remove her hands from the wheel.

But Roxie was a businesswoman, and wasn't the goal of

every successful entrepreneur to build something scalable? Something that could grow without requiring her to sacrifice more and more and more of her own blood, sweat, and tears?

Hmm. The idea of carving out some free time was one she could learn to get behind. In fact—

She bolted upright in her chair.

A noise had come from the kitchen.

Silently rising to her feet, she crossed her small office to retrieve the golf club she kept handy *just in case*.

A metal dish clattered to the ground, and her heart stopped.

She squeezed herself next to the futon, out of view of the intruder, and tightened her grip on the seven iron she held like a baseball bat. Lying in wait, her pulse drummed a deafening beat in her ears.

Footsteps sounded on the linoleum. Her stomach pitched. As a shadow grew in the doorway, she sucked in a breath and prepared to swing. She was going to clock this bastard.

"Roxanne?"

Holy. Crap. The seven iron clattered to the ground. Her legs gave out, and she collapsed onto the futon with a whoosh.

Joe kneeled before her, running his hands over her arms. "Rox? Talk to me, baby. What's wrong?"

"Oh my god, Joe," she said, her voice trembling. She nodded to the golf club. "I almost decapitated you. Again. If you hadn't said anything, I was ready to swing."

Effortlessly, he lifted Roxie and settled her on his lap. Nestling her head into the crook of his neck, she took comfort in the warmth of his embrace.

"I'm sorry I scared you. You weren't home yet, so I figured I'd come by to see if you were still here. I texted you."

She glanced at her desk and frowned. Her phone was somewhere under the pile of paperwork. She was surprised she'd missed the notification.

"How did you get in?"

"Back door."

Her eyes narrowed. "I thought the locksmith fixed it."

"He did, but at the risk of sounding like the bossy bastard I am, you really, really need to remember to use the lock. Especially when you're here by yourself."

She sighed, relieved that the door was fixed but annoyed at herself for being a careless idiot.

"I thought I did," she said, snuggling into him. "I know it's not a good excuse, but it was busy. Nina and the catering staff we use were in and out all evening."

He pressed a kiss to the top of her head, and she smiled. She could sit like this forever. With him.

"So, baby," he murmured against her ear.

Electricity zipped down her spine and settled low in her belly.

"You got any food around here? I'm starving."

She reared back and raised an eyebrow. "Seriously, Buchanan? You're going to bust out the seductive, sexy voice for some food?"

He grinned. "Is it working?"

Laughing, she smacked a loud kiss on his forehead and stood. "Check the walk-in. The shelf on the left is fair game. Get something for both of us."

"Yes, ma'am," he said with a wide smile.

"Oh, and get the box with blue polka dots when you're in there."

As he foraged for their dinner, Roxie headed to her desk to pack up. She grabbed her wallet and phone and tossed them into her tote bag. Then, rummaging through the mail to find a catalog she'd thrown aside earlier, her hand paused over a plain white envelope with her name on it. The edges of her vision grew fuzzy with adrenaline. She didn't want to touch it.

"I've got the polka dot box, a lasagna, and a ham casserole," Joe said from outside her door. "Want anything else?"

Her head shot up, and she sighed in relief when she saw he was looking at the containers of food in his hands.

"No, that sounds good," she said, shoving the envelope into her tote.

She hoped he hadn't noticed the quiver in her voice.

<hr>

Less than fifteen minutes later, Joe opened their front door. With his arms full, he gestured for her to go in first.

She murmured her thanks as she walked past him. Always the gentleman.

Setting her tote bag down with a thud, she began the winter unwrapping—gloves, scarf, jacket.

Joe kicked off his shoes and headed toward the kitchen. "Are you going to tell me what's wrong, or are you going to make me guess?"

She stilled. "It's nothing. I'm fine."

Really? I'm fine? God, if he hadn't known there was a problem before, he certainly did now.

Taking a deep breath, she hung her jacket on the coat rack and switched from work clogs to fuzzy slippers. Only once her clogs were lined up on the shoe rack did she follow him into the kitchen. If it took her a bit longer to do those menial tasks, it was merely a coincidence. Yeah, that was it.

She bit back a groan. Yup, she still sucked at lying. Even to herself.

Joe turned from the oven as she entered the kitchen. "Don't pretend everything's okay, Rox. You barely said a word on the way home, and I'm not quite sure you heard a thing I said."

"That's not true." She was restless, fidgety, so she focused her attention—and hands—on opening a bottle of wine. "I heard everything you said." After removing the cork, she ticked each item off on her fingers. "First, I think the job at Cade's is a great opportunity for you, and for that amount of money—to do something you already love doing—why not, right? It's a no-brainer, really. Second, Nina told me about the self-defense class. Alex is going. Sheila's in as well. Apparently, June, that crazy lady, already takes the cardio kickboxing thing and is looking forward to your class. So, Mr. Buchanan, the Comfort Food staff is all in."

"Okay, I stand corrected. You were listening." He leaned against the island next to her. "So, are you going to tell me what's wrong or what?"

"Joe, there's nothing—"

She was silenced by his lips. They settled softly on hers, not demanding a thing, just offering simple comfort. "I know you, Rox. What's wrong?"

Looking into his concerned blue eyes, she couldn't lie to him. Besides, she didn't even know what was in the envelope. It could be nothing.

"I got another . . ." She sighed. "Hang on."

Stepping around him, Roxie hustled to the living room. She dug through her tote bag and found the offending envelope. Back in the kitchen, she placed it on the counter as if it were a big, hairy spider.

"Son of a bitch," Joe muttered.

"I saw it when we were heading out. I kinda panicked and didn't know what to do. Should I call Quinn?"

She could see him debating it.

"Let's open it first and find out. Besides—"

"It could be nothing," she finished. *Please, please, please let it be nothing.*

"Right." He held her gaze. "It could be nothing."

She had a feeling they both believed otherwise.

Carefully, Joe opened the envelope. She held her breath, waiting. Then he uttered a curse, and her heart sank. *Please, please, please don't let it be something awful.*

Only touching the edges, he pulled out multiple photos. He scanned each one before setting them on the counter for her to see.

Saliva filled her mouth, and for a split second, she feared she was going to be sick, right there in the middle of the kitchen.

Joe was next to her in an instant. He pulled her back to his chest, and his arms circled her in a warm, protective embrace. "I've got you, baby," he murmured repeatedly in her ear, tightening his hold as she trembled.

Three pictures total. All taken the night before. A shudder racked her body.

The first photo showed her hugging one of the knitting ladies goodbye. The second showed her climbing out of June's car with a dippy, drunk smile on her face. The third showed her standing on the front porch as Joe in the doorway, arms crossed over his broad chest, expression irritated.

"We should call Quinn," she said, her voice cracking. "I doubt there's anything he can do, but he should know."

One hour and zero answers later, Roxie locked the door behind Quinn. Between her lack of sleep last night and the stress of . . . well, everything, exhaustion threatened to knock her over right then and there. Her mounting anger was the only thing keeping her upright. She thumped her forehead against the wood.

"It's so damn frustrating. All we can do is sit and wait." She put her back to the door and rested her weight against it. "Honestly, I kind of wish this person would hurry up and do whatever he's going to do already."

Joe's eyes filled with astonished disbelief. "What?"

"I can't live like this, with this constant paranoia that someone's watching me all the time. Someone's taking pictures of me, and I'm absolutely clueless. Who the hell knows what other pictures they've taken? Maybe they have a whole private collection." She waved her hands in a helpless, frustrated gesture. "It's so freaking creepy! If this person would just attack or something, then at least we'd know who it is and what they want."

"I'm sorry, baby." Pulling her close, he looped his arms around her waist and laid a soft kiss on the tip of her nose. "I completely, five hundred million percent disagree with you, though. The very last thing I want is for anyone to go after you. Even if we had you under constant supervision, there are still too many variables. Too many things that can go wrong. You getting hurt again is the last thing I'd ever risk."

She opened her mouth to speak, but he placed a finger on her lips.

"I understand your frustration. I do. Unfortunately, right now we just have to wait. Stay vigilant. And then wait some more." He replaced his finger with his lips for a quick kiss. "Is there anything I can do to help you relax? Draw you a bath? Back rub? Anything?"

Sweet, sweet man.

An idea hit. "Hold that thought."

Roxie slipped from his arms and headed toward the kitchen, motioning for him to follow. She refilled her wineglass that still sat on the island and took a big gulp, then reached for the polka dot box, carefully prying open the lid.

This always had the ability to make her feel better.

Smiling, she cut and plated a generous slice, then scooped a healthy spoonful and held it up to Joe. "Try this."

His lips enclosed the spoon, and in that moment, she would have given just about anything to be that little utensil.

He closed his eyes and moaned. "Pardon the French, Rox," he mumbled with his mouth full. "But holy shit, that's fucking amazing."

Her answering grin was part culinary satisfaction and part female pleasure at seeing such a fine male specimen blissed out. "It's my latest creation. Death by Chocolate. You approve?"

"Oh hell yeah. It's like a freaking party in your mouth. What's in it?" His brows knit together in worry. "Or do I want to know? I have a feeling I'm probably going to have to run an extra mile or two tomorrow."

"It's not *that* bad." She wrinkled her nose. "Well . . . seeing as we're going to eat this whole thing tonight . . . yeah, we should probably add in a few more miles."

Her newest concoction was a decadent chocolate dessert —hence the name. But it was flourless, so it couldn't be too terrible for you, right? Never mind the full pound of butter and full pound of Belgian dark chocolate, or the sweet and tart raspberry sauce drizzled on top.

In fact, the way Roxie saw it, Death by Chocolate was practically a health food. Dark chocolate was good for your heart—thank you, antioxidants—and raspberries were fruit and fruit was good for you in general. At the very least, it was a not-completely-horrible-for-you dessert choice. It was all about balance.

Oh, and it was a dessert that went best with a nice glass of red wine—which was made from grapes, and grapes equaled fruit. Ergo, balance.

Joe topped off her glass and took a lengthy swallow. She arched a brow at him.

"Sorry. I assumed you were sharing."

The corner of her lips twitched, and she nodded.

Without delay, he took another sip of wine and snagged the spoon from her hand, then downed another bite. "Damn, it's even better with wine."

Her smile turned smug. *See. Balance.*

Joe held out a spoonful for her. Accepting the bite, she closed her eyes, allowing the rich, savory chocolate to dance on her taste buds.

"Holy crap, sometimes I even amaze myself."

"Damn, baby."

She looked at him in question. "What?"

Joe shook his head. "I thought the dessert was good, but watching you eat it may be even better."

"Really?" Taking the spoon from his hands, she scooped a large bite and held it to his lips. "That's funny, because I think watching *you* eat this is doing wonders for keeping my mind off the creepy aspects of today."

Mouth full of chocolate, he moaned again. "Damn, that's good. Seriously, I'll be a distraction for you anytime. You need a guinea pig for new recipes? I'm your man."

Her heart squeezed. *Yes. Yes, you are.*

Roxie cleared her throat. "Speaking of distractions, is your offer for a back rub still on the table?"

"Always." A sly smile lifted his lips. "Did you know that ninety percent of back rubs end in sex? Statistically speaking, of course."

She bit her bottom lip to suppress a chuckle. "Is that so?"

"Hey, that's just what I heard. So, if we play our cards right, the back rub may literally end up on the table. Or this counter." He wagged his eyebrows, slapping the kitchen island. "You game?"

"For the back rub, most definitely. For the rest?" She pursed her lips and tapped her chin. "My brain's a little preoccupied tonight. I might need some convincing . . . and probably a softer surface."

He laughed and plucked the spoon from her hand, then tossed it onto the counter. "Challenge accepted, baby."

CHAPTER TWENTY-ONE

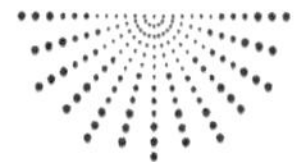

While the temperature was still brisk—it was January, after all—the gray gloom of winter in the Pacific Northwest was noticeably absent. If the Saturday afternoon crowd filling Comfort Food was any indication, the ferry dock was extra busy today. Rare bluebird skies usually led to tourists pouring onto Hudson Island.

At the front counter, Sheila and Nina managed the rush of customers with ease. Roxie covered the back, taking three lasagnas out of the oven and popping in two more, then grabbing a washrag to wipe down the prep counters. She'd thought that with it being so hectic, her mind wouldn't have time to wander. She'd been wrong. A smile—a sappy, gooey smile—spread across her face, and her stomach fluttered. She wanted to kick herself for being such a twitterpated moron, but she couldn't. She was too damn giddy.

The last week had been surreal. She wasn't an overly romantic person—at least when she was talking about herself—but over the last couple of days, she and Joe had fallen into a rhythm that she could only describe as magical.

Their morning runs had been tossed out the window and

replaced with amazing morning sex. Both were forms of exercise, right? God knew she'd take sweaty sex over sweaty runs any day of the week. Her face heated at the mere thought.

Then she and Joe went their separate ways during the day, and at night . . . oh, at night, they performed delicious reenactments of the morning.

Roxie simply couldn't get enough of the man. Of *Joe.*

She shook her head. That was the surreal part, the part she was still trying to wrap her head around. *Joe.* Her childhood friend. The man who had been one of her best friends. Who had then become her enemy. Who was now working his way back to best-friend status. But with sex. Amazing sex. Best-sex-of-her-life sex.

His initial desire to take things slow, like their morning runs, had gone out the window. She didn't regret it for one moment, though she was a bit shocked by the speed at which things had progressed. They'd gone from barely tolerating each other for *years* to screwing like bunnies in a matter of days. She wasn't a prude by any stretch of the imagination, but she did tend to hold out well beyond a few dates before jumping in the sack with a guy.

But Joe . . . there was no getting-to-know-you period necessary. He was . . . Joe.

Roxie had no clue where they were going. So far, they hadn't had any sort of relationship talk. There'd been no holding hands or movie-and-a-dinner dates. They hadn't even gone anywhere together. Because, well, they'd jumped straight to the best-sex-of-her-life thing.

She paused mid-swipe, the washcloth in her hand forgotten. An uncomfortable feeling crept over her. She tried to push it away, but the discomfort grew and soured her belly.

Roxie knew Joe was popular with the ladies. She wasn't a complete idiot. After all, the guy was gorgeous, charming, and a natural flirt. She knew he wasn't seeing anyone else because they'd barely left each other's side. But a little voice in her head whispered that she was getting *way* ahead of herself.

She couldn't define what they were doing, but she knew this was different from anything she'd ever experienced before. It was special. *He* was special. She'd never been with someone whom she'd already cared so much about. And she'd never been with anyone who focused so completely on her.

In fact, for better or worse, she'd never been the center of *anyone's* attention before. Not her parents', not any of her exes'. But when she was with Joe, he had a way of making her feel like she was his entire world. It was mind-blowing. And comforting. And utterly terrifying.

Was she his girlfriend, or was she just a convenient fuck buddy? He'd implied early on that she meant more to him, but then again, he wouldn't be the first guy to spout a crapload of lies to get laid.

Her shoulders sagged. She really, *really* hoped that wasn't the case.

What makes you *so special from all the other women?*

She wanted to tell that nagging little voice to shut the hell up, but it made a valid point. The only thing that differentiated her from all the others was their shared past, their history, their friendship. After all they'd been through—the highest of highs and lowest of lows—the idea that this was just sex to him scared her. But the idea that when he got tired of her—because let's face it, everyone got tired of her—they'd go back to being friends was worse. It made her physically ill.

She squeezed her eyes closed and fought a wave of nausea. *Universe, please don't let this end up being the biggest. Clusterfuck. Ever. Amen.*

"Are you okay?"

Her eyes flew open, and she yelped at the low voice. "Holy crap, Eli," she said, pressing her hand to her thundering heart. With a long, slow exhale, she tried to calm her frazzled nerves.

"Sorry, Roxie. I didn't mean to startle you."

She frowned, and a tingle of unease settled at the base of her spine. "What are you doing back here?"

"I wanted to talk to you about, um, the party for Poppy. Sheila said it was okay to come on back." His face reddened, and he shifted on his feet. "If it's a bad time, I can come back when you're closed."

Yeaaah, or not at all.

"Now's fine." Roxie tossed the dirty washrag into the sink and moved toward her office. "Let me get a notepad, and we can talk."

She retrieved a pen and notepad off her desk, turned, and came to an abrupt halt.

Eli was standing close. Too close.

That tingle of unease crept up her back. "You know what? Let's grab a table up front and discuss this there."

She tried to step around him, but he stopped her with a firm hand on her arm. "It would be best if we talked back here. I'd hate for anyone to eavesdrop. That would . . . ruin the surprise for Poppy."

She eyed him suspiciously. He was saying all the right things. But dammit, there was something else going on.

"Don't touch me, Eli," she said, her tone sharp as she tugged her arm away.

"I'm sorry," he said, raising his hands in front of him.

Again, he was saying the right words, but something flickered in his eyes. It made her uncomfortable.

"I didn't mean to grab you. I would never hurt you, Roxie." He reached out to caress her face.

She recoiled, swatting his hand away. "What the hell?"

"Is everything okay, Roxie?"

At Nina's voice, Eli sprang back a couple of steps.

Her new favorite employee stood in the doorway, hands planted firmly on her narrow hips. It was good to know that she wasn't the only one giving the man a death glare.

"Eli," Roxie snapped. "You need to leave. Now."

He murmured something incoherent and scurried out of sight.

Nina came inside the office and closed the door behind her. "What the hell was *that*?"

Roxie sat on the edge of her desk and shook her head. Chilly all of a sudden, she wrapped her arms around her middle. "No freaking clue. He wanted to talk about a party for his wife, but . . . I don't know. He was acting strange."

Nina grimaced. "The dude's a creeper. I don't know what the hell Poppy sees in him. I'd stay far away if I were you, boss lady."

"That's the thing. I've known him since high school, and he's never acted like this before."

"People change. Sometimes not for the better." Her friend shrugged, and a shadow flickered in her eyes. But then she smiled, so maybe Roxie had imagined it. "Good thing we're going to learn how to kick some ass tonight, right?"

Some of the tension eased from Roxie's shoulders. "More like how not to get *our* asses kicked."

"Whatever. I'd better go freshen up my makeup," Nina said.

"Makeup? For a self-defense class?"

"Uh, hello? Have you seen what those guys look like?"

"Fair point," she said, laughing. When the humor faded, she was left with her lingering unease. She caught Nina's eye. "Hey, let's not mention what happened with Eli to anyone, all right? Especially Sheila. She and Poppy are tight, and I don't want to stir up anything. I mean, it's probably nothing, but—"

"But the creeper vibe."

"Yeah. The thing is, I like Poppy. If this is just us overreacting, I'd hate for it to get back to her."

Nina winced. "I understand thinking it's overreacting if one person gets the vibe, but two people picking up on it?"

She grimaced. "I know. But still, Poppy's nice."

"*You're* too nice, but okay." Nina gave her a pointed glare. "Make sure you pay attention in class tonight."

"Don't worry, I will. I'll pay attention for both of us. You know, since you'll be ogling all the men."

Nina's eyes twinkled as she opened the office door. "You've got that right, boss lady."

CHAPTER TWENTY-TWO

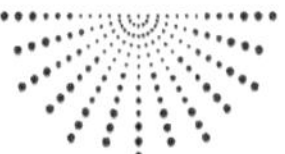

There was a buzz in the air. An electric current of anticipation. The men were on one side of the mat, the women on the other. The divide reminded her of middle school gym class. Granted, the guys were hotter than any awkward seventh-grade boy could ever dream of being.

Roxie returned her attention to what Joe was telling the group. She'd been having a hard time focusing. Her earlier encounter with Eli had shaken her. It had also made her mad. He'd so obviously crossed the line, and she didn't know how to respond. In theory, she should tell him off. But that was in theory only. Reality was much more complicated.

If she told Joe, he'd totally flip out and either confront Eli—which would be a disaster—or he'd tell Quinn, and then the two of them would confront Eli—which would be an even bigger disaster. The loser in both those scenarios would be Poppy.

Selfishly, the idea of Poppy—or anyone—thinking she'd messed around with Eli made her sick. Learning that she'd been the other woman with her ex, Paul, had left an aching wound inside her. A wound that was still too fresh. Too tender. The last thing she wanted was any rumors going around about her and Eli. But the man was sure to leave her alone after what had happened today, right? He had to.

Roxie's skin prickled with awareness. Glancing around, her eyes widened. Everyone was staring at her.

"Rox?"

Crap. She managed a chagrined smile. "Sorry, Joe. You were saying?"

He flashed that damn Buchanan grin at their group. Pointing at her, he said, "That's what I was telling you about, right there. The most important thing is to be aware of your surroundings. Situational awareness is your first line of defense. We'll let Rox slide this time, but that's the only break we're giving her tonight."

She rolled her eyes as half the women chuckled and the other half sighed.

"Here's the thing I want to make really clear to all of you," Joe continued. "The point of this self-defense class isn't to teach you how to kick someone's ass. If you want to do that, then I suggest you take some classes here at Cade's—preferably ones that don't start with the word *cardio*. Don't get me wrong, that class is a great workout . . . but ass kicking it is not."

"Thanks for the plug, bro," Cade said with a chuckle from the side of the room.

Joe nodded at his friend, then returned his gaze to the group. "But in all seriousness, this isn't a class about going toe to toe with an assailant. Because here's a simple fact: men, in general, are physically stronger than women. And if a man catches a woman by surprise, then the scales tip even more in his favor."

"Then why are we here again, gorgeous?" Sheila called out. "Not that I'm complaining about the scenery."

Roxie stifled a gag as Joe winked at Sheila. It didn't matter that she'd thought the same thing; she hadn't said it out loud all breathy-like.

"The point of tonight, ladies, is to learn how to temporarily stun your assailant so you can get away. I can't stress that enough. You're not out to kick the bad guy's ass. Your focus is to get away to safety. Alive. Those are the goals. Now for the basics. Everyone make a fist." He scanned the group, then motioned to Roxie. "Front and center."

Oh no. She arched a brow and gave him her best princess-to-peon look.

With an impatient sigh, Joe tried again. "Please. Will you come up here for a class demonstration?"

Roxie grinned. Much better. She hopped up from the mat and joined him.

"Now, many of you know that Rox and I go way back. So far back that I know our resident baker here once broke our fearless sheriff's nose with a wicked right hook."

She curtsied as guffaws erupted from both sides of the room.

"It's okay, sweetie," Alex called to Quinn. "I still love you."

"So, Rox," Joe said over the din, "feel free to show everyone how to make a proper fist."

Roxie held up her right hand. "You make a *B* in sign language, then move your thumb out. Starting with the tips of your fingers, roll them down to a fist. Finally, bend your thumb back across your fingers. For the love of god, ladies, do *not* wrap your thumbs inside your fists."

"Right. That's the best way to hurt yourself. You don't want to put yourself at any sort of disadvantage." Joe went around and checked the women's fists, correcting them where needed, then returned to Roxie's side. "As I've said before, the focus is to damage the other person enough so you can get away. That means you're going to use whatever you have at your disposal, not just your fists. There are zero rules in defending yourself."

Joe motioned for Cade to join him, and Roxie took that as her cue to leave. She walked toward her spot on the mat, but he caught her by the wrist before she got far.

"Oh, I'm not done with you yet, Rox." Joe grinned and gave her a wink, playing to the crowd again.

"I'd be happy to take your place any day, Roxie," Sheila called out to a few laughs.

Great. Had she known she was going to be part of the entertainment portion of the evening, she'd have stayed home and skipped directly to the girls-night-slash-drinking portion of the evening instead.

Joe yanked her toward him, and she jerked away. Irritation simmered in her gut when he responded by yanking a second time. She opened her mouth to tell him to shove it—she wasn't his pull toy, dammit—but he spoke over her head.

"Wrist control. If the assailant gets control of your wrists, you make sure you do everything you can to break their hold on you. Everything."

He looked at Roxie, one hand still locked around her wrist. "I'm the bad guy—"

"No shit, Sherlock," she muttered.

"Focus, Rox," he said quietly, just to her. Then he turned to the class. "She's going to try to get away from me."

She glared at him when he wrenched her to the side again.

"Go, Rox."

Jackass. This wasn't her first rodeo. She twisted her wrist and tugged.

Nothing.

Joe increased the strength of his grip, and her eyes narrowed.

Squaring her body to his, she punched him in the

stomach with her free hand. His hold eased for a split second, and she pulled free. On her next breath, his hand resumed its clamp-like grip on her wrist.

She gasped as he hauled her toward him. Before she could blink, she was facing the other women, back against his chest, arm pinned between their bodies. The air caught in her lungs when his forearm closed around her neck.

Memories of being held the same way by Preston Woodsworth drowned out her senses. Cologne and stale cigarette smoke filled her nose. Her shoulder burned before bursting into flames. The cold barrel of a gun pressed to her temple.

Roxie couldn't catch her breath; the flashback was too intense. She began to tremble.

"Holy shit, baby," Joe said, immediately releasing his grip. Turning her away from the class, he put his arm over her shoulder, tucked her against his side, and steered her toward the edge of the room.

As her hazy mind waded back to the present, Roxie watched something unspoken pass between the men. Cade seamlessly took over instructing the class, with Gavin and Quinn assisting. Other coaches and fighters moved from their side of the room to stand in front of her and Joe, creating a human wall to shield them from view of the other women.

Cade started talking about wrist escapes and small joint manipulation, but it was all just words, all incoherent. The only thing she heard with any clarity was the pounding in her ears. The only thing that registered was the man beside her.

"Holy shit, Roxanne, I'm so fucking sorry, baby." Joe ran his hands up and down her goosebump-ridden arms. "I wasn't thinking."

She shook her head, willing it to clear. If only she could stop shaking. "It's not your fault."

It had been almost nine months now since her terrifying ordeal with Woodsworth. Nine months. She should be over it. For the most part, she was. She hadn't had a nightmare about it in weeks. But when Joe's arm had locked around her neck, she'd launched back to that awful night when that madman had taken her captive. And just like back then, she'd panicked.

The warmth of Joe's hands framing her face reminded her where she was. "I'm so sorry," he whispered. "Are you okay?"

She let out a shaky exhale and nodded. "It's not your fault. You just surprised me. I'm okay, I promise."

His gaze searched hers, and she saw his blue eyes were clouded with worry.

Needing to reassure him—and needing to not make a scene—she pasted a smile on her face. "Really, Joe. You just caught me by surprise. I'm fine."

His eyes narrowed.

She knew he didn't believe her, but she pressed on. "As history indicates, I obviously suck at self-defense, so let's get back to the class, okay?"

"Okay." He moved his hands to her shoulders and squeezed. "Don't think we're done talking about this, Rox, because we're not."

Well, they were through talking about it now. That's all that mattered to her.

CHAPTER TWENTY-THREE

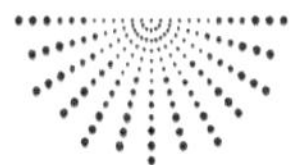

"All right, ladies. Now that the sweaty, don't-be-afraid-to-headbutt-the-bad-guy segment of our night is over, let's move on to the alcohol portion." Roxie set four wineglasses on the coffee table and filled them. Generously. "In the spirit of girls' night, but more importantly, team building—because I'm writing off all the wine and food tonight as a business expense—"

"Of course you are," Alex chuckled.

"Zip it, O'Conner." Roxie grabbed her glass and took a sip. She reveled in the fruity, oak-tinged flavor. "Business first, and here's the deal: Sheila and Alex. I value both of you tremendously, but you guys seriously need to stop being bitchy to each other."

As both women began to protest, Roxie simply spoke louder. "I'm serious, you guys. If I have to play moderator, I will. If either of you refuses to participate or gets out of line, I'll give Nina the okay to kick both your asses. After all, we've seen how she can beat the crap out of a punching bag." She glanced over at Nina. "Frankly, even though you're five foot nothing, I'm a little scared of you."

Nina threw up her hands. "Hey, Alex is short, too."

"Yeah, but I can take her." She returned her attention to both Sheila and Alex. "Now, ladies, what gives?"

Both women remained silent.

Roxie arched a brow. "Do I have to remind you that this is a team-building exercise? Don't make me get new team members."

"Fine," Alex sighed. "Sheila, you have to stop flirting with Quinn. And touching him. You *really* need to stop doing that."

"Okay," Sheila nodded. "I'll give you the touching. I'll stop that. But not the flirting. *Everyone* flirts with Quinn. Why is what I do any different?"

"It just is," Alex snapped.

"Uh-uh-uh," Roxie interrupted, waving an imaginary flag. "Moderator here. You need to explain yourself, missy."

Alex glared at her. "I hate you."

Roxie air-kissed her back. "I know, sweetie. I love you, too."

"It bothers me because of *that*." Alex waved in Sheila's general direction.

"Sorry," Sheila said with a laugh, "but you're gonna have to explain a little better than that."

Alex shifted uncomfortably, then gulped down more than a few swallows of wine. After clunking her glass onto the coffee table, she tapped the rim for a top-off. "It's the boobage, okay? I don't give a rip if other people flirt with my husband. But when *you* do it, it irritates the crap out of me because of"—she waved her hand at Sheila's chest—"all that. I've seen him when you flirt with him, and the poor guy doesn't know where to look." She folded her arms over her smaller chest and sent another glare to Roxie. "Happy?"

"Are you kidding me, Alex?" Sheila looked at the woman as if she'd grown a fifth head. "Have you seen yourself in the mirror? Better yet, have you seen the way Quinn looks at you? I flirt like mad with him because I know there's no chance in hell he's going to do anything. It's like practice for me. If I can make him uncomfortable and have him try to figure out where to put his eyes, then I know that what I'm doing will work on a regular guy." She took a sip of wine and shrugged. "You just need to get over it."

Alex's jaw almost hit the floor, and Roxie began cracking up.

"Baywatch does have a point, Alex," Nina chimed in. "Quinn could look his fill—which he doesn't—but it wouldn't matter because it's pretty obvious to anyone with working eyeballs who stars in the good sheriff's head porn."

Roxie choked on her wine. "Oh my god, Nina, you're killing me! My stomach muscles hurt from laughing so much."

Nina rolled her eyes. "Whatever, boss lady. Like we all don't know that you have a starring role in the personal spank bank of a certain blond-haired, blue-eyed Adonis. Not that I'm insanely jealous or anything."

It was Roxie's turn to have her mouth fall open.

Nina reached over and patted her back. "It's okay. We're off the clock now, so it's totally okay. Spill it."

Heat rushed over her face, and she could only stare at Nina. "I don't have the foggiest clue as to what you mean."

"Bullshit," Nina snorted.

"Tsk-tsk, young lady," Alex said, voice full of glee. "Do you kiss your mom with that mouth?"

Nina grinned. "Not anymore, that's for damn sure. But come on, aren't you guys the tiniest bit curious about what's going on with them? Because let me tell you, Roxie, even *my* panties get wet when Joe does that sexy, smoldering look. And the guy isn't even directing the smolder at me!"

A chorus of raucous laughter filled the room.

"What?" Nina asked, a devious twinkle in her eyes. "Give me a break. Don't act all shocked. I'm just saying what all of you are already thinking. Even you, Mrs. Married-to-the-Smoking-Hot-Sheriff."

Alex leaned back against the couch cushions and tipped her glass to Nina, the wine she'd guzzled a few minutes prior obviously taking effect. "Joe is pretty hot; I'll give you that much. But that's all I'm gonna say."

Roxie laughed and stared at Nina in wonder. "You're hilarious, you know that? To think that sweet, innocent face of yours hides such a raunchy and dirty mouth."

Nina batted her lashes. "Who? *Moi*?"

"Do you knit by chance?"

Nina howled. "Oh hell no. I've got nothing on those knitting ladies. I mean, they even make *me* blush."

Alex caught Roxie's eye and gave her a quick wink. "So, Nina, are you seeing anyone these days?"

God, Roxie loved Alex for shifting the conversation. While she was more than comfortable talking to Alex about her personal life, she wasn't quite there yet with the other girls.

Nina shook her head and took a big gulp of wine. "No, I'm on hiatus from men."

Shelia gasped. "Why the hell would you do something crazy like that?"

"Well, Man-Eater," Nina said, "I've had bad luck in that department, and I've had my fill. Therefore, I'm taking a break."

"Yeah, well, sounds like your last man wasn't *filling* you correctly," Sheila scoffed.

"That, too." Nina's eyes gleamed. "You know, when I moved here last year from Hawaii, I said it was because I needed a change of pace." She shrugged and swirled the wine in her glass. "Well, I may have left out the teeny, tiny part having to do with breaking my engagement and leaving my fiancé. At the altar."

Roxie's eyes widened. "Holy hell! A raunchy mouth *and* the ability to keep a massive secret? Most impressive. Hang on." She scrambled to her feet and dashed toward the kitchen. "We're going to need more wine for this nugget!"

Less than a minute later, Roxie resumed her seat with an uncorked bottle in hand. She topped off everyone's glasses and settled on the couch. "Spill it, sailor."

"There's not much to tell, really. My family is super old-school, snobby Filipino. My dad's a doctor and my mom's 'Dr. Castillo's Wife.' That's a big deal to them and their friends. They were seriously bummed when I graduated from college without my MRS degree, but I got engaged a couple years after graduation, so they were hopeful. Especially since my fiancé was about to attend an Ivy League medical school. He got bonus points for being Filipino, too. Oh, and the coup de grace was that he was also the son of a doctor."

Roxie shook her head. "I don't understand why that's such a big deal."

"Status," Nina answered with an eye roll. "Having two 'Dr. and Mrs.' on the wedding invitation just shouts, 'We're better than you.' My parents are big fans of that."

"Now that," Roxie said, lifting her glass, "I get. My folks are all about being better than everyone around them."

Nina clinked glasses with her. "I'm not going to lie and say I didn't milk it for all it was worth because I sure as hell didn't complain when I got a top-of-the-line Mercedes for my sixteenth birthday. I also may not have complained when they threw me a fancy-schmancy debutante ball on my eighteenth birthday at, of course, one of the fanciest hotels in Honolulu. But the idea of being like my mom for the rest of my life was too much. And Jared was—*is*—a nice guy and all, but he's just . . . blah. Our conversations were blah, the sex was blah—"

Sheila's face scrunched up. "God knows that if it was already blah to start, it was just going to get a whole hell of a lot worse once you got married."

"I know, right? And frankly, being all demure and proper just sucked. I hated it."

Roxie choked on her wine. Again. Sputtering, she said, "You've got to be kidding me. *You?* Demure and proper?"

Nina nodded, lifting her hand in a Girl Scout salute. "I shit you not."

She opened her mouth, but it took a couple of tries for the words to come out. "How can that even be? *Demure* doesn't even come into play when I think of you. You're one of the ballsiest women I know."

"And Roxie's pretty damn ballsy herself," Sheila added.

Roxie smiled. "Thank you. I think."

The woman snorted in reply.

"I mean, seriously, Nina, you say the stuff—*out loud*—that people actually think but are too scared to say."

"Trust me, I wasn't always like this. Deep down, maybe, but I never let myself be bold because it wasn't 'proper.' But I'm twenty-eight, for god's sake. Fuck proper, right? And yes, my timing sucked since I figured all this out the morning of my wedding"—Nina shrugged—"but I couldn't go through with it."

"What did your folks say?" she asked.

Something that looked like a mix of regret and sadness flickered across the woman's face, and Roxie's heart clutched for her friend. She knew all about having a strained relation-ship with your parents.

"They weren't happy. At all. They said I was an embar-rassment to the family, and that I owed them for wasting their hard-earned money. You know, all that good stuff." Her shoulders drooped. "So, I left. I have a friend in Seattle, and I stayed with her for a couple weeks. We came to Hudson to do the tourist thing, and I saw your help wanted sign in the window, and . . . here we are, ladies."

Roxie threw her arm around Nina's shoulders and squeezed. "Awww, sweetie. You made the right choice, and I, for one, am thrilled to have you here with us."

"Roxie's right." Alex nodded. "You made the right choice for you. Yeah, it sucks that people got hurt and embarrassed in the process, but you can't live your life for everyone else. Better to happen now than ten years down the line when there may be kids involved and more at stake, you know?"

"Thanks, you guys," Nina said, affection clear in her voice. She poured more wine into her glass and raised it high in the air. "I'd like to propose a toast to Alex and Roxie."

Roxie lifted her glass, though her brow furrowed in confusion.

"While it's truly been dandy giving you girls the details of my scandalous past, I commend you both. You guys sure do know how to deflect the attention. But don't think I've forgotten what we were talking about before my walk down memory lane. Because the night is young, ladies, and here's to getting the dish on what's really going on with Roxie and Joe. Cheers!"

Roxie rolled her eyes but clinked glasses anyway. "You're a persistent little thing, aren't you?"

Nina laughed. "Oh, boss lady, you have no idea!"

CHAPTER TWENTY-FOUR

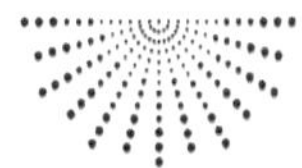

After a nearly sleepless night—who knew such a tiny little baby could scream so loud . . . and for so long—Joe entered his kitchen through the back door. He smiled when he spied Roxie at the kitchen counter. As he approached, he admired her pajama set. The plaid shorts weren't super short, but they showed off a lot of leg. Snaking his arm around her waist, he pulled her against him.

With a gasp, she yanked the AirPods from her ears, spun around, and slugged him in the stomach. Hard.

"Sorry, baby, I thought you heard me come in," he said, rubbing his abs.

Wide-eyed and hand to her heart, she stared at him for a second before her shoulders dropped and the fear drained from her face. "You scared the shit out of me. I didn't hear anything."

"I'm sorry," he repeated, wrapping his arms around her waist again. She relaxed into him as his lips found that spot on her neck he loved, the spot where, if he nibbled juuust right, she'd make the sexiest sound he'd ever heard.

"Joe . . ." Her whisper turned into that sexy moan, and he smiled against her neck.

Mission accomplished.

"It's about damn time those ladies left." His hand snuck under her shirt. Caressing the soft skin of her belly had him going hard in an instant. "I hate to break it to you, Roxanne, but I don't think we're going to make it upstairs to the bedroom. Can we christen the stairs?"

"Time-out," a voice called out.

He lifted his head and found Nina standing in the kitchen archway, one hand holding a coffee cup and the other shielding her eyes. Damn.

"I just need a refill on my coffee and then I swear that Sheila and I will be out of here," she said, peeking out from between her fingers.

Easing his hold, he cleared his throat and grinned. "I spoke too soon, I see."

"Morning, handsome." Nina flashed him a cheeky grin and topped off her coffee before turning her attention to Roxie. "Tsk-tsk, boss lady. You've been holding out on us, but the truth always comes out. Don't worry, I'll get your mug back to you tomorrow so you guys can get on with your bow-chicka-wow-wow on the stairs."

Joe laughed at both Nina's comments and the flush now staining Roxie's cheeks. He slung an arm over Roxie's shoulders but kept her partially in front of him. Because he was wearing sweatpants and, well . . . yeah. "Good morning to you, too, Nina. You guys don't need to rush out of here on my account."

"Oh, we're not, handsome. See, June and I are forcing a day off on Roxie today. So once I'm out of here, you guys can christen the whole damn house." She checked her watch. "But we've got another hour before I need to be at the café."

He stole a glance at Roxie. The flush on her cheeks and the daggers she was shooting at him didn't bode well.

"So . . . should I stay or go?" he dared to ask.

"Stay," Nina said, while at the same time, Roxie snapped, "Go."

Shit. It was barely eight in the morning. How the hell was he already in the doghouse?

While Nina laughed, Roxie pointed to the door. "Out, Buchanan."

<hr>

When the door closed behind Joe, Roxie let out an exasperated sigh.

"I hate to interrupt the broody thing you're doing," Nina said, "but are you nuts? Why the hell aren't you on top of that man right now?"

Heat spread from Roxie's face down to her neck. Why, indeed?

Nina looked at her in obvious disbelief. "That man is sex on a fucking stick. If he had his hands all over *me*, I'd for sure be telling *you* to get the hell out of my house. You're officially nuts, boss lady."

As Roxie watched Nina race up the stairs, probably to gather her things, she knew her friend was right. On any other day, she'd have jumped at the chance—or rather, jumped Joe. No questions, no hesitations.

But since she'd woken up with a wine headache pounding behind her temples, she'd been replaying everything in her head: the residual trauma from the Woodsworth ordeal that apparently still had the power to bring her to her knees, the damn photos that scared the crap out of her, Eli and whatever the hell was going on with him, the confusion that was her non-relationship relationship with Joe . . . All of it. She'd gone over every single minute detail. It had made her grumpy. Not to mention tense.

After her mini freak-out at the self-defense class, she'd been relieved when Joe had pulled her aside. He'd calmed her down. But he would have done that for anyone, right?

That's what nagged at her. He hadn't treated her any differently than he would anyone else. Not really. She'd have preferred him to wrap her in his arms and reassure her the way the hero does in romance movies. And yes, she probably would've bristled because she wasn't a fan of PDA. But that would have been only on the outside, just for show.

On the inside, she would have loved it because then she'd have known where she stood with him. She knew that he enjoyed her in bed. That was obvious. And she knew they got along great because, after all, they'd known each other forever. But did his feelings for her run as deep as hers did for him?

Just now, he'd wrapped his arms around her and acted all sexy because he'd thought they were alone. Then, when they'd gotten caught, he'd let her go and turned on the Buchanan charm for Nina. Like what they had was for behind closed doors only.

From where Roxie stood, the lone thing that had changed between them was the sex. Aside from that, it was business as usual. Well . . . their new usual. They were no longer horrid to each other, and for the most part, they got along. Sure, they made the occasional smart-ass remark or two to each other, but they were back to being . . . friends.

Well, she didn't want to be just friends with him. She didn't want to have no-strings-attached sex with him, either. It was totally stupid of her to want so much—*needy*, as her parents would claim. But she couldn't help it. She wanted more. She wanted to know that she was important to him.

Roxie stifled a groan. *Jeez, how pathetic are you?*

It was the truth, though.

She had seen Joe in relationships before and knew how he operated. He always kept it casual. He never made promises. Ever. But he was an absolute charmer, and as she'd recently found out, amazing in bed, so inevitably, the women he entertained always fell at his feet like little lovesick pups. When that happened, like clockwork, he'd back away, wish them well, and move on to the next woman.

She wrinkled her nose. That had sounded more callous than she'd meant it to. She knew he was always a gentleman during the breakup. Even when some of the women went I'll-boil-your-bunny ballistic on him, he remained a gentleman.

Deep down, Roxie hoped she was different from all the others. She knew that because of their long friendship, because of their chemistry, because they lived together, she was. But only to a point.

Thus far, he'd made no promises to her. Not really. Well, at least not in terms of their relationship . . . or whatever was going on between them. And she highly doubted that any promises were forthcoming. If she got at all clingy, he'd probably take his usual step back and say sayonara.

But she couldn't keep going like this. She couldn't continue to casually sleep with him. That worked for some people, but not for her. Her heart was too involved. She also didn't want to be that couple everyone raised their eyebrows at, the couple who were all hot and heavy for a month before fizzling out.

Roxie strived to be a strong, independent woman, one who was unconcerned about what other people thought. But she wasn't a complete idiot; she knew her public image mattered. She was a well-known business owner. So, given the way gossip spread like wildfire in her little town, she'd not only been discreet in her past relationships, but she'd never seriously dated anyone who'd lived on Hudson. The only reputation she sought was that of a kind and savvy businesswoman. She wanted to be the local-girl-does-good story.

The realist in her was certain what Joe felt for her was lust. And when it faded away . . . because it always did . . . Roxie wasn't sure she was capable of going back to being friends.

Joe was a good guy, and he'd eventually find The One. The thought soured her stomach. She wanted him to be happy, but she sure as hell couldn't—*wouldn't*—sit and watch as he fell in love with someone else. Last time she'd checked, she wasn't a big fan of torture.

"Earth to Roxie?"

Startling, she turned to see Sheila and Nina, overnight bags in their hands.

"Are you okay?" Sheila asked, worry etched on her features.

"I'm fine," Roxie murmured, embarrassment heating her face. She'd gotten lost down the overanalyzing rabbit hole and forgotten they were still here. "Sorry. I zoned out and didn't hear you guys come downstairs."

"Daydreaming of hunk-alicious, no doubt," Nina chuckled.

Sheila sent them both questioning looks.

"I'll fill you in when you drop me off at Comfort Food," Nina said as she dragged Sheila to the door. "We have to hustle, or June will have my head. See you tomorrow, Roxie. Have a good day off!"

Great. Once Sheila heard about what Nina had seen, the gossip train would have its next passenger. Roxie wasn't sure she was up for it. She didn't think she could survive the little comments and passive-aggressive remarks that would be not-so-subtly dropped when things between her and Joe eventually ended. She definitely didn't think she could survive the whispers behind her back when Joe started seeing someone else.

A chill raced down her spine.

Cut and run.

It was cowardly, yes. But like they'd told Nina last night, wasn't it better to end things sooner rather than later? Before the stakes were raised?

Roxie knew it was the best thing. However, it didn't make it hurt any less.

"Is it safe to enter?" Joe asked, peeking his head through the front door.

Roxie nodded. A small smile curved her lips, but there was no humor in her eyes. "All clear. Team Estrogen has left the premises."

He closed the door behind him and stared at her. Something was off, something that had the hairs on the back of his neck rising.

She looked a little tired, but that wasn't it. No, she looked . . . wary.

"What?" she asked.

Yup, definitely wary. Not good. "I didn't say anything."

"Then why the hell are you staring at me like a freaking bug on a dish?"

And defensive. *Shit.* His Spidey-senses went on full alert.

He said nothing. One of the things he'd learned as an undercover FBI agent was the power of silence. If he stayed quiet, she'd eventually tell him what had her so pissed.

"Fine," she grumbled, hopping off the couch. "If you're just going to stare all day, I have better things to do than just sit here."

Or apparently, she'd run. "Whoa, Rox, I haven't said a

damn thing. I just got here, and you're getting all fired up and jumping down my throat. Are you going to at least give me a hint as to why you're pissed at me?"

She aimed a death glare his way. "Like you don't know."

Holy shit. Brick wall, meet head. "Enlighten me, Rox."

"You acted like a Neanderthal earlier."

He frowned, sure as hell not liking where this was going.

"Don't act like you don't know what I'm talking about, Joseph Buchanan. I don't appreciate the caveman routine."

His temper flared. "Really? The 'caveman' routine? Let me get this straight: you're pissed at me because when I came home earlier, I tried to get you into bed?"

"You were groping me in front of my employees!"

His blood chilled. He hadn't seen that one coming. "Okay, princess, first of all, I thought they were your *friends* and not your 'employees.' And second, as you're well aware, I stayed at Quinn's place last night because you kicked me out of my own damn home. I figured that when Alex showed up this morning, it was a good indicator that the other girls had also left. And third, 'groping' you? Seriously?"

"Well, what the hell would you call it?"

His eyes narrowed. Not fucking *groping*, that's for damn sure. "Why don't you tell me? Am I supposed to ask for permission before I touch you? Shake your hand good morning?"

"God, Joe," she fumed, "this is all just a big joke to you, isn't it?"

Anger simmered in his gut, and he clung to it. Because that felt a whole hell of a lot better than the disappointment settling in beside it like a heavy rock. "What's with the hot and cold, Rox? I thought we were done playing games."

"That's just it," she said, tone cutting.

What the hell was she talking about? He crossed his arms over his chest. "I have a feeling you're talking about more than what happened in the kitchen this morning. Why don't you just spit out whatever the hell it is you're really getting at?"

Roxie mimicked his pose and a cold, blank expression consumed her face. She really had perfected that fucking princess look. "This thing that's going on between us, Joe, what would you call it?"

There was no way in hell he was answering that loaded question. "Why don't you tell me? Obviously, you have your own ideas of what it is."

"It's sex, Joe," she spat. "It's going to run its course. And when it does, it's going to be awkward between us. For Quinn, for Alex, for everyone." Her chin raised a notch. "So why don't we cut our losses early and end on a high note? The sex has been great, but we should go back to being only friends."

He clenched his jaw so hard his teeth ground together.

Damn her. What they had was so much more than that. So. Much. More.

He ignored the burn spreading in his chest, the bile rising in his throat, the desperate need to beg her to tell him what the fuck he'd done wrong.

But did he really need to ask? He already knew the answer.

She didn't want him. Clarification: she'd been fine with the orgasms he'd given her—the sex had been "a high note." It was *him* she didn't want. He'd thought she'd begun to trust him again, thought she was giving them a real chance, a real shot.

After everything . . . she didn't want him.

At least now he knew where he stood with her.

Fuck it.

He exhaled and pasted a bored smile on his face. He'd take the kick to the balls like a man. If that's how she saw it, if that's what she wanted—then fine. Yeah, he'd believed they could make it work. Because it had always been Roxie. Always.

But apparently, he was only a good fuck in her eyes. He was the dumbass with his head in the fucking clouds. Not anymore, though. Now his feet were firmly planted on the ground, and he would not be chasing after her. Because chasing a woman only worked if she wanted to be caught. And Roxie clearly didn't.

"If that's how you feel, then fine. We'll go back to being friends," he said, surprised he'd found his voice. He was even more surprised by how steady, how blasé it sounded. "I'm not going to lie, Rox. It's been a lot of fun, and I was hoping it would last longer. After all, it'd been a while for me."

The fire in her eyes dimmed the tiniest bit. His parting shot was a dick move, and it made him an even bigger asshole, but he didn't care. He was more than happy to fall into old habits and lash back. If she was going to stomp on him like a flaming bag of shit, then he'd get a dig in, too.

He was on the verge of taking another cheap shot at her when a loud bang made them both jump.

Joe turned and swung open the door. Quinn stood on the other side, expression grim.

His friend looked past him. "Roxie, you need to come with me. There's been an incident at your café."

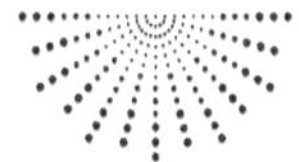

Roxie stared at the hole in her café's front window. Disbelief and horror warred within her. She couldn't believe it. It was only the tiny shards of glass on the sidewalk that sparkled as they caught the sunlight that told her it was true.

She wrapped her arms around her waist, but her hands wouldn't stop shaking. The trembling had started the second she'd buckled herself into Quinn's SUV for the short ride to Comfort Food. She wanted to blame her anxiety solely on the vandalism. However, that would be a lie.

Cut and run.

She closed her eyes. The messy confrontation with Joe had sucked. Torn her apart. She hadn't expected him to put up a big fight, but she'd thought he'd protest. At least a little.

He hadn't. At all.

His silence cut in ways she couldn't have anticipated. His thanks-for-the-lay comment made her feel dirty.

She swallowed past the lump in her throat.

As if her morning hadn't been bad enough . . . Now this.

Taking in the webbed glass with its gaping hole, she

sucked in a few deep breaths. The police buzzed about the scene in a blur of activity. An arm wrapped around her waist and squeezed. Unfortunately, it wasn't the one person she truly wanted to comfort her. Regardless, she leaned against her friend and blinked back tears. "Thanks, Alex."

"I'm so sorry, honey. Are June and Nina okay?"

Roxie nodded, a wave a relief sweeping through her.

"Do they know what happened?"

"No," Roxie said. "Quinn told me they were both in the back when they heard the glass shatter. They ran to the front, and when they saw the damage, they immediately called it in. Thankfully, the front was empty, so no one was hurt. It was horribly perfect timing because no one outside saw who did it, either."

But thank god June and Nina were unharmed. That's what mattered.

"What a mess," she mumbled, pulling away from Alex and stepping toward Comfort Food's entrance. "I guess I'd better grab a broom."

She stilled when a familiar hand settled on her shoulder.

Joe didn't have to say anything. Hell, he didn't even need to breathe for her to know it was him.

He was the one she'd wanted comfort from, but now that the comfort was being offered, she needed to put the kibosh on it. Just like she'd needed to put the kibosh on their fling. For her own sanity, she'd had to. It was the smartest choice. As much as their romantic end hurt now, the reality was they'd been together for less than a week. *One* week. She couldn't risk getting in deeper with him, couldn't risk falling completely in love. Because when it ended weeks or months down the road? It would have been even more devastating.

"Don't worry about the mess, Roxanne," Joe said softly. "I'll take care of it."

"That's okay. My place, my mess." She averted her gaze and tried to walk past him.

"Hey." His grip tightened on her arm. "We're friends. That's what you said earlier, right?"

She nodded, blinking furiously as her eyes watered.

"Then let me be your friend and clean this up for you. Stay with Alex. Check on June and Nina. Let me and Quinn take care of this."

Her gaze stayed locked on her toes, but she nodded.

As he walked away, a fist gripped her heart and squeezed. *We're friends. Let me be your friend and clean this up for you.* Those words had slayed her. They'd shown how quickly, how easily, Joe was able to fall back into being friends. Like what they'd shared this last week meant nothing to him.

Roxie gasped for breath. *Dammit.* The pain proved how far she'd already fallen for him.

She wanted to scream, *Erase! Erase!* and tell him she'd made a horrible mistake. That she wanted to go back to how it had been before she'd opened her stupid mouth, to go back to him holding her in his arms and making all the bad things go away.

Instead, she straightened her spine. She *would* get through this. She'd had an entire childhood—an entire lifetime, really—of doing things on her own. This was no different.

"Roxie?"

Glancing up, she spotted Quinn standing in the entryway of her café, motioning for her to join him. She was at his side in a few strides. His demeanor put her on edge. Her friend was fully in cop mode.

"What's wrong?" She cringed. "Aside from the obvious."

"I'm going to have Deputy Chase and a couple of my other guys clean up here and board up the front window. I want to talk to you at the station." He nodded at Joe, who stood close by. "You too."

"I take it this wasn't some punk kids throwing rocks?" she asked, attempting humor.

"No, Roxie." Quinn's gaze was steady, but the crinkle between his brows had dread swirling in her belly. "You've got a big problem."

<hr>

"He's escalating," Joe said, leaning against the closed office door. He glanced at Quinn, who gave a slight nod of confirmation from his seat at his desk.

Groaning, Roxie dropped onto the guest chair and rubbed her temples. "You think this was the stalker's doing?"

Quinn placed a clear evidence bag on the desk and pushed it in her direction. "That's what broke your window."

"It's a brick." She shook her head, confusion and exhaustion written on her face. "The cylinders aren't all firing right now, Quinn. I don't understand what you're getting at."

Quinn turned the bag over, and the bang it made on the desk sounded like a hammer knocking the proverbial final nail into a coffin. A single word was painted on the brick.

WHORE.

Joe bit back a growl as he watched the blood drain from Roxie's face. Quinn had told him about the brick before they'd arrived, but seeing it for himself was different. And seeing how it affected Roxie—how it sparked fear in her beautiful green eyes—had him wanting to put his fist through a wall. Better yet, he wanted to put his fist through the asshole responsible for this.

Tears shimmered in Roxie's eyes when she looked over at Quinn. She took a deep breath in and lifted her chin. When her lips wobbled, she pursed them into a firm line. She was desperately trying to put on her brave face. The fact that she was failing cut him to the fucking core. It made him want to howl.

"But I haven't done anything," she whispered. Her eyes locked on his, and her voice shook as she added, "I swear to you both, I haven't."

His heart ached. It killed him that Roxie thought she deserved any of this. And dammit, it destroyed him that her self-doubt was his fault.

More than anything, he wanted to wrap his arms around her and offer her comfort, support, anything she fucking wanted. But just that damn morning, she'd called off their . . . relationship . . . or whatever the hell it was she wanted to call it.

She tucked a stray lock of hair behind her ear with a trembling hand.

Fuck it.

And fuck her let's-be-just-friends bullshit. Not now. Not ever.

Without a word, he stormed across the room.

Her eyes went wide, and she let out a tiny squeak as he lifted her off her seat, sat down, and hauled her onto his lap. He pulled her tight against his chest, then caught her chin in his hand and waited until her eyes met his, their faces inches apart.

"All that crap we talked about this morning, baby?" he said, tone fierce. "It's bullshit. I don't want to go back to being friends. What we have—whatever name you want to put on it—is *everything* to me. You were breaking my fucking heart, so I lashed out like the asshole that I am. And I'm so damn sorry. I'm not letting you go, Roxanne. I'm not. Deal with it."

His pulse pounded in his ears, and he held his breath. The slow tick of the clock drove him wild as we waited for some clue as to how she was feeling. At last, by some miracle of miracles, she relaxed in his arms.

"Okay," she whispered, giving him a tiny nod. "And I'm sorry, too. I said some stuff I didn't mean. That wasn't fair."

He sighed in relief and held her closer. Thank Christ.

A throat cleared. Loudly. "Can we get back to the issue at hand?" Quinn asked, his eyebrows raised.

"Give me a second, man," Joe said, kissing her forehead. "She broke up with me a couple hours ago, so let me enjoy this, will you?"

"Well, you probably fucking deserved it," Quinn muttered. "Roxie, I know you said you haven't had any big issues with anyone in town, but what about any smaller disagreements? Maybe something you see as minor could be something big for this other person? Anyone acting differently toward you?"

She remained silent, but her muscles tensed. Joe went on alert. When she shifted on his lap, he loosened his arms around her. "Roxanne?"

She chewed on her bottom lip, a worry line forming between her brows. "It's probably nothing, but Eli got a little close the other day."

Joe's jaw clenched. *Motherfucking shit.* He'd never liked that bastard. "Define 'close.'"

"Jesus Christ, Buchanan," Quinn groaned. "Can it, okay? I'm the sheriff, so *I'll* ask the questions. You get to sit there with your damn mouth shut."

Joe bristled. "You were going to ask the same exact fucking question, so what does it matter?"

"Holy fu—" Quinn cut himself off and inhaled. Looking at the ceiling, he appeared to be counting. After about ten seconds, his friend met his gaze. "It matters, Buchanan. Protocol matters, and this is not your fucking show. So, either shut the hell up or leave. It's your choice."

Fine. Joe gave a brisk nod. He knew he wasn't helping matters, but he felt so damn helpless.

Roxie placed her hand on his chest. "Let Quinn do his job, okay?" When he started to protest, she brought her finger to his lips to silence him. "I need you to just keep doing what you're doing."

"That's the problem, Rox. I'm not doing a fucking thing right now and it's—"

"Stop," she murmured. "I need you to keep doing *this*. Keep holding me. I feel better when you're with me . . . You make it better."

His breath left him. Goddamn, she humbled him like no one else.

Joe took her face in his hands and laid a soft kiss on her lips. "You got it, baby. I promise I'll keep quiet."

She arched a brow, and he could see the skepticism in her gaze

He grinned. "Yeah, okay. I promise I'll *try* to keep quiet."

She kissed him quickly, and then they both focused their attention on Quinn, who was shaking his head. "You guys are sappier than shit, you know that?"

Roxie rolled her eyes. "Please. Don't forget that I see you with your wife on a regular basis, so you can drop the tough-guy routine, Sheriff. But back to business. Like I said earlier, it's probably nothing, but Eli came in yesterday and got too close. We were talking in my office, and when I tried to get by him to leave, he grabbed my arm. I thought he was going to try to kiss me or something."

"Motherfucker," Joe hissed, anger boiling in his gut.

"But he didn't." Roxie shot him a pointed glare before continuing. "Look, guys, I could be totally off base because he didn't actually say anything inappropriate. It was just a creepy vibe I got."

"Then what happened?" Quinn asked.

"Nina popped her head into the office and asked if everything was okay. She picked up on the creeper vibe as well. Then I told Eli to leave and to not come back." She shrugged. "That was that."

Joe caught Quinn's gaze, and they traded quick, subtle nods. Over their long friendship, there had been many times when they hadn't needed to speak to get their points across. This was one of those times. They were going to pay a little visit to ole Eli.

Roxie smacked his arm, startling him. Her eyes were narrowed. "Oh no, you don't, buster. I saw what just happened there. Don't think I don't know what you guys are up to. You two are going to go hassle Eli about this, aren't you?"

He wanted to feign ignorance, but there was no point. The trio had been thick as thieves since they were knee-high, and Roxie had always been fluent in his and Quinn's nonspeak.

Joe's phone rang, and he thanked the universe for the interruption. A glance at the display revealed a phone number and area code he didn't recognize, so he silenced it and turned his attention back to Roxie.

"I have no idea what you're talking about." It wasn't an outright lie. Technically, he couldn't read her mind. "Quinn?"

"Not a clue," his friend said, hands raised.

She glared at both of them. "Seriously, you guys, it's probably nothing and I *really* don't want to stir up trouble for Poppy. Especially if I'm simply blowing it all out of proportion."

"Don't worry about it." Quinn jotted down a couple of notes. "Anyone else you can think of?"

"Jeremy buzzes around once in a while, but he's more of an annoyance than actual trouble. Besides, I haven't seen much of him since the Chamber party at Pacific View." She shook her head, lips pursed in thought. "It couldn't be Jeremy, though, because he was in one of the pictures that was sent to me."

Joe ran his hands over her arms. "Never say never, baby."

"Not everything is a conspiracy, ex-Agent Buchanan," she retorted.

"True, but many things are." He'd seen a lot of fucked-up shit during his time with the FBI.

"Any other instances you can think of, Roxie?" Quinn asked.

She shook her head. "No, that's it. Things have been busy with the café, so I haven't gone out much. I honestly can't think of anyone who would do this . . . or *why* anyone would do this."

The dismay on her face broke his heart. She'd always gotten along with everyone. That was one of the reasons why Comfort Food had been such a success from the get-go. People liked Roxie. Period. When she'd first opened, she'd had the unconditional support of all the locals because they'd wanted her to succeed. The fact that she was a terrific baker and cook had been an added bonus.

Joe would give anything to find out who was behind this. Sending Roxie pictures to scare her was one thing. Threatening her business, her physical safety, and most importantly, her sense of security was another. Whoever this asshole was, Joe would be more than happy to make them pay. He'd use the skills he'd learned in the FBI to keep her safe and assist Quinn in any way he could. Later. Right now, they were getting nowhere.

"Quinn, I'm taking Rox home. She's had enough for one afternoon. Come over when you're done here, and we can talk more if you want."

Quinn nodded. "I know I don't have to say this, but if

either of you think of anything, no matter how seemingly insignificant, call me."

"Of course," Joe said as they rose from the chair. Taking her hand, he laced his fingers with hers. "We'll stick to the house today, so you'll know where to find us."

<hr>

Roxie sank down on the couch, propped her feet on the coffee table, and closed her eyes. It was only three in the freaking afternoon, and she was utterly beat.

She felt like she was on the tail end of a three-day bender. Her head was pounding, her stomach queasy, and if she could crawl into bed, throw the covers over her head, and make everything disappear, she totally would.

Well, maybe not *everything*.

She'd appreciated Joe's support today. She hadn't thought they would recover from their breakup this morning, but life had a way of surprising you. Honestly, she wasn't sure she would have made it through the last few hours without him. They had been the biggest, craziest emotional rollercoaster of her life. Highs, lows, and neck-breaking whiplash. Something told her that there were more monster drops and corkscrews to come. The day was still young, after all.

"Here." Joe interrupted her musings. "Drink this."

She cracked an eye open and glanced at the steaming mug in his hand. "Please say that's not tea."

"Come on, baby," he said. His quiet voice held a hint of laughter. "Give me some credit, will you? I know you have the same opinion of tea as I do."

She wrinkled her nose. "Dirty gym socks mixed with dirt and boiled in water?"

Joe smiled the smile that Roxie loved best. It wasn't that charming, smoldering, somewhat-obnoxious grin that had "player" written all over it. Rather, it was a warm smile that made his blue eyes dance. It only came out when he was genuinely happy, which made it the most dangerous of all. Knowing not many people ever saw this smile made her heart squeeze.

"Exactly," he said, holding out the mug. "Hot cocoa. With milk, not water." He held out his other hand. "Plus four Tylenols."

Sitting up, she held her hands out for the loot. "My hero."

She downed the medicine dry, then took a sip of the hot cocoa. The warm, rich chocolate soothed her soul. Closing her eyes, she waited for the combination to work its magic on her headache.

The couch cushion next to her dipped, and a second later, strong hands began massaging her temples.

"What's going on with us?" Roxie asked before she could think better of it.

Joe's hands stilled at her temples, then fell away.

She took another sip of her drink, set her mug on the coffee table, and turned to face him. Now that she'd kicked off this discussion, she might as well get the rest out. Unsure where to start, she blurted, "Sometimes I really hate being such a needy girly girl."

His eyes scrunched in confusion.

A lock of hair fell into her face, and she impatiently tucked it behind her ear. "What I mean is that I'm not good at just screwing around with someone. If I'm sleeping with someone, I want it to be exclusive and—"

"Whoa, Rox. Time-out." His hands formed a *T*. "First off, I, for one, am glad that you're a girl. Also, by 'girly girl' you better be meaning kick-ass. Second, you are the polar opposite of needy. And third, we're not just screwing around. At least, I haven't seen it that way. You said I was groping you this morning, and that really pissed me off. Is that how you see it? That we're just fucking?"

Did he really need to put it that way? She lifted her chin in challenge. "Aren't we, though?"

His eyes darkened. "Are you trying to piss me off again? I thought we were done with the games."

Somehow, she'd lost control of this conversation. "You don't do relationships, Joe. I know this. You do casual. You do flings. Trust me when I say that I didn't enter into this thinking I was going to be any different." *But a part of me sure as hell hoped I was.*

He stared at her. His face was completely blank. Then, swallowing hard, he nodded. "I'll give you that. I've never done serious. But you didn't answer my question. Is screwing around how *you* see what's going on with us?"

She didn't know how to answer that. Technically, yes, they were screwing around, but that made it sound cheap. Not as crass as "just fucking," but cheap, nonetheless. In either case, that's not what was going on with them. At least not to her.

Maybe it was their shared history, maybe it was their friendship . . . but what they had felt different. What if that was just her wishful thinking, though?

"Roxanne, answer me."

"No. It's not just screwing around to me." She sighed and looked down at her hands. "I don't know where I stand with you, Joe. That's what's making me crazy."

He remained silent, and she wished she'd never started this conversation. The couch cushions shifted, then Joe was kneeling in front of her. Tenderly, he framed her face with his hands, giving her no choice but to meet his gaze. Her breath caught as she looked into his blazing blue eyes.

"You stand on a fucking pedestal with me, Rox. You always have. What's going on with us isn't just screwing around. To me, it's not casual. It's not a fling." He paused, tracing her lower lip with his thumb. "Truth be told, I'm not exactly sure what you'd call our relationship. *Boyfriend and girlfriend* doesn't quite do it justice, and I've always thought *lovers* was creepy."

"Because it is," she said with a soft chuckle.

"But, baby, whatever it is we choose to call it, know that it's just me and you. No one else."

Roxie's heart swelled. She couldn't put into words all that she felt for this man. Because she loved him. She'd always loved him. He'd been her best friend, an integral part of her life, through the good, the bad, the ups, and the downs . . . all of it. But now, there was so much more depth to her love. Maybe there had been for a while.

Until this moment, she'd been scared to feel what she did for him, petrified that she was alone in her emotions. That's why the last few years had been so hard. It was also a big reason why her business had been such a success. Yes, she was driven and a damn fine businesswoman. But without Joe, there'd been a void in her life. His absence had hurt so much, she'd thrown herself into her work. She'd vowed to distance herself from others and to keep her personal emotions safely tucked away.

Because it had always been him, she realized.

"Me and you," she murmured, bringing her lips to his, "I think we make a good team. We'll argue from time to time—"

"Time to time?" He scoffed. "More like more often than not."

She eyed him. "That's because you're so stubborn and bossy."

"No, that's not it." He trailed kisses from her jaw to her ear. "It's because I like make-up sex."

She laughed as he lowered her down onto the couch. "Well now, that makes a lot more sense."

For the fiftieth time that minute, Joe asked himself what the hell he'd done to be this fucking lucky. He was lying on the couch with the girl of his dreams, propped up on one elbow so he could memorize her face. A face he'd known his entire life. A face that somewhere around his sixteenth year, he'd become fascinated with.

Roxie was so damn expressive, and one of his new missions was to get to know all her looks. Right now, he saw happiness, exhaustion, and arousal on her beautiful face. The arousal was a bonus, but the happiness was what mattered. He didn't want to fuck this up. She was too important.

"You know me, Rox. You know me better than anyone on this planet. You know that I can be an ass. I try not to be, but sometimes . . ."

She grinned. "Sometimes you just can't help yourself."

He traced her smile with the tip of his finger. "Right. I'm going to piss you off—and not just for the make-up sex—but know that I don't mean to. I'm just an idiot sometimes."

"You're a guy." She shrugged. "It goes with the territory."

"True, but this is new territory for me. As you so eloquently called out, I've never been in a serious relationship. I'm not quite sure how they work. But me and you? *We* work. I want to make us work."

For as long as he could remember, she'd been the one he'd measured all others against. Which explained why he'd never been in a relationship for more than a few months. Everyone else had inevitably fallen short.

He wasn't one to make promises because life had taught him that you never knew what the next day would bring. But he knew there was one promise he could make her. "I won't lie to you. I don't think I ever have, and I never plan to in the future."

His heart stopped when her eyes welled.

She chuckled and shook her head. The tears escaped down the sides of her face. "Don't look so scared. I've been an emotional wreck lately, but I promise they're happy tears."

He brushed his thumbs over her cheekbones. She was fighting it, but he could see her exhaustion overtaking all else. He laid a kiss on her lips before shifting them into a spooning position.

Draping a blanket over them, he held her close, marveling at the fact that she let him, even after all they'd been through. He took solace in her forgiveness. Her compassion. He wasn't sure she would ever fully understand how much she meant to him.

It was no shocker that he'd loved her his entire life. But *love* love? As in romantic love? He couldn't go there yet. He honestly wasn't even sure what the hell that felt like.

All he knew was that Roxie was vital to him. As vital as the air he breathed and the blood in his veins. He'd made so many mistakes with her—hell, sometimes he still made mistakes with her—but he would work every day to make them right and earn her trust.

After a few moments, her breathing slowed to a soft, steady rhythm. She was asleep.

He tightened his arms around her and relaxed into the couch cushions. The smell of citrus with a hint of honey teased his nose. There was nowhere else he'd rather be.

CHAPTER TWENTY-SIX

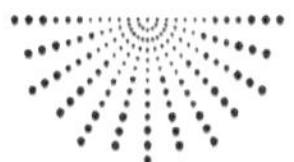

On Tuesday afternoon, Roxie stood behind the counter of Comfort Food on the verge of tears. The support she'd received from the community this week was overwhelming. Everyone had come by and been so wonderful. She was touched beyond belief. She was also dead tired.

Prior to Joe coming home to Hudson Island, her routine had entailed going to bed by ten, waking up at three for her morning run, and then heading over to the café no later than four thirty. Joe's arrival had thrown that all out of whack, but the events of the last couple of days had made things even worse. Not only was the front window still boarded up, but both Nina and June were out sick. Roxie was used to long days and little sleep, but this was something else entirely.

Stifling a yawn, she handed over Deputy Chase's latte. "Thanks for the update."

"I wish I had better news," Chase replied. "But know that we're working on it. Sheriff O'Conner will make sure we find out who's behind this."

She thanked the young deputy again as he headed out. There'd been no progress on finding out who had thrown the brick through her window. She knew the sheriff's department was doing their best, but the lack of movement in the case discouraged her. If she was this frustrated, she couldn't imagine what Quinn was going through right now.

A glance at the clock showed there were fifteen more minutes until closing time. Only a few customers remained, and they were talking with Sheila, who was tidying the tables.

"I'm going to be in the back," Roxie called out.

A large stack of mail sat on her desk. Her eyes zeroed in on two large manila envelopes. To her relief, the top envelope was insurance paperwork. Putting it aside, she scanned the second. No return address. In fact, no markings at all.

Dread pooled in her belly, but it was quickly replaced by anger. She was so damn tired of this. If she ever figured out who the hell this coward was, she'd kick his ass. Well, maybe not personally, but she'd hold him down so Joe and Quinn could kick his ass.

Satisfied with the mental image of the nameless, faceless asshole getting pummeled by her two favorite guys, she tore open the envelope and poured its contents onto her desk.

Her breath lodged in her throat, and her stomach turned. *Damn.* The nameless, faceless asshole was getting creative. She picked up her phone and dialed Quinn.

As she waited for the call to connect, she stared at the picture. A shiver ran up her spine and her dread returned. Feeling queasy, she took a deep breath, hoping it would steady her.

It didn't.

The photo showed a naked woman lying on her back in the snow, her long auburn hair spread out around her. Her legs were spread eagle and her arms lay at unnatural angles. Blood-stained snow surrounded her, and she stared up at the sky with cloudy eyes. Those eyes . . .

Hers. The face was hers.

Knowing the woman's appearance had been doctored didn't make Roxie feel any better, didn't make it any less shocking. If anything, it made her feel worse. The picture seemed like an omen, like an unspoken promise from this crazy, obsessed nutjob.

It fucking scared her.

"Sheriff O'Conner."

She jumped at the sudden voice and fumbled the phone. Pressing it back to her ear with unsteady fingers, she said, "It's me. I got another photo in the mail. Can you come to the café?"

He mumbled a reply, and the line went dead.

Setting the phone down, she continued to stare at the disturbing photo. She knew she shouldn't, she knew that the longer she stared at it, the deeper it would penetrate her subconscious and be locked in her brain. But it was like a train wreck. The biggest, worst train wreck ever. She couldn't look away.

"What do you have?" Quinn asked from her office doorway.

For the second time in a matter of minutes, Roxie jumped. Watching him with unfocused eyes, she realized she wasn't sure how much time had actually passed since she'd hung up with him. She'd been transfixed by the damn photo.

Nodding to the picture, she said, "Whoever he is, he's got really good Photoshop skills."

"Fuck," he murmured, reaching for it with a gloved hand. "Stop looking at it, Roxie."

"Too late. The image is seared into my brain." She propped her elbows on the desk and massaged her forehead, hoping the soothing motion would alleviate the tension headache she felt coming on. No luck. A sudden thought gave her pause. She whipped her head up to look at

Quinn. "Holy shit. Do you think the woman in the picture is real?"

"I hope to hell not, but I'll check around. That's for damn sure." His lips pressed into a tight line as he studied the photo. After placing it into a clear evidence bag and discarding the glove in the garbage bin, he took the chair in front of her desk. "Are you okay?"

"I don't know." She shrugged and crossed her arms over her chest. "I'm a little spooked, I'm not gonna lie."

"Look, Roxie, I know your independence is really important to you, but until this is figured out, you may want to consider having someone around at *all* times."

"Like a babysitter?" She'd meant the remark to sound flip, but her voice shook as an image of *her* sprawled in the bloody snow flashed in her mind.

"More like safety in numbers."

She rubbed her eyes. "I know. Part of me balks at needing a babysitter, but this guy has me creeped out."

"You're not alone in this. You know that, right?"

Roxie sighed as a wave of fatigue plowed through her. "I do. You know me, though. I hate feeling like an inconvenience to everyone." *Thank you, childhood.*

"You're an idiot," he said, glaring at her. "That's coming from someone who loves you, by the way. So, stop being stupid."

"Gee, thanks." She smiled at him, but it was all teeth. Quinn really was the annoying big brother she'd never had. Emphasis on *annoying.*

"I'm serious, Roxie. Over the last couple of days, how many people came through your doors to check on you? *All* those people care about you. But me, Alex, and Joe? We fucking *love* you. You're not alone, and you're not a damn inconvenience. Get that shit out of your head."

God, she loved him. He could be frustrating as all get-out, but she knew she could always rely on him.

"Thanks, Quinn." To her horror, tears flooded her vision, and her throat grew thick. She grabbed a tissue. "I swear, I've been an emotional disaster these last few days. I blame sleep deprivation."

Quinn's eyes went wide with panic. He was one of the strongest men she knew, but tears were one of the few things that, without fail, sent him scurrying.

"Relax, Sheriff," she teased. "I've been able to keep it under control."

"I'm glad you think this is funny." He squirmed in his chair. "Speaking of emotional disasters, how are things with Joe?"

She chuckled. "I wouldn't necessarily call him an emotional disaster, per se. He's more like . . ."

"A guy," Quinn stated. "Hence, he's an emotional disaster. Trust me on this."

"Joe's good," she said with an eye roll. "He's been busy with Cade and Gavin the last couple days. He's made some suggestions for the new program and they're tweaking some other things, so he's pretty excited. "

Quinn nodded. "That's great and all, but you know that's not what I'm talking about. How are the two of you doing?"

It was her turn to squirm.

Outside of work, she and Joe had been inseparable—in more ways than one—ever since the craziness on Sunday. The sex between them was still ridiculously hot, but they hadn't talked more about their relationship. It was as if neither of them wanted to be the first one to bring it up again. She knew she didn't. He'd already said he wanted to make it work between them, and she didn't want to push her luck by being *that* girl.

She doubted Quinn wanted to know any of that, though.

"We're good. It was a little rocky at first, but one day at a time, right?" She shrugged. "I think it's a bit different for both of us. Neither of us have ever dated anyone that we were friends with first."

Quinn scoffed. "Uh, that would be the biggest understatement of the year. There's friends, and then there's *us*. Aside from the shit show of the last few years, we're like the Three freaking Amigos."

"That's just it, Quinn," she said, worry starting to roil in her gut. "What Joe and I are doing is risky. I think in the back of our heads, we're both worried about messing up our friendship, not just with each other, but with you, too, you know? But . . ."

But they couldn't help themselves. The attraction between them was explosive, their connection unlike anything she'd ever experienced before. It scared her. But high risk, high reward, right?

Joe had the ability to destroy her. Completely.

Roxie tended to play it safe with her heart. Except with him, she simply couldn't.

"But the risk is worth it," Quinn said quietly, a knowing look in his eyes.

Butterflies took wing in her stomach.

"Yeah." Her heart pinged, and a small smile tilted her lips. "It's worth it."

CHAPTER TWENTY-SEVEN

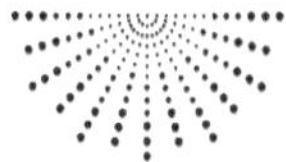

Roxie threw her head back and moaned. With her hands braced on Joe's chest, she rocked her hips harder, riding him. The friction, the pressure, had her seeing stars.

"That's it, baby," he murmured. His hands gripped her hips and worked her up and down his thick cock. She was teetering on the edge when he abruptly pulled out.

"No," she groaned, eyes flying open. She'd been so close. But before she could protest further, he flipped her onto her hands and knees and pressed between her shoulder blades. She dropped her chest to the mattress. Tingles shot up her spine. *Oh, fuck yes.*

He pulled her hips up and slapped her ass. The crack of his palm was loud in the near-silent room. Her heart raced, and wetness flooded her pussy. She moaned his name as he slammed into her.

"You're so fucking hot, baby," he praised, his hands squeezing and molding her cheeks.

She clenched and throbbed around him as he pounded into her. Her thighs began to quiver.

"More, Joe. Harder," she begged.

He pulled her upright, bringing her back to his chest as he continued to pump into her. His hand dipped to where their bodies met, and his fingers rubbed tight circles over her clit.

"Come for me, baby," he growled in her ear. "Come all over me."

Electricity shot through her body, and when he pinched her clit, she screamed. Detonated. He slammed into her pulsing center and groaned his own release.

Trembling, they collapsed back onto the mattress in a sweaty heap of tangled limbs. Her pulse was racing, and her bones were jelly. Her core throbbed with aftershocks. *Oh my god, this man . . .*

Joe lay atop her, limp with exhaustion, pressing her deeper into the mattress.

"Can't breathe," she mumbled into the sheets.

"Sorry."

Before she could blink, she was on her back, and Joe was on top of her again.

"Not sure this is any better," she said with a laugh.

He shifted, displacing some of his weight so she was no longer squished.

"Better," she said, kissing his shoulder. Slowly, she trailed her nails down his spine, all the way from his delicious neck to his firm ass. She smiled when he shivered.

"Rox, baby," he said against her hair, "if you keep doing that, you better be ready for round three."

She smacked him on the rear. "Still can't breathe."

With a grunt, he rolled fully off her and onto his side.

Goosebumps prickled her flesh at the loss of his heat. With her arms high above her head, she stretched. "Now, what were we talking about before you distracted me?"

"*I* distracted *you?*" Joe nuzzled her ear. "I think you have it the wrong way."

She didn't. He'd distracted her from her horrible day. Well, the day had been fine until the photo . . . Nope. She wasn't going to think about it. She was going to focus on the here. The now. On the man who calmed and steadied her.

Her breath hitched as he ghosted his fingertips down her neck, over the valley between her breasts, and around her belly button. She shuddered. It should have embarrassed her how much she wanted him. He'd been inside her only a few minutes before, and yet she still craved more. She craved *him*.

Arching up, she brought her lips to his. His arms wrapped around her and—

The doorbell chimed.

"Ignore it," he said, rolling her under him and settling between her thighs. "I want to eat you."

Roxie pushed against his shoulder. "We can't just ignore it —" Her protest fell short when his fingers dipped inside her and his lips found that perfect spot on her neck. She moaned.

"Joseph, you up there?"

They froze.

Her eyes went wide when footsteps sounded on the stairs.

She slapped at his chest, her heart racing in panic. "Holy shit! Get off me, Joe," she hissed. "Your dad's here!"

***

Joe couldn't help but laugh. Of course his dad would choose this exact moment to visit. And use his key. Considering the man owned the damn place, Joe couldn't complain.

"Seriously, you idiot, get *off* of me!"

He looked down at Roxie and laughed again. Her face was flushed, and mortified horror filled her eyes as she glanced at the open bedroom door. She gave him a weak shove.

Then she slugged him in the gut. Hard.

He winced. Apparently, Roxie had yet to find the humor in this situation.

"Give me a few minutes, Dad," Joe called out, rolling off her. "We'll be right down."

"Are you crazy?" she hissed. "I can't face your dad right now!"

He watched—well, more like ogled—as she scrambled back into her yoga pants and tank top. It was the yoga pants that had distracted him earlier. He'd been in the kitchen, and Rox had been in the living room. They'd been talking about god knew what when he'd rounded the corner . . . and found her in the downward dog pose. Wearing yoga pants that fit her like a second skin. No man on earth could fault him for getting distracted.

Joe grabbed his sweatpants and T-shirt off the floor. Pulling them on, he said, "Come down when you're ready, baby."

She glared at him.

Damn, she was gorgeous when she was mad. He snaked an arm around her waist and drew her to him. Crushing his lips against hers, he teased her mouth until she opened for him. Their tongues tangled in a kiss that was more heat than finesse. With a groan, he broke away.

"Damn, Rox." He couldn't get enough of this woman. He brought his lips to hers again, gentle this time, then kissed the tip of her nose. "You know you have to come say hi to my dad. It would be weird if you didn't."

She grimaced. "I know. But talk about awkward."

They walked down the hallway, and he slapped her on the ass as she turned toward her room. Descending the stairs, he knew he sported a shit-eating grin.

He found his dad seated at the kitchen island. "Hey, Dad, what's up?"

His father looked up, and his face turned beet red. "Sorry, Joseph. I didn't mean to barge in."

Joe shook his head, baffled by his dad's embarrassment. "It *is* your house."

"Yeah, well . . ." He shifted in his seat. "I should have called first."

"You don't need to call, Dad. Like I said, it's your house."

"I know, but still." He cleared his throat. "I have to remind myself that you're a grown man now, and if you're . . . um, entertaining a lady, I don't want to interrupt as I . . . uh, obviously have."

"Really, don't worry about it." Joe's face grew hot. Yeah. Talk about uncomfortable. Desperate to do something with his hands, he grabbed a bottle of cabernet and began the process of opening it. "You'll stay for a drink?"

His father's eyes shifted to the stairs. "Um, only if you're sure."

"I am." Joe poured three generous glasses, then cleared his throat. "This is pretty awkward, huh?"

"You have no idea, son. No idea." Chuckling, his dad shook his head and reached for a glass. "Is your . . . uh, friend . . . going to be okay with me joining you two for a drink?"

Joe bit back a grin. "She'll be fine with it."

"Okay. But if you want me to split, I will. It's not a prob—"

"Hey, Doc!" Roxie called from the bottom of the stairs.

Joe watched his father's eyes go wide. His glass of wine was held mid-air, halfway to his lips, forgotten.

"How are you?" Roxie asked, entering the kitchen. She leaned against the island an arm's length away from him. He knew she was attempting to look nonchalant, but her shoulders were tense, her smile too bright. She reached for the remaining glass of wine and took a healthy swallow.

He held his breath as his father's gaze ping-ponged between him and Roxie. When the man lifted his glass the rest of the way to his mouth and took a sip of wine, Joe exhaled.

"I'm doing good, Roxie," his dad said with a smile. Humor flickered in his eyes. Something else, too. It looked like satisfaction, but that made no sense. "The question is, how are *you* doing?"

Joe grinned when a light blush stole across her cheeks.

She cleared her throat. "Um, I'm good."

"I'm glad to hear it. I've been over in Seattle the past couple days and only just got back. When I got off the ferry, I heard about what happened at Comfort Food. That must have been awful. That's why I came right by."

Roxie's eyes widened, and her blush spread down her neck.

Well, well, well. What he'd do to be a little fly on the wall of her brain . . .

"Right. Of course," she said, speaking fast. "It was a shock for sure, but everyone has been so great. Everyone's stopped by to check in on me. Like you. Quinn and his guys still don't have any leads, but I know they're working on it."

Joe suppressed a cringe. His girl was nervous. She hadn't paused once to breathe between sentences.

"Well, I'm glad the community has supported you," his dad said. "You're one of us, Roxie. You always were and always will be. Now, my dear, could I bother you for a slice of pie?"

Rox lit up like a freaking Christmas tree. He was sure she was relieved to have something to do, something to distract her.

Taking another large sip of wine, she walked to the refrigerator. "What would you like, Doc?"

"What have you got?"

With her back to them, she rattled off the pies she had in the fridge. He caught his dad's gaze and mouthed, *Thank you.*

His father nodded, a smile playing on his lips, and reached across the island to clink glasses with him. "I'll have blueberry, my dear. As you know, that's my favorite. If you've got any, why don't you add a scoop of ice cream, too? I did go running this morning, after all."

Joe's smile grew. His dad was awesome. There was no other way about it.

"Oh hey, that reminds me," she said over her shoulder. "Quinn, Alex, and baby Annie are coming over on Thursday for dinner. You gentlemen in?"

His father shook his head. "As much as I'd love to, I'll be back in Seattle. I'm doing a stint at UW Medical Center for the next few weeks."

"I can't either, Rox," Joe said. "We have a couple of Joint Base Lewis-McChord boys coming in that night for a training workshop on Friday. Cade, Gavin, and I are taking them to dinner."

"Okay. More food for us then." She placed two plates of blueberry pie à la mode in front of them. "Where are you guys going?"

"Watermark, probably."

Roxie's brows rose. "A Michelin three-star restaurant? Isn't that a little fancy and romantic for a dinner with the guys?"

His father chuckled. "Yes, what exactly are you fellas planning to do with the JBLM boys again?"

"Ha-ha," Joe said, deadpan. "I'm surrounded by smart-asses. The chef there takes a few classes at Cade's, so he gives Cade a good deal on private dining rooms and other stuff."

"Sure, okay." Roxie wagged her eyebrows. "If you say so."

He put his spoon down and stood. She yelped when he hauled her against him so they were chest to chest.

"Joseph Buchanan," she warned, blushing furiously now.

"Don't 'Joseph Buchanan' me, baby." He kissed her on the lips, then nodded at his dad. "Like he hasn't figured it out already."

"I knew before you kids did." His father laughed and took a sip of wine. "Took you damn long enough, son."

CHAPTER TWENTY-EIGHT

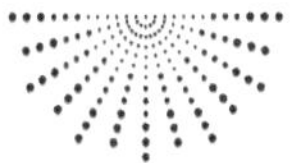

The doorbell chimed. It was Thursday night, and Roxie and Alex had started on their lasagna dinner since Quinn had called to say he was running late.

"Hold that thought, Alex." Roxie rose from the dining table and leaned close to Annie. Tickling the sweet little chubster's drooly chin, she said, "Of course your silly daddy has to interrupt us right when we're in the middle of a juicy story."

Hurrying to the front door and swinging it open, she called out, "Since when do you use the doorbe—"

It wasn't Quinn.

The attractive woman standing on the porch had long blond hair, was roughly Roxie's height, and wore the most amazing pair of leopard-print Louboutins.

She shook her head and brought her attention from the stilettos to the woman's face. "Sorry, I was distracted by your fabulous shoes. Can I help you?"

"No worries, I completely understand. I just splurged on them and have been staring at them ever since." The woman smiled and held out her hand. "You must be Roxie."

Unease crawled up her spine, but she shook the woman's outstretched hand, anyway. "I am. And you are?"

"Candie. With an *ie.*"

By some stroke of luck, Roxie managed not to roll her eyes. Of course it was with an *ie.* "It's nice to meet you, Candie." It wasn't. She couldn't put her finger on why, but it really wasn't. "I'm sorry, but you seem to have me at a disadvantage. Have we met?"

"No, we haven't. Joey mentioned on the phone that he has a housemate, so I assumed that's you." Candie looked over Roxie's shoulder into the house. "Is he ready?"

Joey?

Roxie's heart clenched. She really didn't want to ask her next question, but she had to. "Ready for?"

"Our date. We're going out to dinner."

It was like someone had sucker punched her in the gut. But a part of her had expected Candie's answer, so she shouldn't have been surprised. The woman was exactly Joe's type: blond, beautiful, and impeccably put together.

However, there was a part of Roxie that had hoped, prayed even, that her intuition was wrong. It was the same part that said Joe wouldn't do such a terrible thing to her.

Apparently, that part was a complete idiot.

The smile on Roxie's face was beginning to hurt. No. *Everything* was beginning to hurt.

She cleared her throat and ignored the pressure building in her chest. "Joe's actually not here."

He'd said he needed to work late tonight. He'd said that not only in front of *her*, but also in front of his *dad.*

Joe's earlier words echoed in her mind, and the pressure in her chest grew until she felt like a balloon that was about to pop.

I won't lie to you. I don't think I ever have, and I never plan to in the future.

She'd bought it. Hook, line, and fucking sinker.

God, she really was an idiot.

"Oh, that's right!" Candie sighed and cast her a sheepish look. "We were supposed to meet at the restaurant. I'm so sorry!" She fished her keys out of her purse. "Do you know how I can get to Waterford, Water . . ."

"Watermark?"

Candie's eyes lit up. "That's it!"

Of course it was. Why go to a high-end, romantic restaurant with a bunch of dudes when you could go with a woman who looked like Candie?

Smile still plastered on her face, Roxie nodded. "You follow the road back into town and then follow the signs for the Pacific View Resort. Watermark is at the resort. You can't miss it."

"Thanks," Candie said with a wave. "It was so nice meeting you, Roxie."

She waved back. Because it was the polite thing to do. It wasn't Candie's fault. It was hers.

Roxie held her breath until she could no longer see the woman's taillights. The pain started in her heart, then radiated out. Pressing a hand to her belly did nothing to stop the turning in her stomach. She feared she was going to be sick right then and there.

Stepping out onto the porch, she closed the door behind her. Her blood chilled, and she began to tremble. Neither reaction had anything to do with the frigid temperature.

Taking a seat on the porch's top step, she looped her arms around her shins and pressed her forehead to her knees. Then she did everything in her power to will away the tears.

Please, universe, make it stop hurting. Amen.

Joe had made no promises. He'd made no commitments. All he'd said was he wanted to make it work. Apparently, his definition of *make it work* was different from hers.

But that was her fault, not his. She should have seen the writing on the wall. She really should have, dammit. They'd never even been on a date. She was good enough to fuck, but not good enough to take out.

Unlike Candie. Who was on her way to a date. With Joe. At a restaurant that had been voted Most Romantic Restaurant in the whole entire freaking Pacific Northwest for the past three years.

Roxie had thought that the time they'd spent with his dad a couple of days ago was proof they were in a real relationship.

She'd been wrong.

Dammit, she would *not* cry over this. She would not cry over *him*.

She'd pushed him away earlier. But they'd moved forward. Together. Or so she'd thought.

Wrong. Yet again.

With her eyes closed and her head still pressed to her knees, she took in a deep breath and exhaled slowly. When she was sure her emotions were under control, she sat up. And saw Alex walking out onto the porch.

Alex settled next to her on the step, putting a supportive arm around her torso. "I'm so sorry, Roxie," she whispered.

That's all it took to break the dam. The tears started as a trickle, but in an instant, they became fierce sobs. The sharp pain in her chest was surely her heart breaking. She covered her face with both hands and wished that someone would just take a knife and gut her, put her out of her misery.

Roxie hadn't thought it would hurt so much. But it did. So. Damn. Much.

A pessimistic part of her had predicted this night. She tried to remind herself of that. Because if she'd known it was coming, it *had* to hurt less. Right?

The problem was that deep down, beneath the

pessimism and doubt, she'd begun to hope. To believe that she and Joe would have their happily ever after—with the kids and the dogs and the house with the freaking white picket fence.

Well, add that to the pile of things she'd been wrong about. After all, what the hell did she know?

Joe smiled at the woman across from him. It was probably more of a grimace than a smile, actually, but he didn't care. From the looks of it, she didn't, either.

He wasn't quite sure what he'd been thinking when he'd taken her call. No, he knew exactly what had happened: he'd been a fucking dumbass. He'd assumed the caller was Roxie, and not bothering to check the display, he'd answered the phone with his customary, "Hey, baby. What are you wearing?" Because he was an immature dipshit like that and enjoyed teasing her.

However, instead of Roxie's customary response of "Get a life, perv." or "How old are you, again?" he'd heard a high-pitched giggle. And now here he was, sitting across the table from "Candie with an *ie*!"

Fuck.

Right before she'd called, Gavin had canceled tonight's dinner with the JBLM guys. Somehow, Joe had ended up offering to meet her at the restaurant. Truthfully, he was still a little fuzzy on how it had all happened. She'd wanted to talk with him about a boutique hotel her company was considering opening on Hudson, and she'd hinted heavily that she could meet him at his house. Since *that* would have been a horrible idea, and since he'd already driven to the north side of the island, he'd figured it would be safer to meet at the restaurant.

But for fuck's sake, if she giggled one more damn time, he'd take the damn butter knife and jam it into his eye socket.

A shadow fell over their table, and a throat cleared. Joe glanced up.

It was Quinn. Towering over them. Giving him a death glare.

Actually, *death glare* was putting it lightly. His friend looked like he was two seconds away from murdering him.

"I'm sorry to interrupt," Quinn said, schooling his expression to a blank, steely gaze, "but I need to talk to you, Buchanan. Now."

The hairs on the back of Joe's neck rose. Something was wrong.

With a murmured apology to Candie, he followed Quinn out of the restaurant. "What's wrong? Is Alex okay?"

When Quinn finally stopped and turned to look at him, Joe reeled back in shock. The disappointment he saw in his best friend's eyes was palpable. And it was directed at *him*.

"What the fuck are you doing, man?" Quinn asked.

Confusion furrowed his brow. He was missing something. Something big. "What's wrong? What's going on?"

"Fuck, Joe," Quinn said on a sigh. "Don't play dumb. I thought you were serious about Roxie?"

What the fuck? "I am."

"Yeah?" Quinn scowled at him. "If you're serious, then why the hell are you on a date with another woman?"

Alarms blared in Joe's head. *Holy shit.*

"No, no, no, man," he said, gesturing toward the restaurant's entrance. "This is *not* a date."

"Really? You're having dinner at Watermark with another woman." Quinn shook his head, his impatience evident. "But that doesn't matter. What matters is that the woman inside there? *She* thinks you're on a date. And she told Roxie exactly that when she came to the house looking for you earlier tonight. And you, asshole, told Roxie you were having a business dinner with *Cade* and *Gavin* tonight."

Fuck. Shit. Fuuuck. Joe's breath left in a whoosh, and he squeezed his eyes shut in self-disgust.

"It's not like that," he said, voice quiet but firm. His eyes flew open when Quinn scoffed. "I swear to you, man."

"You're talking to the wrong person, Buchanan."

Growling, he scrubbed his hands over his face. This was the biggest clusterfuck ever. "Is Rox at the house?"

"Last I saw."

He cringed at Quinn's sharp tone. "She's completely pissed, right?"

"Not that I saw."

Ice crawled up Joe's spine. "What's that supposed to mean?"

"It means it was hard to tell how pissed she was since she was crying, you fucker."

Joe's stomach sank. *Holy shit, no.*

He had to see her. He had to explain to her what a colossal, fucked-up misunderstanding this was. Once he explained, surely she'd see how he was *not* on a date with Candie.

She had to.

Patting his pockets to make sure he had his keys, he left Quinn standing at the front of the restaurant and raced to his car. Minutes felt like hours, but he finally made it home. The downstairs lights were all on when he rushed through the front door.

"Rox?"

"She's upstairs. She wanted to be alone."

He jumped at the quiet voice, his gaze flying to Alex, who sat on the couch, a sleeping Annie snuggled against her chest.

He bolted up the stairs and came to an abrupt halt in

front of Roxie's closed door. For a split second, he hesitated. Then he knocked. "Rox?"

Silence.

Taking a deep breath, he turned the knob and peered into the dark room, careful to leave enough space to duck in case she threw—or swung—something at his head. "Roxanne?"

His skin prickled. *Dammit.* He flipped on the light switch, knowing what he'd find.

An empty bedroom.

He checked the remaining rooms on the second level, just to be sure, and came up empty.

"Alex," he called, racing back down the stairs. "Rox isn't here. Did she mention—"

"What do you mean Roxie isn't here?" she asked, frowning.

"She's not here. I'm going to check the café. Did she mention wanting to go anywhere?"

"No. She just said she wanted to be alone." Alex's eyes filled with worry. "I'll stay here in case she comes back. I'll text you if she does."

With a nod, he snagged Roxie's spare keys from the entryway table and ran back out to his car. Three minutes later, he arrived at Comfort Food. The café was pitch-black, locked tight, and secured for the night. Letting himself in, he went to her office and confirmed his sinking suspicion.

No Roxie.

Dammit.

He slammed his fists on his hips and groaned as his gaze shot around the empty space.

Where the hell are you, Roxie?

CHAPTER TWENTY-NINE

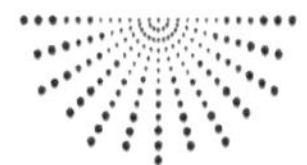

Roxie's lungs burned, and her legs grew heavier with each step. She'd been running—sprinting, really—for over an hour now, along the wooded trail that followed the island's western coast. The only sounds were her ragged breaths, her racing heart, and the slap of her feet on the packed earth.

The longer she'd sat in her room, the more claustrophobic it had become. She'd asked Alex for space, but her friend had remained downstairs. The thought of Alex giving her a pitying smile had been too much. Sitting in her room with her swirling, overanalyzing brain had been too much. Staring at the bed that she and Joe had repeatedly shared had been too much.

She'd needed out, needed to escape, needed to push her body so freaking hard that she couldn't think. Tossing on her running clothes and sneaking out had been a no-brainer. At least she'd been conscious enough to clip a running light to her jacket and toss on a headlamp. That was something.

The terrain she was navigating at breakneck speed could be treacherous if she wasn't careful. For that, she was grateful. It took all her concentration to maneuver the uneven path and left no time to think about what had happened. About how, at that very same minute, Joe was out having a romantic dinner with Candie and her fancy designer shoes.

She grimaced and pushed her pace faster. That floozie had called him *Joey*, for Christ's sake. *Joey*. No one called him that. Ever.

Roxie's foot caught on a root, and she slammed into the dirt face-first. Violently. Her headlamp exploded upon impact, and the hard ground knocked the wind from her lungs. For a few seconds, she gasped for air, unable to catch her breath, chest seizing.

Holy shit, that hurt.

She held still as her entire body smarted. When her pulse had slowed and her oxygen levels had recovered, she rolled onto her back with a groan. Her forehead ached, and a wet trickle slid down the side of her head. With an unsteady inhale, she sat up. Everything swayed.

Holy hell. That fall had served her right for not concentrating on the damn path.

Roxie didn't know how long she sat there in the dirt, but when she felt pretty sure she was no longer at risk of passing out, she gingerly made her way to her feet. A glance at her Apple Watch showed a cracked screen of flickering nonsense. She patted the side pocket of her leggings for her phone and came up empty.

God, she really was too stupid to live. *Shit.*

Yeah. A solo, high-speed run on a dangerous trail through the woods at night, while she was distracted by spiraling thoughts and emotions, might not have been the best decision she'd ever made. But at least now her mind wouldn't wander, that was for damn sure. Because if the awful throbbing in her ankle was any indication—and her whole damn body was throbbing, so that said a *lot*—it was going to take every last bit of her focus to get back to the main road.

Walking at a snail's pace for what felt like days, she finally spotted the trailhead in the distance and let out a sigh of relief. She supposed only a couple of hours had passed since she'd snuck out, but dammit, she was exhausted. The trailhead meant there were still roughly two more miles between her and the house. But she wasn't going home. There was no way in hell she could go back there.

By now, *Joey* and Candie were done with dinner. He would either be home alone now . . . or with her.

Roxie's chest stung, and it had nothing to do with her fall.

No, dammit! Screw Joe. She'd find somewhere else to stay tonight. *Anywhere* else would be preferable.

After the longest two-mile walk of her life, at a speed that had made her earlier snail's pace seem downright gazelle-like, Roxie settled onto the futon in her office. Her body screamed with every move, every breath. The futon was still in the couch position, and she didn't care. She was too drained to think about adjusting it.

Even glancing at the clock seemed tedious, but she managed to do that, at least. Her frown deepened upon seeing it was almost eleven. Just like old times, when she'd been too tired to make it home after an endless day at work. Tonight, however, her right ankle was swollen to triple its size, her jaw ached from clenching her teeth, and the headache pounding at her temples had her eyes watering. But the good news was her forehead had finally stopped bleeding.

Damn. Who was she kidding? She was a wreck. Everything hurt. Her foot, her shoulder, her head . . . her heart.

Gingerly adjusting her position, Roxie attempted to

swing her legs onto the futon. She yelped as a lightning bolt shot through her right ankle, up her leg, and into her hip. *Holy shit.* Grinding her teeth, she wheezed through the pain, willing it—hell, *begging* it—to subside.

She should probably call Doc. He'd come see her.

Looking around, she frowned. The office phone on her desk required her to get up—that sure as hell wasn't happening—and her cell was still on her nightstand at home.

Home.

Her frown deepened, and a lump lodged in her throat. It wasn't really her home, now was it? It was Joe's. How could she go back there? And dammit, how could she have been so wrong about him?

Thinking of Joe—recalling his expression when he'd told her that he wanted to make it work, make *them* work—had her eyes filling. She'd believed him. Why wouldn't she?

Low in her belly, anger stirred. She embraced it. What the hell was he doing going out with the Louboutin chick? The woman had called him Joey, for fuck's sake. *Joey.* The last time someone had called him Joey, they had been in elementary school. That kid had gotten punched in the face.

She pursed her lips as she felt an itch at the back of her mind. Something was nagging at her. Something didn't make sense. But she didn't know what.

Closing her eyes, she let out a breath. Her swirling thoughts settled, and a moment later, it came to her: Joe detested the nickname Joey even more than she detested Roxanne. Well, as much as she detested Roxanne when anyone other than Joe said it. There was no way in hell that woman really knew him if she was calling him Joey. Right?

Dammit. Could she have been wrong? Completely off base? Did she just have the biggest overreaction ever recorded in freaking female-dom?

"Holy crap," Roxie muttered.

With a groan, she threw her arms over her eyes and winced when her forearm connected with her bruised forehead. Ugh. She was so damn tired and couldn't think straight. Was she overanalyzing things again or was it all exactly as it appeared? She was just . . . so freaking confused.

With everything so vague, she needed to focus on the two facts she knew for sure.

Fact number one: Joe had gone on a dinner date with a blond, perky, and fabulously dressed skank. Okay, fine. Whether the other woman was actually a skank or not, Roxie didn't know or care. Whether it had actually been a date or not, she hadn't a clue. She hoped with all her heart, all her mind, all her freaking being, that it hadn't.

Fact number two: Joe had kissed her in front of his dad. His *dad*. That had to mean *something*. Right?

Maybe, but she had a hard time believing it. Because there was a part of her that still doubted him. Doubted the depths of his feelings for her. It was completely selfish and untrusting and paranoid of her. But there it was.

Truth be told, she was scared. She didn't want to lose him. Especially since she'd only just gotten a taste of what they could be together. Roxie was completely herself with him, and there was something liberating about that. He made her feel safe, and she craved him like no other. She'd never loved anyone the way she loved him.

The thought gave her pause. She loved him. No, she was *in love* with him.

Coming to that realization should freak her out. Instead, it calmed her. Steadied her.

She closed her eyes and sighed. What she needed to do was talk to the man. There was no use stewing and worrying when she could simply ask him her questions directly. Namely, did he love her, too?

"Yeah, right," she murmured to herself, rolling her eyes.

She could imagine how the blood would drain from his face at the question.

But . . . what if it didn't?

Shaking her head, Roxie pursed her lips. She needed to get a grip. She needed to squash the hope blooming in her chest. There was no hoping allowed until she talked to the guy, dammit.

Lifting her arms from her eyes, she confirmed that her landline was still indeed across the room on her desk. Her office wasn't big. At all. But with the way her ankle burned, it might as well have been the length of a football field.

She massaged her sensitive temples again. The pounding in her head slowly dulled to an angry, pulsating throb. The futon was uncomfortable as hell, but her limbs grew oddly heavy with exhaustion, as if she were sinking into the mattress.

She was physically spent—and a tiny voice in the back of her mind wondered if she'd hit her head harder than she'd realized—but she was also so damn tired of her own thoughts. This does-he-or-doesn't-he crap was getting to be too much. She was beginning to sound like a heroine in a high school romance novel. The last time she'd checked, Joe didn't sparkle in the sunlight.

Ugh, kill me now.

Sending up a little prayer that she didn't have a concussion, Roxie gave in to sleep, promising herself that she would talk to Joe later. She needed to get to the bottom of what was going on.

CHAPTER THIRTY

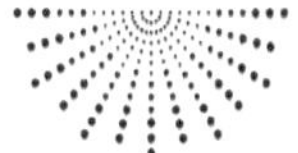

Roxie's eyes flew open. A few heartbeats passed before she recognized the lumpy office futon beneath her. Once her vision adjusted to the dim light, a glance at the clock showed it was a little past midnight.

Something had woken her up, but she wasn't sure what.

She stilled. There it was. A splashing, sloshing noise. But that didn't make any sense.

Her eyes narrowed as she heard it again. What was that?

Sitting up on the futon, she groaned. Her head was screaming, and her body was protesting every movement. She tried to put pressure on her right foot and nearly howled. Sweat dampened her brow as she leaned back against the unforgiving cushions.

What was she supposed to do now? She could barely move, and the splashing sounded like it was coming from the kitchen area. Good god, if she had a flood on top of everything, wouldn't that just be the proverbial straw and camel?

Metal clanged onto the floor.

Roxie froze, her heart in her throat. Not a flood. *Holy shit.* Someone was in her kitchen.

Sinking her teeth into her bottom lip, she hauled herself up and ignored the fire shooting through her ankle and leg. She hobbled to her office door, which she'd left ajar, and peered out.

What. The. Fuck?

For the life of her, she couldn't process what she was seeing.

Sheila. With a red gas canister in her hands. Dousing the kitchen with gasoline.

The woman looked up, and their eyes locked.

Roxie's face warmed, and she felt light-headed as Sheila—her *friend*—grinned back, a maniacal gleam in her blue eyes.

"Well, well, well. Looks like it's my lucky day." Sheila giggled, sounding like Minnie Mouse's evil twin sister.

Roxie gripped the door as Sheila approached, leaving a trail of gasoline in her wake.

"You just had to have it all, didn't you, Roxie?" The woman paused, shaking the gas can. Determining it was empty, she tossed it to the side. Then she slapped her hands together as if she were dusting off flour.

Roxie's heart knocked hard in her chest. What the hell was going on?

As Sheila walked by the prep counter, she picked up a rolling pin. "You weren't happy with just Jeremy's attention, were you? No, no. Of course not. You're greedy. Selfish."

Roxie was at a loss, and her stomach twisted. Who was this woman coming toward her? Because it surely couldn't be the same person she'd just had over for girls' night. It couldn't be.

Backing out of the doorway and into her office, Roxie slipped and put pressure on her right foot. Burning pain brought immediate tears to her eyes. *Suck it up, Roxie, and focus!* Her gaze shot around the tiny room in search of a weapon, a way out . . . anything. She spied her just-in-case golf club, but it was well out of reach. And Sheila kept getting closer.

"Then you had to go after Eli, too, didn't you? Was he like an extra challenge? A bonus? He loved me, Roxie. He swore it. He was going to leave Poppy for *me*! But you couldn't handle that, could you? You need all the attention, all the time. You had to go and throw yourself at him. You couldn't stand to see me happy, could you?"

Holy. Fuck.

Roxie knew you couldn't reason with crazy. Crazy would only hear what crazy wanted, but she had to give it a shot.

"Sheila, I don't know what you're talking about. I promise." She truly, truly didn't.

The other woman cackled, and the grating sound sent chills running down Roxie's spine.

"Right," Sheila spat. "Let me guess, you know nothing about turning Quinn and Cade against me. Gavin and Matt, too, right? Don't bother lying. I *know* you said something to them. Because you were jealous. Jealous of how they looked at me. Wanted me. Just like how Alex is jealous. But the difference is, Alex didn't try to take anyone away from me. You did. You took *Joe*. How *dare* you?"

Roxie tensed, and her eyes widened in surprise. Before she could take her next breath, Sheila rushed toward the office door. Roxie yelped and tried to push it closed, but the madwoman threw her shoulder against the wood, forcing it open.

Knocked off balance, Roxie staggered backward. Pain shot through her leg, and two pops in her ankle had her crumpling to the ground.

In a flash, Sheila was straddling Roxie with a hand clamped tight around her throat. Colorful spots danced in Roxie's vision, but she bucked and thrashed, clawing at the hand holding her down. Her fingernails tore flesh, but she couldn't get Sheila off of her. Holy hell, the other woman was a lot stronger than she looked.

"Guess what, Roxie? This is *my* lucky night. Not yours. Everyone will finally see you for what you really are. A greedy whore. *I'm* going to be the one everyone loves."

Roxie's lungs burned. The circles of color flashing in her vision grew. She gasped for air, but it was futile.

Sheila raised the rolling pin and swung.

Roxie tried to brace herself, but the rolling pin came at her like a bullet. Fire exploded in her head with a deafening crack.

Her vision faded, and everything went peacefully black . . .

CHAPTER THIRTY-ONE

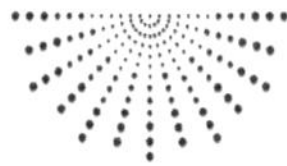

Joe paced the length of his kitchen. Again. Frustration, worry, and self-loathing warred within him. "Where the hell could she be?"

Sitting at the kitchen table, Quinn pushed a bag of chips in his direction.

He shook his head, nausea turning his stomach. The last thing he needed was to puke all over the floor. "I've called everyone I can think of, and no one has seen her."

"Your pacing isn't going to make Roxie come back any faster, you know."

He shot Quinn his middle finger. "I don't think you're taking this as seriously as you should, Sheriff. Maybe you should get up off your lazy ass and get a group out to look for her."

Quinn's jaw clenched. "Fuck you, Buchanan. I'll let that one slide because I know you're really worried about her, but don't push your luck, asshole."

Joe knew he wasn't being fair to Quinn, but dammit, he needed to see her. Needed to see with his own eyes that she was safe. Because his gut was screaming that she wasn't, that something was horribly wrong.

Grabbing Roxie's phone off the counter, he held it up. "When was the last time Rox ever, *ever* went anywhere without this damn thing?"

Quinn nodded.

Joe fumed. "That's it? You're just going to fucking nod?"

"What do you want me to say? Huh? Yes, I can't remember the last time Roxie went anywhere without her phone glued to her ear. And yes, that fucking worries me. But you know what, Buchanan? I also don't recall the last time she got her heart ripped out because some dumb fuck she was dating also happened to be dating someone else."

"Holy fuck!" Joe exploded. "How many times do I have to tell you that it wasn't a goddamn date?"

"You can keep saying it until Roxie walks back through that damn door. Then you can keep on saying it until *she* fucking believes you." Anger radiated from Quinn as he rose from the table. "You fucked up. So don't stand there and play the damn victim in—"

"Quinn, stop," Alex said, her voice calm but firm. She rested her hand on her husband's arm, and he flinched. "Look at me," she murmured, moving her hand to the side of his face. When he finally met her gaze, she said, "Stop. Sit. And breathe."

The big lug did as he'd been told, and the tension visibly drained from his muscles. Alex turned her death glare on Joe, who'd watched the couple's interaction in awe. Now that he was the one snared in the woman's gaze, however, he flinched.

"You're both being stupid," she said, knotting her long, wavy hair on top of her head. "I get you guys are both worried about Roxie, but stop blaming each other. Roxie's impulsive. You both know that. She probably just went for a walk to clear her head."

"In the dark?" Joe scoffed. "Without her phone? Without letting anyone know? That's completely—" Reckless, hasty . . . impulsive. "Fuuuck!"

"There's nothing you guys can do except wait. Bickering like eight-year-olds isn't going to do anyone any good." She sat primly on Quinn's lap. "It only makes me irritated."

Joe knew Alex was right, but dammit. "I just can't sit here."

She nodded. "Who did you call?"

"Nina, Sheila, June, my dad, Cade, and Gavin."

"And?"

"And nothing. Nina and June haven't seen her. Sheila and Gavin didn't answer. Nothing from my dad or Cade, either."

"You went by the café?" Quinn asked.

His eyes narrowed. "What the fuck do you think?"

Alex groaned. "Boys, boys . . . stop already."

"Don't blame me, sweetheart," Quinn said, hands raised in innocence. "He started—"

A cell phone rang.

Quinn's expression sobered as he glanced at his phone's display. "Sheriff O'Conner."

Joe fisted his hands at his sides as he waited for any clue as to what was going on. If Quinn's clenched jaw was any indication, the caller wasn't delivering good news.

Ending the call with a grunt, Quinn moved Alex aside and stood. "Stay here with Annie, sweetheart," he said, laying a quick kiss on his wife's forehead. "Joe, let's go. Now."

His stomach sank. The command in his friend's voice left no doubt. Something was definitely wrong.

Joe grabbed a coat, shoved his feet into a pair of shoes, and climbed inside Quinn's SUV in under thirty seconds.

Quinn shifted into Drive and tore down the street before Joe had finished closing his door all the way.

"What is it? Is it Roxie?"

"I don't know," Quinn said, sounding hoarse.

"Then what the fuck is going . . ." The words died in his throat as they turned the corner and parked.

Holy. Fuck.

The entire front of Comfort Food was engulfed in flames.

Joe's heart stopped, and his lungs seized in his chest. He leaped from the car and raced through the chaos—lights, sirens, hoses, water—toward the burning building. Two firefighters halted his progression.

"Hold up, Joe."

"Sorry, man, but this is as close as you can get."

He glared at the two men. He recognized them as fighters at Cade's gym.

"She's not in there, is she?" Panic clawed at his throat when the men looked at each other. "Tell me she's not in there!"

Joe tried to lunge past the firefighters, but he was hauled back by unseen hands.

"Stop, Buchanan. You gotta stop."

He turned, fists clenched, ready to pummel whatever asshole had grabbed him.

It was Quinn. Joe stiffened at the somber look on his friend's face.

"Shut up and just fucking listen, okay? I talked to the chief." He blew out a breath, then nodded to the group of firefighters attacking the blaze at the front of the building. "There's another group around back. Fire's not as bad there. They were able to enter the building, and they . . ."

Joe's stomach dropped as he watched his friend try to control his emotions.

"Holy shit, man," Joe murmured. "What is it?"

"Roxie," Quinn said, tears filling his eyes.

Joe's blood ran cold. "She's in the fucking building?" It was on the tip of his tongue to ask if she was alive. But no. He refused to put that thought out into the universe. Because Roxie *was* alive, dammit. She had to be.

When Quinn nodded, the relief that flooded through him turned his knees weak.

"They see her," Quinn said. "She's on the ground, but they weren't able to get to her. They're going back in now."

If Quinn said more, Joe didn't register it. All he could hear was the whooshing of the hoses and the pounding of his heart. All he could think about was Roxie in that blazing building.

She had to be all right. She had to.

Chaos swirled around him, but Joe stood rooted. From his spot in the middle of the street, he could see the front of the café as well as the right side of the building—which was where the firefighters would walk on their way to the awaiting ambulance. His eyes never left that side.

She had to be all right. She had to.

It was the mantra he repeated in his head. Because dammit, if he said it enough, the powers that be would hear. He just hoped they'd listen. Not for him, because let's face it, he'd fucked up, but for Roxie.

Because she was so damn perfect. She was also possibly the most exasperating woman ever, but fucking perfect nonetheless. For him.

Tears fell unchecked from his eyes. The only image in his mind was her. His beautiful, exasperating, perfect Roxie.

She had to be all right. She had to.

Seconds felt like minutes, and minutes felt like hours. Slowly, the firefighters managed to bring the blaze under control. He wasn't sure how much time had passed when he noticed growing activity on the side of the building.

Quinn and a couple of his deputies went to join the commotion. It took all of Joe's willpower to stay where he was. The last thing he wanted to do was get in the way.

But then a pair of firemen rounded the building. One carried a bundle in his arms.

Joe was moving toward the ambulance before his brain made the connection.

Roxie.

He could only watch in horror as they loaded her limp body onto a stretcher. She was covered in soot, and her auburn hair was matted against her head.

Quinn appeared at his side and put an arm around his shoulders. "They're taking her to the hospital. They may airlift her over to Seattle, depending on how bad she is."

Nodding, Joe opened his mouth to speak, but he couldn't find his voice. He cleared his throat and tried again. "She's alive. That's what matters."

Quinn gestured toward the ambulance and the medics prepping Roxie for transport. "You going with?"

"You better believe it, man. Holy shit."

When they reached the back of the ambulance, Joe blew out a breath and turned to give his friend a hard hug—without the usual manly slap on the back. They'd both come so close to losing her tonight. Roxie was their best friend, their third Amigo and Musketeer. But to Joe, she was also much more. She was everything. "I'm not letting her out of my sight. Fucking ever."

"I hear you." Quinn ran his hands through his hair and left them atop his head. "I can't imagine how you feel right now. I'm about torn in two because that's *Roxie*. I know you love her the way I love Alex, and . . . Holy shit, brother."

"It feels like shit being so damn helpless." Nodding to the medic, Joe stepped into the back of the ambulance. While he waited for the okay to sit down next to her, he turned back to Quinn. "But I'd rather be helpless next to her than helpless and not knowing where she is. That's for damn sure."

CHAPTER THIRTY-TWO

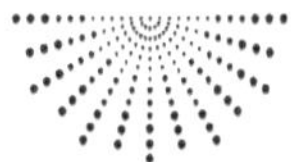

Roxie blinked open her eyes. Then she quickly closed them. The hammering in her head was unlike anything she'd experienced before. It was like the worst hangover. Ever. Only amplified a thousand times over.

She couldn't help the groan that escaped, but she immediately regretted not trying harder to prevent it. That one little noise from the back of her throat had set off a blaze of fire in her lungs and brought tears to her eyes. Apparently, on top of achieving the worst hangover ever, she'd also managed to smoke five entire cartons of cigarettes in one sitting.

Holy freaking crap.

If she could, she would have curled into fetal position and whimpered. But whimpering would hurt her throat too much. Hell, everything hurt too much right now.

"Morning, sunshine."

For a brief moment, those two little words wiped all her pain away. Just poof—it was gone.

She felt Joe take her hand in his. When the pain returned, it was still god-awful . . . but somehow, it was also a little more bearable.

Roxie peeked open her eyes and there he was. There were dark circles under his bloodshot blues, and his hair stood on end as if he'd been running his hands through it. His clothes were rumpled. Hell, *he* was rumpled. And he was still gorgeous.

Tears sprang to her eyes. She'd never been happier to see anyone.

"Hey," she croaked.

He held out a cup and bent the straw toward her. "Drink."

She did as she'd been told, and the water was a cool balm to her raging throat. With his free hand, Joe wiped away a tear that had escaped. When he tucked a stray lock of hair behind her ear, she flinched. The throbbing in her head returned in earnest.

"Sorry, baby, didn't mean to touch that spot."

She moved away from the straw. "What happened? I don't remem—" She froze, and her eyes went wide. "Oh my god. Sheila. Joe, you don't underst—"

His fingers gently touched her lips. "Shhh. It's all right. You need to rest your throat. The smoke—"

"No," she interrupted, her heart racing. "You don't understand. Sheila—"

"Is a nutcase," he finished. "Don't worry, baby, they got her." She opened her mouth again, but he brought the straw back to her lips before she could speak. "I'll explain everything to you. You've just got to stop talking."

She took another sip of water. And then another. Who knew water could feel so good?

"How do you feel? Honestly, Roxanne."

"Like I was on the wrong end of a meat tenderizer." She frowned. "Make that a rolling pin."

"Holy shit," Joe said. "Too soon, baby. Too soon."

Her lips quirked, and she took a moment to scan the hospital room. "Where am I?"

"Virginia Mason Medical Center."

She raised a brow. "In Seattle?"

"Yeah." He leaned toward her, caressing the side of her face. "After the fire, they airlifted you to Harborview in Seattle. You had pretty severe smoke inhalation."

She frowned. "Then why am I at Virginia Mason?"

"Because while Harborview is the only level-one trauma center in the region, they don't have a hyperbaric unit like they do here."

That seemed like a lot of moving around. Her frown deepened. "What day is it?"

"It's Sunday, baby."

Her jaw dropped, and her mind scrambled. Three days. She'd been out for *three* freaking days?

"The doctors kept you sedated so you could heal. Not only for your lungs, but . . . you also got bashed in the head pretty badly."

Sheila and the damn rolling pin. The memories flashing in her mind had goosebumps rising over her skin. "Am I going to be okay?"

Her heart stuttered when he kissed her softly on the lips. "You'll be good as new. You sprained your ankle too. Now, you just have to rest. Dad should be here any minute and he can explain all the medical jargon."

"And Sheila?"

"She's in jail. The person who called in the fire saw Sheila and reported it. Quinn said when they went to her apartment, she confessed to all of it. Breaking into your café, knocking you out, and starting the fire. She admitted to sending you the photos over the last month. Said she'd seen your folder of press clippings and that you deserved to be taken down a few notches."

The muscle in his jaw twitched, and she squeezed his hand.

Joe cleared his throat. "Apparently, she didn't believe she'd done anything wrong. Ranted about how it was *your* fault for telling lies about her, stealing men away from her. Me, Jeremy, Eli, Cade, Gavin . . . even Quinn. He said when they searched her apartment, she had a room filled with photos of you."

The hairs on the back of her neck rose, and she shivered. "Oh, wow. I worked with her practically every day, Joe. She just spent the night at our house . . ." Her heart hurt.

"I know, baby," he soothed, running a hand up and down her chilled skin. "She fooled everyone. She's not right in the head, Roxanne. None of this is your fault. At all. Do you hear me?"

Roxie nodded. Holy crap, she was lucky. So very, very lucky to be alive. She caught his steady gaze and held her breath. "And us, Joe? Are we okay?"

He framed her face in his hands and kissed her on the lips again. "You have to believe me when I say that I was *not* on a date with Candie. I know it looks bad, but I swear to you it wasn't like that. The JBLM guys missed their ferry, so dinner was off. She happened to call right after I got off the phone with them and wanted to talk about some business thing. I was hungry and thought I'd kill two birds with one stone. I figured she and I could eat and talk at the same time."

Roxie fought a smile. That *did* sound exactly like Joe's brand of logic.

"You know me, Rox. You may not like me all the time—which I completely get—and I know I can be an asshole, but you know I'm not a cheater. You know that's a deal-breaker for me." A blush bloomed over his cheeks, and he covered his embarrassment with a cough. Then, tipping his lips up in a playful smirk, he shrugged and added, "Besides, I'm lazy. I've never dated more than one woman at a time. That takes too much planning and deception and effort."

There it was. He'd tried to cover it up, but she'd seen it. The tender heart he kept hidden behind the bluster and sarcasm.

"Truly, Rox, why the hell would I date anyone else? I have you." He cringed. "Er . . . I hope I still have you?"

"You do," she said, her heart filling. "I'm so sorry I doubted you."

He flashed her that charming Buchanan grin, and for the first time, she didn't find it annoying. At all. Because in that charming grin, she noticed something different. She saw his wariness, his fear that she'd say no and turn him away. She damn near saw his heart on his freaking sleeve.

"You're everything to me, Roxanne. Everything. You've been my dream girl since I was sixteen. You're the one I want to be with. Forever. It's always been you. Always."

Her breath caught. She hadn't been expecting *that*.

"Joe," she whispered as tears welled in her eyes.

He took her hand and laid his lips on the back of it. "You don't have to say anything, baby. And don't worry, I'm not planning to officially declare my love for you in a hospital. Just like I'm not going to ask you to spend the rest of your life with me while you're still wearing that fabulous hospital gown."

A sly, lopsided smile spread across Joe's face as he reached into his pocket and pulled out a little wooden box. Her mouth fell open in shock. Was he serious?

"What's that?" she asked, heart pounding.

"Oh, this?" He showed her the box, then shook his head. "You don't get this until it's check-out time."

Her eyes narrowed. "What are you playing at, Joseph Buchanan?"

He kissed her again. "I'm not playing at anything, Roxanne. I love you. I've always loved you. And I will continue to love you until the day I die."

"I love you, too," she said, tears spilling down her face. She draped her arms around his neck and pulled him close, ignoring every ache and twinge of pain in her body. With a watery laugh, she said, "I thought you weren't going to declare your love and all that while I'm still here."

He chuckled. "I said I wasn't *planning* to. Change of plans, Rox. Besides, I should have told you I loved you years ago." He shrugged and brought her hand to his lips again. "I'm a little slow. What can I say?"

She grinned, then tugged on his hand. "What do you say you squeeze in here and hold me for a little bit?"

A smile lit up his face, and his blue eyes twinkled. Moments later, she was wrapped in his arms.

She sighed and leaned into him. "I love you, Joe."

"I love you, too, baby." She felt his lips press to the top of her head. "But you're still not getting the box until discharge time."

EPILOGUE

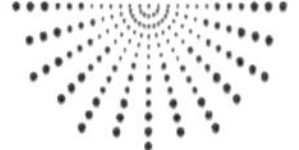

THREE WEEKS LATER

The whirl of a bandsaw and the thudding of hammers drowned out the classic rock blaring from the dusty portable speaker. Wood, sawdust, and paint thinner scented the air. From the kitchen archway, Roxie surveyed the work taking place in the front of her café, and a lump formed in her throat.

Her landlord had been mercifully quick to bring a crew in to rebuild Comfort Food. New counters, new walls and windows, new flooring . . . new everything. The fire had done a number on the front of the café, but only minimal damage to the kitchen area. And thankfully, it hadn't spread to the neighboring buildings.

She'd been touched when the community had rallied around her after the brick-in-the-window incident. But the way they'd come together to support her after the fire? It humbled her beyond belief and brought tears to her eyes on a regular basis. If she hadn't been an emotional mess before the fire, she certainly was now.

Glancing down at the air-cast around her ankle, she smiled. Her bruises and injuries would heal. And her café was a week away from its grand re-opening.

She was lucky. So damn lucky.

An arm snaked around her waist and gently pulled her backward. Familiar, spicy aftershave cocooned her like a warm blanket. Soft lips landed on her neck, and she leaned against the man behind her.

Joe. He'd been by her side since she'd come home from the hospital.

Another smile lifted her lips when she glimpsed the thin, light-blue silicone band on her ring finger. The sneaky man had indeed given her the little wooden jewelry box upon her release from the hospital, and her heart warmed at the memory.

After she'd been discharged, Joe had helped her settle into the hospital wheelchair. But before wheeling her out of her room, he'd presented her with the little box. Upon opening it, she'd been surprised to see the silicone band nestled in the cushion. When she'd glanced up at him, she'd laughed at the sweet, sheepish smile that had spread over his handsome face.

"I haven't had the chance to get you a proper engagement ring, but I wanted to give you something now. It's a promise that when I ask you to marry me for real, I'll do it right. You won't be on pain meds, I will have showered, and we'll—"

She'd yanked him down for a kiss. Pain meds and all. And she'd been wearing the simple, but perfect, silicone band ever since.

"Can I sneak you out?" Joe asked, bringing her back to the present.

She turned in his arms. "Can we get lunch? I'm starving."

He nodded toward the back door. "Let's get out of here."

Roxie linked her fingers with his. Waving to the construction workers, she followed him out. The air-cast had her walking slowly, and he helped her into his truck.

"Where to?" she asked as he drove by Ray's Diner. Then her brows turned inward when he drove them out of Hudson's quaint downtown.

"How's your ankle?"

Her eyes narrowed as she studied him. "What are you up to, Joseph Buchanan?"

"Lunch." He shot her a wink.

"Yeah, but where?"

He simply smiled in response, and she rolled her eyes.

After a few minutes, he turned off the main road toward a familiar trailhead. Her curiosity climbed as he drove past the small parking lot and pulled onto the gravel service road. "Uh, Joe?"

He shot her the sweet and mischievous grin she loved. "You trust me, baby?"

"I do." Her heart squeezed. And then her stomach growled. "There is food planned, right?"

"Hang on," Joe said, chuckling as he put the truck in Park. He hopped out, hustled around the hood, opened her door, and helped her down.

Holding hands, he led her to a short trail. The late-February chill had her thankful for her scarf and Joe's body heat. Recognizing the familiar area, she smiled. She'd run this trail countless times and knew it led to one of her favorite views on Hudson Island.

They ambled down the path in companionable silence. When the trail opened onto a grassy bluff, she let out a reverent sigh. Ahead, the Pacific Ocean's Puget Sound shimmered beneath gray and cloudy skies, the water calm and smooth despite the season. In the distance, the silhouette of the Pacific View Resort loomed atop its own bluff.

Tearing her gaze from the view, she looked up at Joe. "What are we doing here?"

"Lunch."

He nodded toward the edge of the bluff, and she gasped. How had she missed the picnic blanket? When she turned back to him, her jaw dropped.

Joe was on one knee, that little wooden box in his hand. The lid was open, and in it sat a sparkly, beautiful diamond ring.

"Joe," she said, struggling to find her voice. Her throat was thick with emotion.

"I'd planned on doing this at your grand re-opening party. Everyone was going to be there. Alex and Nina were both in on the surprise. They were talking about balloons and signs and some sort of confetti." He shrugged, and the smile on his face melted her heart. "But I'm a selfish guy, Rox. You know that. I didn't want to share you—share *this*—with anyone else."

Tears welled, and her pulse kicked up when he took her hand.

"Roxanne Elizabeth Jameson, I have loved you my entire life. I promise you I will never stop. We'll have our ups and downs, but I promise I'll always fight for us. I won't lie to you, and I'll never stop working to prove how much I love you."

Her heart swelled. "You have my love, Joseph Buchanan. You always have. I think I fell in love with you when I was eight." She laughed, and a tear spilled down her cheek. "We've had our ups and downs, and I'm sure we'll have more. I promise I'll always fight for us, too. It's always been you, Joe."

"I love you, baby. So much. I promise to do everything I can to deserve you." His eyes shimmered as he brought her hand to his lips. "Will you marry me, Roxanne? Please be my wife?"

She nodded, more happy tears falling in earnest. "Yes," she whispered, her heart singing.

Joe jumped to his feet and slipped the ring onto her finger. Then his hands were in her hair, and his mouth was on hers. Passion and love. That's what they'd found together. But they would be best friends first . . . and forever.

ENJOY THIS BOOK?

Reviews and ratings encourage other readers to try out a book & I would love your help spreading the word! If you could take a quick moment to rate or leave a review on your favorite book site, I would be forever grateful! You can do that on Amazon, Goodreads and/or Bookbub. Thank you!

ABOUT THE AUTHOR

Christina Sol is an award-winning author who writes what she loves to read—romance books filled with heart, heat, and suspense.

An avid reader from the get-go, Christina was obsessed with The Babysitters Club, Sweet Valley Twins, Sweet Valley High, Christopher Pike, and all things V. C. Andrews. Her love for romance started with the Sunfire books, a YA historical romance series. Caroline by Willo Davis Roberts was her favorite of the series, and a copy of the 1984 novel is one of her most treasured possessions. Then she discovered Danielle Steele and Nora Roberts. And never looked back. She's still a voracious reader and enjoys all genres of romance but leans toward romantic suspense and dark romance.

She lives in the inland Pacific Northwest with her husband and two kids. When she's not writing, reading, or knitting, she's watching football or fueling her planner, sticker, and washi-tape obsession.

To find out more, visit: www.christinasol.com

ACKNOWLEDGMENTS

My wonderful readers: thank you! I know life is busy and time is so very precious. I am forever grateful to you for choosing to spend your valuable time reading Roxie & Joe's story. It was so much fun writing them—and digging Joe out of the giant hole he'd made for himself. I hope his grovel was satisfying and that you ended up rooting from them as much as I did. Again, thank you for taking the time to read Shattered Illusions.

Heather G: this one has been in the works for a long, long time and I can't thank you enough. I hope I was able to redeem Joe . . . at least a *tiny* bit more. lol

Jen C & Danielle R: I hope you know how much I value you both. Your comments, feedback, honesty, and the support you've given me means so, so, SO much! Thank you!

Megan S: Simply put, these books would not be what they are without you. I appreciate your expertise more than you'll ever know. Thank you!

LJ at Mayhem Cover Creations: your covers are stunning—thank you!

My family & friends: from the depths of my heart—thank you! Your enthusiasm and support have truly meant the world to me.